THE TAKEOVER

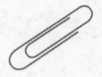

Also by Cara Tanamachi

The Second You're Single

THE
TAKEOVER

CARA TANAMACHI

ST. MARTIN'S GRIFFIN
NEW YORK

First published in the United States by St. Martin's Griffin, an imprint of St. Martin's Publishing Group

THE TAKEOVER. Copyright © 2024 by Cara Tanamachi. All rights reserved. Printed in the United States of America. For information, address St. Martin's Publishing Group, 120 Broadway, New York, NY 10271.

www.stmartins.com

Designed by Jonathan Bennett

Library of Congress Cataloging-in-Publication Data

Names: Tanamachi, Cara, author.
Title: The takeover / Cara Tanamachi.
Description: First edition. | New York: St. Martin's Griffin, 2024.
Identifiers: LCCN 2023036032 | ISBN 9781250842282 (trade paperback) | ISBN 9781250842299 (ebook)
Subjects: LCGFT: Romance fiction. | Novels.
Classification: LCC PS3612.O258 T35 2024 | DDC 813/.6—dc23/eng/20230814
LC record available at https://lccn.loc.gov/2023036032

Our books may be purchased in bulk for promotional, educational, or business use. Please contact your local bookseller or the Macmillan Corporate and Premium Sales Department at 1-800-221-7945, extension 5442, or by email at MacmillanSpecialMarkets@macmillan.com.

First Edition: 2024

10 9 8 7 6 5 4 3 2 1

For PJ, the love of my life, in this life and the next.
This story, and all love stories, I dedicate to you.

When she asked the universe for her soulmate,
fate delivered her hate mate instead.

THE TAKEOVER

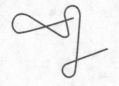

ONE

Nami

Employee birthdays shall be celebrated with cupcakes and 50 Cent.
#UNOFFICIAL-TOGGLE-EMPLOYEE-HANDBOOK CHANNEL
TOGGLE INTERNAL CHAT

I hate birthdays like most people hate toilet paper hoarders.

It's probably because when I was six, I scarfed down four pieces of cake, downed a dangerous mixture of extra-large fountain drinks, and then went into a sugar-blasted frenzy at Lotza Cheese Pizzeria, which ended with me hurling in the ball pit in front of a dozen horrified kids and their parents.

Apparently, even at age six, I suffered an existential crisis about aging. My feelings about birthdays haven't improved with time.

I hate them more than ever. And I really, really hate milestone birthdays. Like today. I'm turning thirty, and the very thought makes me a bit queasy as I slide through the revolving doors of my Chicago high-rise building on the Magnificent Mile. The blissfully cool air-conditioning washes over me as I swim out of the swampy late-July heat and into the white marble lobby. My sleeveless linen olive-green jumpsuit clings to my sweaty lower back and I'm a tad worried the thin camel-leather soles of my strappy sandals might have begun to melt during the five-block walk from the L across the blistering concrete. I mentally cross my fingers my mascara isn't running down my face as I lift up my long dark hair, letting the AC hit my hot neck.

Is this what happens when you're old? You can't tolerate heat anymore? Ugh. I want to be twenty-nine again. I don't remember sweating this much when I was twenty-nine.

Then I remember I don't have time to worry about aging or what milestone birthdays might mean. I'm busy trying to keep my tech company, Toggle, afloat.

My phone pings as I walk amidst the swarm of people heading up to their offices or to the coffee kiosk nearby. *Forecast for Series D: cloudy with a good chance of never happening.*

That's Imani. My partner who's part finance magician and part trailblazer. She put the boss in girl boss. When people told her she couldn't get funding for a company run by women of color, she said *Watch me.* Then she proceeded to nab three rounds of funding in the many millions. She's meeting with our venture capitalists today, hoping to get an idea about how plausible Series D funding could be for Toggle, our app that connects people who want to share or swap cars, vacation homes, or parking spaces.

Things really that bad? I text.

Worse, Imani says, and I feel a pit forming in my stomach. *This time, they're not going to just throw a Dell at us and call it a day.*

After our last round of funding, one of the venture capitalists, Dell, came on as our third partner and member of the board. His hobbies are money flexes and casual misogyny. Imani and I didn't like it, but it was the price we paid for the investment cash.

What are our options? I ask her. Sixty employees are counting on us.

Not sure yet. That's not like Imani. Usually, she has about forty different angles she's working. This worries me.

We just need a little more time, I type. Not long ago, we were set to go public, grace the cover of *Business Tech* as trailblazers, but then the pandemic changed everything. Everyone stopped traveling. Nobody wanted to share a car with possible plague germs clinging to the steering wheel. We just need another round of funding to float us until we can get back on our feet again.

Preaching to the choir, sister.

I'm headed to the elevator bank when I realize a new set of ads have gone up near the coffee kiosk in the lobby. I'm focused on the biggest poster: a couple laughing together in matching pajamas, little foam hearts in their cappuccinos.

Even worse, the model looks like my ex, Mitch. Brown hair, the build of a former athlete, the smirk of a man who believes the world owes him everything.

No.

Not today, Satan.

I hurry away from the giant poster of Doppelgänger Mitch, trying not to think about my empty apartment with the moldy takeout in the fridge waiting for me at the end of the day. I duck into an elevator, fighting back bitterness. All my well-laid plans—publicly traded company by twenty-eight, married by twenty-nine, have a baby by thirty, or at least be baby-adjacent by thirty—have been waylaid by forces beyond my control. In my twenties, I used to think nothing was out of my control. If I studied more, worked harder, and hit the gym like a Peloton instructor, every goal was within reach.

And now I think we're all pinballs pinging around at random, hoping that when we collide with something, it's good.

Soon, I'm at my floor, darting away from the elevator and out into the happy buzz of our bustling tech firm. The Toggle office might be in Chicago, but it's got the Silicon Valley vibe: bright colors, open floor plan, Ping-Pong and foosball tables in the break room. Free cans of soda in the clear-door fridge, and a fully stocked juice and espresso bar. Ridiculously smart twentysomethings in Vans and faded concert tees roam the halls. At least four of them toss a Frisbee back and forth down the main corridor, riffing on new app functions, while others lob a Nerf football. Another pair have their heads together trying to solve a glitch, or arguing about who was the better *Star Trek* captain: Kirk, Picard, Sisko, or Janeway, and an "official" vote of the matter is currently open on the break room whiteboard. These developers and programmers are loud, boisterous, and hilarious, and I love them. I breathe a little sigh of relief, the tightness in my chest loosening.

"Nam-eeee!" Priya Patel, a senior software engineer, shouts, her bright blue hair impossible to miss as she stops, mid-Frisbee throw. A few others swivel around in their chairs and join my senior engineer in the chant. "Nam, Nam, Nam, Nam-eeee!"

They chant like I'm a gold-medal Olympian and not their boss. These are my people. They love me and I love them back. I've spent a lot of time and effort building a community, not just a regular old workplace, making sure that Toggle is the kind of place people feel good about working for. In fact, our tagline on a bunch of employee shirts last year read: TOGGLE: FUN. NOT EVIL. REALLY. WE MEAN IT.

Arie Berger, my chief technical officer and Priya's boss, slowly rises from his desk. He's got his TV Dad vibe on hyperdrive today with his short, curly, sandy-blond hair; a brown plaid shirt; khaki shorts; leather hiking sandals; and his company ID around his neck in a Toggle-logoed lanyard. He's the only employee on the floor to wear his ID, and some of the other programmers joke it's because—at age forty-five and the oldest employee at Toggle—he's getting too old to remember his name. He's got a wife and two kids in the suburbs, proudly drives a silver minivan, and listens exclusively to old-school hip-hop from the early 2000s.

He nods sagely at Priya, who hits the volume button on the portable cube speaker on her desk.

The first bars of 50 Cent's "In Da Club" boom out. The engineers slip on sunglasses and turn their baseball caps backward, some wearing bling in the form of paper clip and Post-it Note necklaces and immediately start a poorly planned group dance. They might be able to create the most complicated code from scratch, but coordinated they're not. I slap my hand over my mouth to suppress a giggle.

The engineers unfurl a banner that says "It is your birthday." It's decorated with two limp brown balloons—ode to *The Office*. Arie hands me a small box wrapped in Toggle flyers.

"Go on! Open it!" Priya cheers.

I open it, slowly, and pull out a ceramic mug.

It reads *World's Best Boss* on one side, and on the other *We Mean This Un-Ironically*. This mug instantly becomes my most favorite thing in the world. Everyone applauds and cheers. My face hurts from smiling and my heart feels like it might burst. I couldn't ask for a more perfect present.

"Aw, thanks, everyone!" They almost—almost—make me like birthdays. But it's right now, as I'm glancing at the words *World's Best Boss,* that I start to wonder if I am. Am I the world's best boss if I can't keep Toggle afloat?

"And we have . . . cupcakes!" Arie grabs the big pink box from beneath his desk, distracting me from the panic threatening to take over my brain. He's barely got the box open when Priya dives in, grabbing two, and reaching for a third.

"Hey, watch that sugar intake," warns Jamal, head of Quality Assurance, as he rolls his wheelchair toward the cupcakes. He's wearing a black polo, per his usual uniform, and comes to a stop, adjusting his black Clubmaster glasses on his nose.

"You're not the boss of me," she says and sticks out her pierced tongue.

"No, but we basically share a desk, and if you're hyper all afternoon, you'll be shaking it with your bouncing knees and your sugar nerves," he says.

Jamal and Priya are polar opposites: Jamal being reserved, serious, and quiet, and Priya being flamboyant, dramatic, and loud.

"You know you love it when the desk vibrates," she coos, winking at him as she flips a bright blue piece of hair from her forehead. Jamal just sighs and rolls his eyes.

"Arie? Help, please?" Jamal asks.

"That's enough, children," Arie says in his best TV Dad voice. "Be nice. And Priya—one cupcake! Nami hasn't even gotten hers yet."

"Sorry," Priya says, sheepishly handing me one.

"No worries." I take it and grin. It's all so freakin' sweet. "What did I do to deserve all of you?"

"Signing bonuses?" a programmer shouts from the back of the crowd.

"Breakfast Mondays!" another adds.

I laugh. "Thanks so much, everyone. There would be no Toggle without you. And I mean that. I'm so grateful for all of you, your brilliance, and your hard work. Thank you for all you do to make Toggle good."

"Fun, not evil!" another shouts.

I raise my mug in a toast to them as I glance around their goofy, oddball, perfect faces, shining back at me. My heart expands in my chest. Who needs a Mitch when you've got an army of eccentric tech nerds who love you? "We're not just a company. We're a family."

Everyone claps their approval.

"And thank you for the 50 Cent," I add. "I really needed that today."

"You can repay us by giving us your official vote. For best *Star Trek* captain . . . Captain," Arie says, crossing his arms across his ID tag and nodding back toward the whiteboard, visible through the glass wall of the break room.

"My vote is Janeway," I declare. "She explores a new dangerous quadrant with a ship full of enemies, and still gets the job done."

The Picard, Kirk, and Sisko fans groan and boo, good-naturedly, and the Janeway fans, including Priya, cheer.

"I knew it. Hear that? I told you!" Priya gloats, looking at Jamal.

"She doesn't have a catchphrase!" complains Jamal, throwing up his hands in disgust. "Every good captain has to have a catchphrase."

"She does," I counter. "It's . . ." Priya and the other Janeway fans join me. "Do it!" we shout together.

"That's a marketing slogan, not a catchphrase," grumbles Jamal as he balances a cupcake on his knee, and then rolls back to his desk, shaking his head in disapproval.

Arie, by my side, laughs. "Okay, redshirts, back to work."

"Really? Redshirts? We're expendable now?" Priya asks.

"Always," jokes Arie as he runs a hand through his short, curly hair. "You all are beaming down to the hostile planet first." Arie glances at me. "You sure you don't want to quit being the boss and come back to code with us? Look at all you're missing."

He says it with some sarcasm, but I actually think it is a tempting offer. Some of my happiest days were early programming time when I got to throw my own Frisbees. Back when I was both programmer and corporate lawyer, melding my two favorite things together: complicated code and even more complicated contracts.

The programmers resume their games of Frisbee and football and working out age-old pop culture debates as I walk to my glass office, setting the birthday cupcake down. Arie lingers, trailing me to my office.

"By the way, got a second?" Arie asks as I dig my laptop out of my bag and plug it into the port on my desk.

"Not if you're going to talk to me about block chains and crypto again," I tease. Arie is so into NFTs that he gifted both his kids their own when they were born.

Arie rolls his eyes. "You *asked*."

"I asked 'what is it'? I didn't expect a four-day-long PowerPoint presentation."

"This is not about NFTs," he assures me, fidgeting a little with his ID tag. "Though you are absolutely missing out on those. I want to talk about benefits."

"Isn't that technically Paula's domain?" I glance at our office manager and HR's office.

"She's on vacation, remember?"

"What about Dell?"

Paula technically reports to Dell, so he should fill in for her when she's out.

"Running on Dell time." Arie doesn't bother to keep the disapproval from his voice.

Right, Dell time. Disappearing for hours. Sometimes, skipping entire days without explanation. Yet he'll be the first to complain about the staff's work ethic because he can't keep an assistant, since they keep quitting. If I had to work for Dell, I'd quit, too. He only ever has two modes: bragging about his vacation properties and his multiple Teslas, or being totally unreasonable about job expectations, including not being above asking a senior software engineer to go fetch his dry cleaning. It's no wonder the entire staff spend at least a quarter of their time thinking of ways to prank him. Last December, after word got out that Dell was lobbying to slice everyone's bonuses, they wrapped his entire desk in Grinch wrapping paper—including his stapler and every single pen. The cherry on top was someone hacked his phone, setting his ringtone to play "You're a Mean One, Mr. Grinch." He went for a whole month with that blaring from his phone before he figured out how to change it.

"He wasn't here at all yesterday," I mumble, almost to myself.

"Don't worry," he says, and glances at me. "We can hold down the fort."

I grin at him. "I know you can."

"I was hoping to ask you about some extra paid leave for Maria."

Maria Lopez, one of our best programmers, had a few complications after delivering her baby via C-section last month. An infection kept her in the hospital longer than she wanted, and her healing was progressing slowly. We'd sent her a ginormous get-well bouquet from the office, but I also know flowers don't pay bills.

Normally, I wouldn't hesitate to approve the extra time. Then I think about our lopsided balance sheets and pause. I'm not 100 percent sure I can cover employee expenses for the next six months, and I hate to make a promise I can't keep. We have reserves—for right now. How long those reserves last depends on how much new business we can get. Arie clocks my hesitation.

"We're all willing to donate vacation time . . ." Arie begins, fiddling a little nervously with his ID badge.

I feel awful and immediately wave off my money worries.

I shake my head. "That's sweet, but no need. She can have all the leave she wants." Maria is an amazing coder, and I don't want to lose her. "What kind of family would we be if we didn't take care of our own?"

Arie looks relieved. "Good. Because Dell was dragging his feet on that and said we couldn't afford it," he says. "At least that's what Paula told me before she left for vacation."

He looks slightly uneasy. Everybody has been lately. It hasn't missed anyone's notice that revenues are down, and while they've started to tick back up, we've got a long way to go before we're whole. And who knows if we'll ever get there. Just when we think the pandemic is in the rearview, a new strain or outbreak sets us on our heels again. Not to mention, there are grumbles about the economy slowing down, and the looming threat of recession. And then there was Imani's worrisome text thread earlier. The investors might not be able to save us this time. I push the thought from my mind. No need to invite bad news inside before it's even in the driveway.

I frown at Dell's darkened office.

"Let me deal with Dell," I say. If I have to donate my own sick time, I will. If I have to just pay for her paid leave out of my 401K, so be it. It's a Band-Aid solution, I know, and it's not like I have unlimited resources, since I put most of what I had into Toggle. I'll just keep hoping Imani can work her magic.

I know better than anyone how the unexpected can change your life forever. Like the week my father died of a heart attack. It had come out of the blue nearly three years ago, right smack dab in the middle of us raising venture capital. No one plans for crappy things to happen. But they do anyway.

"Thanks, Captain," Arie says, looking at me like a proud dad before he saunters back to his workstation. While he could've opted for his own office, he picked a desk in the middle of his programmers. He said it was to keep an eye on them, but I know our resident TV Dad/CIO loves to toss the occasional Frisbee. I get to work digging through the mountain of emails that have piled into my inbox just during my commute time. My watch pings. It's a message from a number I don't know.

Happy Birthday, Namby.

Namby?

My blood runs cold.

Only one person ever calls me that annoying nickname.

Jae Lee.

My former high school nemesis. The boy who barely beat me out for valedictorian and two different scholarships I wanted. Badly. The boy rich enough, it was rumored, to pay someone to take the SAT for him. Twice. Jae was always about *Jae.* To make matters worse, he isn't even a nerd. He was stupidly, wildly popular in school, a popularity I could never hope to achieve with my penchant for gobbling up extra credit and always raising my hand in class. His popularity continues today on all major social platforms, which I'm absolutely, positively not following him on.

Jae? I write, even though I know it's him. Nobody else calls me Namby.

Who else would it be, Namby?

I don't know . . . the antichrist? Whenever you're around it does feel like end of times, I type back. *And how did you get my number?*

I'll tell you when I see you.

Oh, no. Not in this lifetime.

I thought you were in San Jose. Supporting bro culture. Setting wildfires. Antichrist stuff.

Not anymore. I moved back to Chi-town.

Since when?

I'll tell you all about the move when we catch up. I'll see you very soon, he types.

Not if I see you coming first, I type back.

He sends me a laugh-crying emoji. And a devil emoji.

I don't have time for this nonsense. I've got a company to save.

Leave it to Jae to have rotten timing. I haven't talked to him since high school graduation. And I've been carefully avoiding him for years. I glance at the devil emoji on my phone. See me soon? I glance around as if he might pop out of my filing cabinet. Why on earth does he want to see me? And *why* is he tracking my birthday? It makes me think he's been working on some kind of horrible prank that'll be filmed and showcased at our next class reunion. There can be no good reason he remembered my birthday.

Maybe there are clues online. I could check his social.

I glance at my laptop. I've been largely avoiding every platform ever since I announced the wedding with Mitch was off. I asked for privacy eighteen months ago, but of course, it was just like pouring gasoline on the fire. Nobody gave me privacy. Somebody even unearthed a blurry video of Mitch, enthusiastically getting familiar with a blonde in the back of his bachelor party neon bus. A couple of people posted it and tagged me, along with their weak condolences and barely disguised gloating. The worst part was it was shared, gleefully, again and again . . . and again. I've always known that I was not popular in school (someone has to be hall monitor), but honestly, until this last year and a half, I never actually realized there were so many people out there rooting for me to fail.

I was the smoldering roadside wreck everybody gawked at for months.

But I have to look at the social media I've been avoiding now. I have to see what Jae's doing. Maybe there's a clue on one of his accounts about seeing me "soon." Maybe something less nefarious like a mutual friend's wedding?

I haven't checked up on Jae in years. For a split second, I imagine maybe his life isn't as perfect as I imagine it to be. Maybe he is also whiffing at his social life. Although I can't imagine Mr. Prom King ever having that kind of issue. Maybe he has a gambling problem. Maybe even a rare, nonfatal disease. Or even an untreatable recurring rash. On his face. My mind goes down a terrible rabbit hole of bleak outcomes for Jae, anything that might make me feel better about my own life.

I'm not proud of this, okay?

I get that I shouldn't wish bad things for people. Even for people like Jae.

I pull up his account and peer at his public posts. Immediately, I realize my mistake. There will be no gleeful tale of woe in Jae's profile. Why would I think that? The golden boy is still . . . golden. And worse, he's gotten better-looking with age. Brilliant-white dimpled smile still perfect. Not one missing tooth. Not one. And he still has all his thick, black hair.

Look, he just got a new car. A sleek, expensive-looking silver Audi that would make Tony Stark jealous. Fantastic. And look there, that's him *moving back home to Chicago*. Did he really write #SweetHomeChicago like a tourist fool? Ugh. There's him relaxing on the balcony of his obscene Gold Coast condo in the brand-new high-rise everyone's talking about overlooking Lake Michigan. His place makes my Old Town two-bedroom apartment look like the dark, wet corner of a dumpster.

Also, why are almost all his posts public? Braggy, much?

I scroll through more posts. Where is he even working? He doesn't say in the public posts I can see. But whatever he's doing, it pays well enough to frequent all the Michelin star restaurants. I feel nauseous. There seems to be a new gorgeous influencer model on his arm every week, even though he only moved here less than a year ago. Of course. Jae Lee never went dateless in his life. And all his ex-girlfriends beg to be friends with him afterward, too, based on all the hearted messages. Wait. I peer at my phone. He went on safari? In Africa? Posed with wildlife conservationists? There's an actual lion in this picture. A lion!

And . . . Paris.

Wait. He went to freakin' Paris.

I feel hollowed out and sad as he's perched near the base of the Eiffel Tower, arms outstretched, huge smile on his face.

My stomach twists with envy.

Paris was where I was supposed to go on my honeymoon.

I shut my laptop with an irritated sigh, envy burning a hole in my gut. Jae's account should come with a warning label, like all those random prescription drug ads. *Looking at Jae Lee's profile might bring on a severe and untreatable case of Life Envy. Some patients experience feelings of despair, wanting to jump out the nearest window, scream as loud as they can, pull out all their hair, and/or murder Jae Lee. If you have Life Envy lasting more than eight hours, or sudden, violent homicidal thoughts, contact your doctor immediately.*

Might as well rehash how he was state tennis champion, and I didn't even make it past the first round of regionals. How he won prom king by leading a viral flash mob dance, while I was never even asked.

Despite being an egomaniacal jerk for most of high school, he was never the smoking wreckage that people cheered to see burn.

My phone pings again.

Can't wait to catch up—in person, Namby, Jae texts. *Bye for now.*

TWO

Jae

Voted most likely to succeed.

Voted Most Popular.

Voted Best Dance Moves.

Voted winner of the talent show (with brothers) for Best Boy Band.

Voted most likely to form his own boy band.

Voted Most Likely to Be Internet Famous.

Voted Most Likely to Be Just Plain Famous.

Voted Most Likely to Be Freakin' Awesome.

Voted Most Likely to Throw an Amazing Party.

JAE LEE, CLASS OF 2010

Voted most likely to spend Saturday night in the library.

NAMI REID, CLASS OF 2010

So, texting Namby might've been a jerk move. But I'm kind of known for jerk moves, so it's on-brand. Besides, it's fun playing mind games with the former Hall Monitor from Hell. She gave me so many tardy slips senior year, I could practically paper my bedroom wall with them. Honestly, she was rumored to be the queen of killing a party vibe, for good reason. If she showed up at your kegger, the police weren't far behind.

Except for that one time. My graduation party. My parents had taken a trip to see my uncle in South Korea, and my brothers and I took the opportunity, as all adolescents would, to throw *the* party of parties that everyone talked about for months. I have a flash of her, hair askew, hiccupping after downing a half cup of rum and Coke, as she performed her version of the running man before she stumbled straight into my mom's hydrangea bushes. If I'd ever seen that version of Namby again—the one that stops lecturing everyone else long enough to let loose a little—we might have been friends. But she went to the University of Chicago, and I went to the University of Pennsylvania, and that was that.

But it's her drunken version of the hustle that I thought of when I arranged a meeting with Namby's partner, Dell. I'd heard through the grapevine he was unhappy at Toggle. And as I expected, he had a laundry list of complaints. Nami, he says, doesn't care about the bottom line. She's got pie-in-the-sky dreams about utopian workplaces, but no one will have a place to work if she keeps it up. She asked the partners—the *partners*—to forgo dividends and pay when the pandemic hit! Just to keep the lights on and make sure employees were paid. Dell was really hot about that one. How dare she care more about the staff than the owners? Was she a Communist? He was actually worried.

It doesn't surprise me that Namby is all too concerned about the rules, and doing what's right, and, more importantly, *telling* everyone she's right. In high school, Namby's black-and-white view of the world (tardy is tardy, no exceptions) was annoying, but even I can admit I've never met a competitor as fierce or as unrelenting as she was. I haven't faced such a worthy adversary in . . . I don't know how long.

I actually thought landing my dream job as the youngest VP of acquisitions for Rainforest, the company everyone loves to hate, would be more challenging than it actually turned out to be. But the job is . . . kind of easy, and more than a little boring. I should be thrilled to be paid what I am, doing what I'm good at, and yet, lately, I'll admit, I've lost my lust for it. I've found myself thinking more and more about the days before Rainforest, before my MBA from Wharton, back in high school when Namby's razor-sharp competition kept me on my toes.

Lately, I've begun to think one of our AI assistants, Treely, could do my job. Just like now, sitting in this cramped little conference room of the AI company Hal. We're buying them because we heard Joust was interested in them, and anything Joust wants, we have to get first. Joust is our single biggest tech competitor, gobbling up new tech faster than we gobble up big-box stores. Joust is the Rainforest of tech and social media.

But Rainforest wants to be the Rainforest of everything. Some people call it world domination.

I call it winning.

Like all Rainforest acquisitions, this should be an easy deal. We should just be signing the purchasing papers and moving on with our lives. Except one of the owners suddenly found his conscience at the eleventh hour.

I get it. Who wants to sell to the Big Bad Company Everybody Loves to Hate, Yet Still Orders from Anyway? We'll gut the company, steal the goods, and probably lay off half the staff—half if they're lucky. We're not going to win any Nobel Prizes.

But if you want to keep your little piggy house, then don't invite the wolf over for dinner. That's all I'm saying. Hal's partners—all of them—sent the wolf a gilded invitation. That's why I'm here.

And before you get on me about being a wolf, there are just two kinds of people in this world: wolves and pigs. I'm not going to apologize for being higher on the food chain.

One of Hal's partners is in mid-impassioned plea to the other four about why they should consider rejecting my deal. My *very* generous deal. Overly generous, if you look at their projected third-quarter earnings. The deal means everybody at this table will get promoted to the top 1 percent with a single instant wire transfer.

I hate wire transfers. Honestly, I think if I got to bring big cartoon bags full of money, then nobody would have a last-minute change of heart. They'd look at the big burlap bag with the green dollar sign on it and not say one word.

Because I already know all of this is just for show.

"I just don't think Rainforest aligns with the values we set up when we began this company, and do we really want to sell out—" the partner is saying. He's wearing a hemp poncho, a man bun, and gladiator sandals to a business deal. He wants people to think he cares about things like a livable wage, but I'd bet my stock options he only uses progressive talking points to impress his dates. When it comes to his own lifestyle, he's more than happy to be in the 1 percent of the 1 percent and complain about the capital gains tax.

I clear my throat. "Jim—"

"It's Jake."

"Right. Jake." I flash an apologetic smile. I got his name wrong on purpose. It's my way of keeping him off balance. After all, wolves don't need to know piggy names. I'm not here to network.

"What's wrong with selling out?" I ask.

Poncho Jake looks at me, confused.

"No, I mean it. What's wrong with selling out? Do you plan to offer your employees permanent work? Their children work? Their grandkids? Where does the obligation end, Jake?" I chuckle, as do a few others. I glance around the table, meeting the eye of Rainforest's legal counsel, Maureen. She's been at a million of these deals and knows what's coming next, but she shuffles the contract papers before her, dark hair up in a French twist, face impassible behind her thick, clear glasses. "I mean, come on, this isn't a noble's lands in the Middle Ages."

Two of the other partners smile. One chuckles.

"As we've discussed, Rainforest will keep some of your employees." Key word: some. Maybe, technically, a handful. Until we get the knowledge we need from them, and then they're gone, too. "Or you can keep the company. By all means, don't sell. Go ahead straight into that third-quarter earnings report, which will completely tank your ability to go public in the fourth quarter. Ask yourselves: Will your investors back you for one more round? What do *they* want? And if they don't back you, then what? You'll have to come right back to us, Jake. Right back and ask us to buy you. But by then, maybe we've bought your competitor, Aragon. We don't want to do that. You're better than Aragon, and Rainforest wants the best, but if you play hardball with us, then we'll have no choice. Then we buy Aragon. And we're not interested in buying you anymore. Then where are your employees? Out of work and still out of options. And now, even you can't help them."

Jake goes pale. Worried murmurs pass between his other partners at the table. I know I sound like an asshole. But I'm actually just telling some hard truths. The thing is, I've known a million Jakes. They're not really hung up on principle. They're just virtue-signaling with no real intent on follow-through. In the end, he wants to take the money—he just wants to feel good about it. That's all. He wants to be able to tell everybody that he had no choice.

That's where I come in.

I don't give him a choice. I give him an out. It's all he really wants.

"So, this way, some of your employees continue on. Others leave. You and your partners get aptly compensated, and you have the freedom to, say, fund severance packages for those who don't want to work for us or who can't. Or you want to be really innovative? Set up your own fund to help your employees who want to start their own companies."

I lean forward in my chair, elbows on the table, and make deliberate eye contact with each of the partners, lingering the longest on Poncho Jake. "You can still be the good guys here."

I know Poncho Jake won't share his proceeds for severance funds or microloans. In the last year, only one person ever did that. One. Out of probably two dozen companies. But they like to *think* they would.

My phone vibrates. It's Dad calling. I consider sending him to voicemail, but this would be a good time to let Poncho Jake marinate.

"You all think about it. I've got to take this." I head to the conference room door. "Hello?"

"Jae-Yeon." Dad's stern, deep voice feels choppy in my ear. He always uses my full name. There's no informality, hardly ever. He worked hard to lose his accent since immigrating from South Korea for med school, but it still lingers despite his best efforts.

"Hi, Dad."

"You will be at Sunday dinner." Dad never asks a question. He always speaks in definitive statements, just like he does in the operating room where he performs general surgeries, repairing hernias or taking out an appendix.

"Yes, Dad. I'll be there. Wouldn't miss our monthly Lee family gathering—or your delicious bulgogi."

Dad grunts, almost derisively. He never accepts a compliment. It's kind of like praising a stone wall. Also, his childhood in South Korea with his ultra-traditional and conservative dad who escaped from North Korea means that he thinks accepting compliments is the same as bragging, a cardinal sin. He moved to the U.S. after he met my Hawaiian-born mom, who was teaching his English class in South Korea. They both moved to Chicago, so Dad could go to med school and Mom could teach at a local Korean school.

"You will be bringing a date."

"Uh, no. Sorry, Dad. No date." I haven't actually brought a date to family dinner in years. Because anytime I do, Dad, Mom, and my brothers turn it into a nightmare game show, called "Who Wants to Be Jae's Wife"? Also known as "Let's Ask Uncomfortable Personal Questions" like: *Will you use Korean names for your children? And . . . but why not?*

Yeah. No thanks.

"You need to bring a date. Your brothers have . . ."

"Dates. I know." But they're not the oldest. There's less pressure on them. Nobody cares if they marry. It's somehow all about me. About *me* carrying on the family name, when the last I checked, we all were Lees. I glance through the big glass window of the conference room. Poncho Jake is weakening. The other partners are convincing him. One even pushes the contract papers over for him to sign. "Dad, I've got to get back to my business meeting."

"Business." Dad snorts the word in distaste. "It's for men who like the sound of their own voices. You should go to med school." Dad doesn't believe any career is worthwhile unless it requires a medical or law degree. "Like Cheol-Yeon."

Charlie, the youngest, a hotshot cardiovascular surgeon who blares Metallica in the operating room.

"Or law school—if you must. Like Sang-Yeon."

Sam was the black sheep in the family for about a second when he broke the news he'd be taking the LSAT senior year, and not the MCAT.

"Not interested, Dad." Never mind that I'm probably making *twice* Dad's surgical salary in my job. But Dad has rigid views on careers. He doesn't want to understand companies like Rainforest. "But trust me, I'm doing just fine in my career."

"You should do something meaningful with your life, Jae-Yeon. Delivering boxes isn't doing *good.*"

"We do more than deliver boxes," I say.

"Working for Rainforest is not how you'll attract a good wife."

Dad speaks about dating as if we're all peacocks, and need to preen our feathers to attract a mate. I glance at Poncho Jake through the glass walls, signing the papers, as expected. I'm a little sad he caved so easily. "I'll be fine, Dad."

"Business come and go, but everyone always needs a doctor. Or a lawyer. These professions have longevity. They help you contribute. To society. This company you work for. What does it really do?"

"You mean aside from employing more than one million people?"

Dad makes a disapproving sound in his throat. "Bigger isn't necessarily better."

The worst part of this conversation is that part of me agrees with him. When I took the job at Rainforest, I thought I might be able to have more influence inside the company, change the dynamic and make the culture better for employees, and even for the companies we take over. But then, I just realized the world is full of Poncho Jakes. No one really cares about making the world a better place. They only care about the bottom line. And it would be foolish to believe different. My job now feels predictable. In some ways, kind of sad. I never thought about cartoon bags of money before Rainforest.

"You should do something more worthwhile," Dad says now. "Besides, you are the oldest, Jae-Yeon. You have responsibilities. You have to carry on the family name."

"Yes, Dad. But, sorry. I have to go. I'll call you."

I hang up before Dad can launch into his full *You're failing me as my eldest son* speech. I tuck my phone in my pocket and try to shake off Dad's disappointment. I don't know why it should bother me: I've been disappointing Dad for as long as I can remember, for the crime of not being a carbon copy of him. I wonder if I'll ever stop caring. Part of me worries that I won't. Part of me worries I will.

I exhale out my frustration and head back into the boardroom. I tell myself that even though this job might bore me, what I do is still worthwhile. After all, they pay me well enough to do it.

Besides, Dad won't ever understand what I do, and that's okay. It's just like trying to explain to him what trick-or-treating is on Halloween.

They give candy for free if you dress like the fool, he once said. *A piece of candy? Is your dignity worth so little?*

Some things he'll never truly understand.

I push through the conference room doors. "Do we have a deal?" I ask, confident we already do. The usual buzz of anticipation I used to feel on the edge of the win is notably absent. It's what I've started to call the Rainforest Effect.

Poncho Jake reluctantly reaches out and shakes my hand, but there's a smile on his face. "Yes," he says. "We have a deal."

"Glad to hear it." I clap him on the shoulder.

Go on then, spend your yacht money guilt free, Jake. And you're welcome.

I should feel elated, but instead it just feels like an empty win. The partners are in high spirits now, with more handshakes. Someone busts out a champagne bottle from the mini fridge in the corner and pops the cork with a celebratory panache. Plastic flutes are quickly filled and distributed.

I feel less like a victorious wolf, and more like a caged Pomeranian.

My phone dings in my pocket.

It's Namby.

> No need to come see me. My status? Still think you're the Evil Undead. Now you can save yourself a visit. We're all caught up.

I have to laugh. Good old Namby. She hasn't changed a bit. Something warm and bright lights up in me. There's nothing about Namby that's easy or predictable.

I type a quick response. *Can't wait for you to tell me that to my face.*

In your boardroom. With one of your partners and at least half the board wanting to sell, and the other seriously thinking about it.

And their votes will cancel yours. Or will they? It's been a long, long time since I wasn't sure of an outcome of an offer. The challenge of it lights the fire of competition in me. Someone might be letting the wolf out of his cage.

> *Why don't you let me know where and when?*
> *Then I can make sure to bring a crucifix and holy*
> *water.*

My fingers slide quickly across my screen.

> *What? And spoil all the fun? FYI: Vampires*
> *are sexy now.*

> *Ha. Right. Only a rabid werewolf would swipe*
> *right on you.*

> *Jealous?*

Namby's answer appears almost instantly. *Of your sad zombie self? Please. We both know that the only way you'd ever get brains is to eat them.*

I bark a genuine, surprised laugh.

I forgot how much I used to love our mutual insults. We clashed like this all the time in the hallways, lobbing insults at each other faster than anybody else could keep track. Nobody could keep up with me like Namby. And it never felt so good to land an insult. She was always so determined to prove she was better than everyone else. Bringing her down a peg will be delicious.

You say I don't have brains, but you're the one who has no clue. Have you guessed when I'll see you yet? I can't help teasing her.

> *Who says I care?*

Please. Namby. You wouldn't be texting
right now if you didn't.

I see the dots appear, and then disappear. As she types and probably deletes her response. Then . . .

Glad to see you've managed to find some
humility after all these years. And you're right.
I've been dreaming up reasons to text you
for a decade. This is all working out exactly
as I planned. Also, I might be the bearer of
bad news, but the universe does not, actually,
revolve around you.

Oh, this is going to be good. So, so, very good.

You can try to humble me when you see
me.

She whips back quickly: *Game on.*
Oh, yes, please.

THREE

Nami

Live every day like it's Taco Tuesday.
Because a day without tacos won't kill you, but why risk it?

#DAILY INSPIRATION CHANNEL
TOGGLE INTERNAL CHAT

My stomach ties itself into knots on the way to Mom's house that very evening. I've convinced myself Jae might be coming to the surprise (not such a surprise) party Mom and Sora are throwing for me tonight.

And, yes, I know about it. Neither one of them can keep a secret. Sora nearly blurted out the truth when she awkwardly asked for my friends' contact info, and Mom made me swear—three separate times—to text when I was on my way. If the Illuminati ever want to go public, they should just text my sister or my mom and ask them to "keep some cabal stuff quiet." It would be public domain within two hours.

They know how I feel about birthday parties (See: Lotza Cheese Pizzeria). Technically, if they'd told me in advance, I might have suddenly come down with a mystery fever an hour before. This way, I can't duck out of the party without admitting I already know about it. Catch-22.

Will Jae be there? I'm starting to really, seriously worry he will be. And yet, I don't know why I care. But I do. All those weird cryptic messages about seeing me? I mean, I couldn't ask Mom or Sora if he's coming without *also* admitting I know about the surprise party. I feel exposed. Unnerved. I almost want to take out my phone and ask Jae point-blank if he's here tonight. But I know I won't get a straight answer. Never from him. He's the same cocksure jerk he was in high school.

My rideshare pulls up near Mom's driveway, which is already crowded with cars (subtle, much?) and my stomach twists into a tighter knot as I try to press out the wrinkles in my linen jumpsuit. I don't hop out right away, and instead just sit. I know none of my Toggle family is going to be there, because they tried to get me to join them after work for a birthday drink. When I told them about the surprise party, they were more surprised than I'm supposed to be, which means they weren't invited. Which again makes me worry about who is.

"Um . . . miss?" My rideshare driver, a silver-haired grandfather named Julio, makes eye contact with me in the rearview mirror as we sit in my mother's driveway. "Uh, is this the right address?"

"Yes." We're sitting in front of Mom's adorable little bungalow, her green grass and neatly trimmed shrubs showing how much she cares about the place. I glance at the cars in the driveway, recognizing Sora's, and my aunt and uncle's car. Family is here in force. The heat that began this morning just got worse over the course of the day, and even the breeze from Lake Michigan nearby won't offer too much relief from the thick wall of humidity. I'll take all of Julio's weak AC filtering through his gray sedan for as long as I can, especially since I already have an impressive nervous sweat going.

Maybe Jae won't be there. But then . . . if he's not . . . who will be? College friends? Law school? High school? The same ones who greedily gobbled up all the posts about my canceled wedding, gleefully whispering behind my back?

"It's a surprise party for my thirtieth birthday and . . . I just want to give everyone time to hide."

"Oh! *Feliz cumpleaños!*" He grins. "You do not look thirty! My goodness!"

"Aw. Thank you." The blowout was worth the money even if it dies a slow frizzy death in the humidity.

"You will . . . not be surprised?" Julio seems sad for me.

"I'm okay with it. I've had enough surprises this year."

Like having to eat the deposits on my wedding venue and caterer. Like missing my honeymoon in Paris. Like not being able to return my already altered dream wedding dress, so I have it, hanging in the closet at home in a plastic black death shroud, an eight-thousand-dollar reproach of my life choices.

Me—the perfectionist—reminded at all times: my life is nowhere close to perfect.

And Jae will probably be there just to rub my face in it.

"Uh . . . Miss Birthday Girl?" Julio shoots me a concerned glance in the rearview. He's trying to be nice about it, but the man has other people to pick up.

"Sorry, Julio. Yes, I'm going." I double his tip since he's wasted so much time in the driveway, and I give him a five-star review.

His phone dings. "Oh, *muchas gracias!*" he gushes, holding up his screen.

I open Julio's back door and slide out where the heavy July heat wraps me up like an electric blanket set on high, reminding me that there truly are two seasons in Chicago: winter and July. I watch with dread as Julio backs out of the driveway, waving at me as he goes. I fight the urge to run after him. Maybe I could still catch the Toggle developers at happy hour.

No. Not worth upsetting Mom. Or Sora.

I take a deep breath and head to Mom's back fence. I'm already starting to sweat as I traverse the short bit of asphalt, wobbling in my platform espadrilles, late to my own surprise party. Which, I guess, is better than being early.

My throat feels thick. I stare at Mom's fence latch. I just need to open the door to the backyard. I think about my ex, Mitch, angry that he's not here to push me into this party with a firm, steady hand. *Go on, babe,* he'd say. *The beers aren't going to drink themselves.* He might have been lazy, self-centered, and unfaithful, but he was a dependable plus-one.

I grab the latch like it's his throat. I jiggle it loudly.

Mitch isn't here. It's just me. All alone. Per usual. If life has taught me anything, it's that the only person you can ever really trust is yourself.

Okay. Deep breath. Ready, set . . . I swing open the gate.

I'm met, as expected, with a small throng of people shouting, "Surprise!"

There's my sister. Her fiancé, Jack. Mom. Grandma Mitsuye. Aunt Aiko. Uncle Rod. Our bevy of mainland cousins (half redheaded from the Scottish side, half jet-black from the Japanese, looking like some patchwork United Nations subcommittee meeting). And . . . no Jae.

Okay, good.

Except, I'm kind of disappointed.

I tell myself that it's only because I wanted to get whatever sick plan Jae has in store over with as quickly as possible.

"Surprise! Happy birthday!" Mom calls, jumping out at me from behind the grill on her deck, her sleek black bob bouncing, as she looks her ageless, Japanese-American self. I realize, belatedly, she's filming me. From my worst possible angle.

"Oh! Wow!" I try to act surprised.

"We're *livestreaming*!" she singsongs, pointing the lens at me. "Isn't this great? Aren't you so happy? We worked so hard on this, and we just knew you'd love it. You love it, don't you?" Mom is so hopeful. Her need is so clear on her face: *I need you to be happy about this, Nami. Be happy or I'll be unhappy.* When things in my life are going well, this isn't hard to deliver. But since the breakup with Mitch, it's all become harder. Mitch was a jerk, so it's not like I miss him exactly, but I do miss all the things I planned to do with him: tour Paris, buy a house, have a family. But being unhappy around Mom isn't really an option. It's been the same undercurrent of extortion since I was little. *My job is to make you happy, and yours is to pretend, even if you're not.*

Those thoughts are terrible and selfish, so I push them way down inside and vow never to let them out again. Mom is amazing. She's dealt with so much in the last three-plus years, losing Dad and the future retirement they'd planned. The least I can do is pretend everything in my life is perfect and that this party is exactly what I wanted.

I plaster on a fake smile. "Aw, thank you, Mom. This is . . . so awesome. Really. Awesome. Awesome!" How many times am I going to say "awesome"? Too many more and she'll start to catch on that I don't think it's awesome at all. I never even normally use that word. My fake smile is starting to hurt my cheeks but we're livestreaming, so I can't let down my guard.

Sora steps forward, followed by her lumberjack baker boyfriend—er, I mean fiancé—Jack. Sora looks gorgeous, per usual, without even trying. She's curvy and perfect, and I don't even think she's wearing makeup. She's got on a petal-pink sundress that's defiantly wrinkle-free, and makes it look like she walked out of a Renaissance painting. She throws on the first thing she randomly grabs from her closet and always looks amazing. I frankly both admire and envy her *c'est la vie* attitude. She never overthinks things like I do. She's got that blush of love on her cheeks—still. Not to mention the gorgeous carat-and-then-some princess-diamond engagement ring on her finger, which nearly blinds me in direct sunlight. I send her a silent mayday message with my eyes.

"That's enough livestreaming, Mom," Sora says, tapping Mom on the shoulder. "Happy birthday, sis." She pulls me into a hug, holding on a bit too long. Sora's really been the one to treat me with super kid gloves since Mitch. I lived with her a bit after the breakup, when I was an emotional wreck who'd burst into tears about the most random things, like a freshly opened box of Cheerios. At that time, everything reminded me of Mitch. I'd spent months apologizing for how I'd behaved planning the wedding. I'll always be grateful to Sora for not holding that time against me—when I lashed out at everyone about wedding details. Now I can see I was so unhappy because I knew Mitch wasn't right for me. I funneled all my doubt and fear into bridesmaids' dresses and cake selections.

While Mom wants to hurry right past any emotional discomfort, Sora's the opposite: she worries endlessly that I say I'm okay when I'm actually not. Growing up, we couldn't be more different. Sora was calmer and more Zen. I was always the one losing my temper or crying, whipped around by my emotions that always seemed Category 5 to Sora's low-grade tropical storms. The rage, heartbreak, and borderline depression following Mitch scared her. Reminded her that I was more temperamental, like Dad, than she was.

I squeeze her back in the hug, a nonverbal assurance: *I'm okay. Really.*

She pulls back, doubt in her eyes, even as I glance around the crowd, thinking again about Jae. Maybe he's hiding in the hydrangeas.

"Are you looking for Fatima?" Sora asks, looking pained. She pulls me over away from Mom's camera.

Actually, right up until Sora mentioned it, it didn't occur to me to look for Fatima Bibi, my best friend since sixth grade. We bonded on the mathletes team when we realized we both hated big crowds and loved Sour Patch Kids. Sure, we haven't been as close since she got married and moved to the suburbs, but I thought we always had an unspoken pact to show up for each other at things like this. But she's actually not here.

"Her baby's got a fever. She called just a half hour ago."

"Oh."

"And Desmond and Ramone were going to come, but their adoption went through," Sora explains quickly. "They had to fly to New York this morning to pick up the baby." As Sora talks, I realize, glancing around the party, that I'd been so fixated on finding Jae, I missed the fact that nearly everybody else here is a blood relative. "And Ava had a house closing today that's running long. She's going to try to come after."

"She's coming late to a surprise party?" I glance around, suddenly realizing the crowd in Mom's backyard is barely a throng.

"Yeah." Sora looks pained. She hugs me, too tightly. She releases me, eyes pleading. "We really tried. We did. Really."

It really hits me then.

The dwindling followers on social media and the giggly shared posts of my downfall weren't just coincidences.

I might actually not have any real friends—outside of Toggle—anymore.

"I guess this is what it means to be thirty," I say, but the joke falls flat, and Sora and Jack study me with concern.

"No, thirties are great," Sora declares quickly. "Really."

"Oh, yeah. Better than the twenties, for sure," Jack adds. And then they both stare at each other with complete adoration, making me wonder if they think that only because they met each other in their thirties. I want to believe my thirties will be better than my twenties, I do. But then I'm reminded life is a pinball machine, set to tilt.

"So-dah?" I hear the voice of my eighty-seven-year-old Japanese grandma behind me, calling my sister. She says her name with the Japanese *r*, which almost sounds like the *t* in "water." "So-dah? Where's Nami?"

"She's right here, Grandma," Sora says, leading her to my side. Mom hovers nearby, too, thankfully with her camera stowed.

"Grandma Mitsuye!" I say, brightening.

"Ah! Nami!" She sounds so excited I can't help but be touched. When she bustles out to the edge of the deck, she's wearing a short-sleeved blouse that's bedazzled with blue gem-topped buttons and her silver hair falls to her chin in a sleek bob. She beams with pure love as she walks to me, arms out. She's soft and tiny, and smells like jasmine.

"You've gotten so tall!" she says, stepping back, as if I'm ten again. I don't want to tell her I think she might be shrinking.

"Heels, Grandma," I explain, pointing down to my cork wedges that give me an added three inches.

"Oh!" She laughs good-naturedly. "Silly me!" Then she frowns. "Where's that boy of yours?"

Dread pinches my stomach. "Boy?"

"Mitch?"

Oh no . . . Even Grandma Mitsuye misses Mitch's bland agreeableness as a plus-one.

Sora and Jack exchange a panicked look. Mom, nearby, jumps in like a battlefield medic. "Mama!" she chides. "Remember, I told you. Nami and Mitch broke up." Confusion passes across Grandma Mitsuye's face, but the damage is done as Mom leads Grandma away to the snack table.

"Nami. Wine. Stat," Sora says, grabbing me by the arm. She and Jack usher me away from Grandma Mitsuye, the two of them urgently working triage, as Jack grabs the nearest bottle of white from the beverage table, and Sora digs around for the wine opener.

"It's okay. Really," I say, even as I feel a wave of regret thinking about Mitch, and the years of my life I wasted on him. Putting him first, and my own friends second. It's really no wonder none of them showed, if I'm honest.

"Do you want wine? Or tequila?" Sora asks, concerned. She's about to issue a weather alert on my emotional hurricane. But I'm okay. I want to tell her there's no need to worry or fuss about me. I'm okay. Well, not totally okay. But okay . . . enough.

"Wine is fine. Really."

Jack expertly slides the cork out. Sora grabs a glass, and before I know it, I'm holding a generous pour of some unknown white.

"To Nami!" Jack says, clinking his glass to ours. The two of them have been a lifesaver for me this last year, and I'm grateful for them. They were both so patient, letting me be the third wheel on countless dinners and dates. Jack is like the big brother I never had, and he's good for Sora.

"Thanks, team. Cheers." We all drink. The wine is crisp and dry and just what I need. What do I have to be sad or mad about? My family is here. Jae isn't. And neither are any social media gawkers. Isn't that a better-case scenario than I'd imagined in the rideshare?

"How is the wedding planning coming?" I ask Sora, hoping to think about something other than my wreckage of a life.

"Badly," she admits, voice low. "Mom is . . ."

"Taking over?" I already know this too well. Mom means well. She thinks she's helping, but if you let her, she'll simply plan the wedding *she* wants. We had a dozen fights about my failed wedding. I let her have the expensive dress boutique, even though I wanted to go to a trunk show outlet to save a few bucks. Now, the big zippered garment bag taking up a third of my closet reminds me I'd be at least eight thousand dollars richer if I'd stuck to my guns.

"Yes," Sora sighs, looking pained. "I don't know how to tell her no."

"You've got to be firm and direct. If you give Mom wiggle room, she'll take it."

The look on Sora's face tells me she's already given Mom more than wiggle room, and she's now moved in, unpacked all of her belongings, and claimed squatter's rights.

"It'll all be okay," Jack says, sliding his arm protectively around Sora. "We'll work it out."

Sora glances up at him with grateful, adoring eyes, and Jack beams down at her, too. I feel a pang of envy. What's it like to have a solid partner in your corner? One to help you tackle life's Big Problems? I wish I had someone like that to help me navigate the mess that is Toggle funding. The fear that everything I've built is balancing on a knife's edge is never far from my mind. When I think about Toggle and how close it might be to failing . . . I feel a dark, deep dread that threatens to choke me.

I wish I had a Jack to talk to about it. Because when someone looks at you the way Jack is looking at Sora, you just know that no problem is too big for them to tackle together.

I don't think Mitch ever looked at me like that. Given that he was always staring at the first-person shooter video games he played every night, I know he didn't.

From across the lawn, Mom waves at us. "Oh, that means it's cake time," Sora says. "Jack?"

"On it," Jack declares, heading toward the freestanding garage, where Mom keeps her second fridge.

"I'll get the paper cake plates," Sora pipes in. "They're inside."

"I'll get them," I offer. "You go help Jack."

"You don't have to . . ."

"Really. I don't mind." Keeping those two apart feels like a crime. I head inside and my phone vibrates in my pocket.

Jae has sent me a gif of a dancing zombie. I feel laughter bubble up in my throat. What does it say about my life when getting a text from my nemesis perks me up? I send back a gif of a samurai-sword-wielding zombie killer.

I glance up, noticing Mom waving at me from the patio door. Jack, award-winning baker, is putting candles in a cake. I grab the stack of paper plates from the island and hesitate.

Give me a hint, I text Jae, and immediately regret it. Why am I even asking?

Sure. Wear sunscreen. Then you'll be less likely to get skin cancer.

That's not a HINT. That's a TIP.

Same difference? Then laughing face emoji. Devil face. Damn him.

What is the cryptic you'll "see me very soon" mean?

                         I could tell you, but then it would spoil all the fun.

I hate surprises.

I know. Devil face again. Dammit.

If it's not my birthday, then . . . what? I hate not knowing. I glance out at the party and notice they're still setting up the cake.

Imani pings my phone then. *It's official. No series D.*

My heart sinks. That deep dark dread fills my throat. My stomach feels like one dark pit of panic.

     For sure?

                         I did what I could. I just couldn't work the magic this time.

I glance at the phone, feeling all the hope drain out of me. We have two options now: sell or go public. And with our earnings the last year, going public would be a disaster. I sink into the loveseat, paper plates in hand. I hadn't realized until right this moment how much I had really been counting on that funding to come through. Imani's always been able to work miracles.

The sliding glass door opens again, and I glance up and see Grandma Mitsuye.

"Oh, there you are, Nami!" She bustles in and sits down right next to me. "You're smart to be in here with the air-conditioning." She fans her face and smiles at me, her adorably wrinkled face impossible not to love. She pats my knee. "I am sorry about . . . earlier." She shakes her white-gray head. "I forget things sometimes!" She pantomimes giving her forehead a slap. "I'm not young like I used to be." She shakes her head. "I have to remind myself to slow down. Be careful with what I say. I'm not in my seventies anymore."

At this, I have to laugh. Not in her seventies anymore?

"How did you feel about turning thirty, Grandma?"

"Terrible," she says, swiping at her face as if she's trying to shoo off a fly. "But the thirties aren't that bad. You still have your face and your figure. The forties? Eh . . ." She sighs. "At least, if you put on makeup, you'll look good."

"What about the fifties?"

"It's a slow downhill slide from there." She laughs, though, and slaps her knees, as if it's a wonderful inside joke that she'll share with me someday. Her laugh dies down, and her eyes shine with concern as she looks at me, *really* looks at me. I remember all those times when I was a little kid when she babysat Sora and me after school, all those scoops of cold red bean ice cream on her porch in the summer, all the times she'd spray antiseptic on my skinned knees and blow on my boo-boos. Grandma was always the soft place to land. "Are you doing all right?"

Am I? Am I doing all right? "I don't know," I admit. "I'm going to have to sell my company. Or it might go under. I worked so hard to build it, and so many people—good people—are counting on me, and now, I just . . . I don't know. If it fails, it'll be like . . ." I think about Mitch. ". . . everything I ever tried, I failed at."

Grandma makes a disapproving sound in her throat. "Since when do you let a little setback get you down? You've always been tough. I remember you—the daredevil, insisting on taking the training wheels off your bike *way* before anybody thought you were ready!"

Grandma Mitsuye had this amazingly long, sloping driveway,

where you could build up speed, and it's the place I learned to ride my little pink bike with the white tassels hanging from the handlebars. Of course, if you took the final lip of the driveway wrong, you'd be headed to the gravel. I did, more than once.

"You were like that saying: *Nana korobi ya oki.* Fall down seven times, get up eight, except you'd fall down twenty times, get up twenty-one! Do you remember? You stayed out in that driveway until the sun went down. You were so determined. And you learned to ride."

I try to drum up that amazing feeling of flying, balancing on the bike, no training wheels, nothing to catch me if I tottered. Now, it seems like everything is so much riskier. It's not just me flying off the bike if I fall. It's my whole team.

Grandma smiles at me. "That brave little girl? She's still in there." She points to my heart.

That's Grandma. Always in my corner, no matter what. "So, you'll make the right decision about your company. And your workers." She smiles at me. "In the meantime, I know what you need."

"What?" Wine? Xanax?

Grandma leans in, voice low. She raises a white eyebrow. "Cake— and ice cream."

I laugh. "Fair play, Grandma."

"So, what do you say? Help an old lady outside to go get dessert?" She nods to the door.

I stand and offer her my hand. Grandma takes it, heaving herself to her feet with some effort, though her knees do not creak. I follow her outside into the sticky July evening, where the sun is setting and purple dusk has settled on everything. A big white moon hangs over the tree line. The partygoers start up a chorus of "Happy Birthday." Jack is holding a beautiful white cake, flecked with gold leaf, and covered in lit golden candles.

The singing dies down.

"And many more!" Mom adds at the end, phone camera once more trained on my face. "Okay, make a wish!"

"Do I have to?" I joke.

Jack's eyes grow big. "You *have* to. The ancient Greeks put candles on cakes to honor the moon goddess, Artemis. If you don't make a wish, you might piss her off."

"Really?"

"Probably not. I mean, it's something a teacher at culinary school told me once." Jack grins at me. "But still. Make a wish. Wish big. You deserve it, kid."

I should wish not to have to worry about Toggle. I should wish for a miracle round of funding to save my company and my people. But then I glance over at Sora, who's smiling at Jack, their love brighter than the candles on my cake. They stare at each other with those amazing adoring eyes. I want that. Someone to look at me the same way Jack is looking at Sora. Like he's staring at his favorite person on earth. Because she is.

And they know that because they've known each other since kindergarten. Isn't that kind of amazing? Meeting your soulmate in kindergarten, and then bumping into each other as full-fledged adults, falling in love, and feeling like you've known each other nearly all your lives, because *you have*?

Maybe that was my problem with Mitch. I never really knew him. And that's why he disappointed me so badly.

I feel an ache in the very center of my chest like someone punched me there. I've spent the last year and a half throwing myself into work, convincing myself that I didn't care if I was single, but the stark truth is, I do care. There's a nagging terrible question bubbling up in my mind: What's wrong with me? There has to be something wrong, because people just keep leaving me. Mitch, social media friends, even people I thought were good friends, who didn't show tonight. The rejection, just another in a long line, stretching back through high school, back to the playground, the lingering hurt of not being good enough.

I squeeze my eyes shut.

I wish for my soulmate.

I blow across the little flames of light before I can change my mind, before I acknowledge how silly that wish is. Soulmate? I'm not even sure I believe in them. I might as well wish for a unicorn.

When I open my eyes, I've blown out all the candles, and a puff of smoke floats up to the ether, taking my wish with it.

"Hooray!" Grandma Mitsuye says joyfully, and applauds. "Now, let's eat cake!"

FOUR

Nami

No matter what, I'll always be here to catch you.

THE FLOOR
#DAILY INSPIRATION CHANNEL
TOGGLE INTERNAL CHAT

My surprise birthday party is far behind me the following Monday morning when I rush into the cool air-conditioning of the lobby of my building. Did I really wish for a *soulmate*? I should've wished to win the lottery so *I* could fund Toggle all by myself. Imani is back today from New York, ready to unpack the reasons why we're likely between a rock and a hard place. Why did I waste a wish on my stupid love life? Just because I felt lonely? Everybody's lonely. It's the modern condition.

What does it matter anyway? Birthday wishes don't come true, Artemis or no. If they did, I'd have gotten a life-sized Barbie pink Corvette for my eighth birthday.

I hurry away toward the elevator bank, which takes me straight up to the Toggle offices. I expect to see the whirl of activity, the throwing of Frisbees, the loud voices of happy programmers. Instead, it's eerily quiet. And all the programmers are sitting solemnly at their desks, eyes trained somberly on their screens. No Frisbees.

No tossed footballs. No loud debates about who should headline the next Comic Con.

Something is up.

I glance across the office and see that Dell's light is on.

Huh. So, he's in. But surely that doesn't account for all the glum faces. The Dell Effect isn't usually this drastic.

Arie sees me and slowly rises from his desk, fidgeting with his ID tag. Priya catches his eye and joins him as they both move to meet me.

"What's going on?" I ask, glancing around.

"We heard a rumor," Arie whispers.

"What kind of rumor?" Now, all the hairs on the back of my neck stand up.

Arie nervously untangles the cords of his ID lanyard as he glances at Priya. "We're being bought."

"Bought? By whom?" Panic runs through me. And why don't I know?

"We don't know who," Priya adds, voice low. "But they look intimidating. They're in our conference room." We all swivel at the same time to glare at the glass-walled conference room on the east side of the floor, which overlooks Lake Michigan. I see the backs of a few intimating-looking men already sitting at the table. There's just one woman among them. They're all wearing suits. Not even just blazers and jeans. Full, matching suits. Like they're all going to a funeral. I just hope it's not ours.

What the hell is going on?

Jamal wheels over. "Are we talking about the breakfast thieves?" he whispers.

Arie and Priya nod.

"Breakfast thieves?" I ask, confused.

"They already raided Breakfast Monday in the break room," Arie explains.

"Rude," I exclaim, and they all nod. Breakfast Mondays are sacred.

"The monsters hit the bacon breakfast sandwiches first." Jamal shakes his head mournfully.

"It's unacceptable," Priya says, and then she drops her voice. "And I don't know if it was them or Dell"—she says his name with added disgust—"who erased the *Star Trek* captain vote on the whiteboard."

"What?" I glance at them all, horrified. "That is not okay."

"So not okay!" Priya exclaims as everyone else circles around, nodding in hushed agreement.

I feel a hot flush of anger. Nobody treats my people this way.

I glance at Dell's office to see him lean against his desk. Dell is barrel-chested and doughy in the waist, and wears his thinning blond hair tucked under an SAE baseball cap. He's not alone in his office, either. Imani sits in one of his office chairs, looking her impeccable, Girl Boss self. She's got a decided style: bright patterns; thick, colorful-rimmed glasses; hair twisted into thick bantu knots. Today she has on bright yellow glasses and a yellow striped shirt. Her nonbinary spouse, Court, always jokes that you could find Imani from space, given her love of bright primary shades.

But why are they having a meeting without me?

"I'll be right back," I tell the team.

I march straight to Dell's open door.

"What's going on?" I ask, glancing from Imani to Dell and back. "Who stole the breakfast sandwiches and who's in the conference room?"

Imani crosses her long legs. "They're reps from Rainforest."

Rainforest. I feel the cold hand of fear grip the back of my neck.

Rainforest is the place where employees are disposable, and each user is a data mine. Their tagline might as well be: *Not Fun. And Definitely Evil.*

I feel like I've flown off my bike in Grandma Mitsuye's driveway, the asphalt knocking the wind out of me.

"Can we still go public?" I know it's a long shot. Part of me has always known selling might be the only option. But to Rainforest?

Imani sighs. "Our third-quarter earnings aren't going to be great so going public isn't the best option. We needed Series D to keep afloat, and since that's a no, selling might be our best option."

"B-but . . ." I stammer. I glance at Imani and Dell, neither of whom will meet my gaze. "Rainforest is evil."

"Please. Don't get your panties in a bunch." Dell sighs and rolls his eyes.

And there it is: the casual misogyny I love so much.

"We all know you want to be the little princess here, but you've got to stop being a Karen, and be realistic. We all have to live in the real world," he lectures me. I mentally tick off "princess" and "panties in a bunch" and "Karen" on my imaginary I Hate Women bingo card.

"Is the 'real world' the place where you ditch all your principles and betray your employees and app users for a quick payday because you're too lazy to look for other options?" I ask in my most lethal tone. "Just checking if we're on the same page, Dell."

Dell glares at me, silenced. He's not quick enough to come up with a retort because the wittiest banter he ever learned was in the basement of a fraternity house. His face goes splotchy and red, and right now, his beady, petulant eyes tell me that he wants to call me a name that would instantly win Misogyny Bingo.

Dell exhales, his eyes calling me that name. Again. And again. "Rainforest," he grits out, "could be our *only* option. And . . . our buy-sell agreement . . ."

"I know what our agreement says. I wrote it," I snap, annoyed, Dad's temper ignited in me. If two of the three partners agree to sell, the other has to sell. With approval from the board, of course, but as they're more than half investors, I can't see why they wouldn't approve a sale that would put money back in their pockets.

Still, I always imagined Dell to be the outlier, not me. I always thought Imani and I would be on the same page.

"Imani," I plead. "We can't sell to Rainforest. We don't need to listen to any of their arguments. They'll dismantle the company. Lay people off. Turn us into a data-mining machine and alienate all our users. We're Fun. Not Evil. But we'll *be evil* if we do this."

Imani looks pained, but determined. "There's no harm in listening to their offer," she tells me, but looks at Dell as she does. "The travel downturn killed us. And Joust has really eaten into our market share since they bought Vacay. We've got to do something."

"How about we just ask Joust if they're interested in buying us?" Joust isn't my favorite company of all time (see: questionable social media platforms that might be increasing teen depression and misinforming grandparents) but they do have a pretty good track record of treating their employees humanely. And they are Rainforest's only real competition.

"They already own Vacay. Why would they want us?" Dell crosses his arms across his chest.

"Total market domination?" I offer. "Besides, Vacay is trash. They have no safety checks in place. They don't even do background checks on their users! A convicted felon rented out his lake house and attacked someone there last week!"

"So, this is the argument you make that Joust is holier than Rainforest? Please." Dell rolls his eyes.

"At least Joust doesn't strip every company they buy," I argue. "If we're trying to protect our employees . . ."

"That's what you never understand," Dell says, shaking his head. "They're just *employees*. People get laid off all the time."

"They're not *just* employees, Dell," I counter. "They're family."

Dell lets out a disapproving sound like air leaking from a tire.

"We're *better* than Rainforest. *We're* good," I plead, which I know sounds like something a kindergartener would say, but still. "We stand for something. Don't we?"

"I get it," Imani tells me gently. "This isn't my first choice either. But we need to listen to them. If we shutter our doors, everyone is out of a job, and not just some of our employees. We do owe it to them to listen."

I know times are dire, but I never really wanted to believe a solution would come at the expense of all our values.

Dell stands. "Well, they've been kept waiting long enough. I'm headed in there."

I'm not ready.

"Meet you there," I say, thinking fast. "Going to grab coffee first." I leave Dell's office and put my bag in my office and grab my tablet and my empty coffee mug.

Arie hustles to my side, straightening the ID card around his neck.

"How bad is it?"

"It's Rainforest bad," I whisper.

Arie lets out an audible gasp. "The Borg? NO. We can't be bought by the Borg."

I nod, agreeing. Rainforest does kind of just take over everything and turn it into mini versions of themselves, bleaching out all individuality or dissent or . . . good. "I'll do what I can, I promise."

Arie nods, still shell-shocked as he walks back to his desk to break the news to the others.

I take the long route to the conference room straight by the break room, just to clear my head. Anger bubbles in my stomach, and that won't do me any good. I've got to stuff down my feelings and be clear-eyed and ready for whatever they throw at us.

Except I know what they're going to throw at us. Money. It's the only thing they have. And, unfortunately, they have plenty of it.

I see the corner of the Ping-Pong table and the big, oversized flat-screen on the wall, against the thick red-and-yellow stripes painted across the room. Two programmers, the knit-cap-wearing, clean-shaven variety, are staring at the near-empty buffet table, looking sad. Jamal and Priya were right. The tray of bacon breakfast sandwiches sits empty, save for a few measly crumbs. They left the egg-white ones with blanched kale untouched, I notice. And our whiteboard, which had been covered with votes for captains and laundry lists of reasons they're the best at going where no one has gone before, wiped clean. One programmer reaches for a tiny piece of broken bacon from the tray and eats it mournfully. He glances up at me, a crumb flaking down his shirt.

These are my people, and I can't let them be treated this poorly.

"Sorry about this," I tell them. "We'll have another Breakfast Monday tomorrow with extra bacon sandwiches." Even if I pay for it out of my own pocket.

The programmers smile weakly. I head to the end of the espresso bar, and hit the button on the machine that dispenses a quick mug of coffee into my World's Best Boss mug. I hurry off, following the bright orange line in the blue carpet toward the conference room, or Fishbowl as it's lovingly called by everyone, since it has only glass walls on all sides.

Dell's standing at the head of the table, glaring at me as I sweep into the room, that insult he can't say aloud beaming in his eyes as I take one of the only empty chairs near the door. Imani, already sitting, is nervous and that makes me nervous. A person who knew her less well wouldn't be able to tell, but I know what the rapid tapping of her fingers on the glass tabletop means. And when Girl Boss is nervous, the rest of us should be terrified. Behind her sit the conference room windows, showing a beautiful view of sparkling Lake Michigan, and the rooftops of shorter high-rises along the Magnificent Mile.

No one, however, is taking in the amazing view. I can't help but notice we Toggle partners seem underdressed. Imani and I are business casual, while Dell has outdone us in his cargo shorts and flip-flops and baseball hat. The Rainforest representatives sit solemnly on the other side in their funeral suits. We look like we've rolled in for a timeshare discussion because we all took the free airfare to the Caribbean. Rainforest looks like they're here to settle a billion-dollar lawsuit.

Six representatives, one woman, five men, all strangers except . . . Jae Lee.

His gaze meets mine as he swivels his chair to face me, the smug smile tugging at the corner of his mouth.

If anything, his perfectly angled Life Envy–inducing photos on social media don't do him justice. He's not only maintained his lean, state tennis champion self, if anything he's put on more muscle since high school. He's wearing an expensive crisp dark blue suit with a tasteful yet trendy windowpane pattern. Oxford shirt, no tie, unbuttoned at the neck. Slim handkerchief folded in his breast pocket, and a smartwatch on his wrist, everything about him screaming money and success. He looks annoyingly amazing.

Then it hits me all at once.

He works for Rainforest.

And *this* is what he meant by "See you soon."

Oh God. It isn't a social visit at all. It's a hostile takeover.

A slow, sly smile curves his mouth. "Hi, Namby," he says.

FIVE

Jae

I've never seen Nami Reid look so shocked—and so angry—to see me in all my life, and that includes the morning Principal Khan announced in his office that I'd edged her out for valedictorian by .25 points. I kind of want to take a picture, blow it up, and put it on my wall. I've missed her fury face all these years.

It's nice to see some things never change. That Nami is wound just as tightly as ever. She's also, I have to note, still breathtakingly beautiful. It's the one thing I forgot about Nami until now. She's like an aloof Asian goddess or *Vogue* cover model: lithe, willowy, and graceful; heart-shaped face perfectly symmetrical, hair too thick and too straight and too glossy to be real, eyelashes too unbelievably long, skin too perfect. Just like high school. It's why she always had a trail of lovesick puppies following her every move. It was no accident that the army of volunteer hall monitors under Nami's thumb were breakout-prone nerds who worshiped the ground she walked on.

"What the hell are you doing here?" Nami hisses at me, voice low, and her dark eyes sparking pure hate.

"My job," I reply easily, and my smile stretches bigger. Oh, this is even better than I imagined. I reach into my breast pocket and pull out a shiny, thick business card.

JAE LEE, VICE PRESIDENT OF DOMESTIC ACQUISITIONS, RAINFOREST

It's got our little Rainforest tree with the smiling monkey hanging out of it. Nami's mouth curls in disgust.

"Rainforest. Of course you work for them. Vice president? Was Abuser of Orphans taken? Chief Kicker of Puppies too?" Nami grumbles, voice barely a murmur, as she sets her tablet on the table in front of her.

"Those are hobbies," I whisper back, staring at my fingernails and not her. "What I really like to do is gut small little start-up tech companies, and sell them for parts."

I side-eye her. Nami's nostrils flare.

"Really—" Nami's voice is louder than she intends. Dell glances up, noticing. Imani, too, who raises a quizzical eyebrow. Nami grabs her phone, and bangs out a text.

> *Really, son of the devil? Seems small beans for you.*

Fine, we can play this game.

> *Endtimes needs to start somewhere. Might as well be with Toggle.*

Her lips press together in a thin, white line of pure rage. Her fingers curl so tightly around her coffee mug that I worry she'll burst the cup with her bare hands. Before she can bite out a reply, Dell stands and clears his throat.

"I'd like to personally thank Rainforest for joining us today," he begins. I nod at him. He glances uneasily at Nami. "We're so grateful you're here."

Nami chokes on her coffee. I glance at her mug. *World's Best Boss*? Seriously? Was that a joke? I can't even imagine it. Tattletale Namby?

She takes a sip and I see the other side. *Meant Un-ironically.*

Huh.

Nami catches me staring at her mug and covers it with both hands and glares at me. Then she notices my bacon breakfast sandwich, sitting on a small paper plate in front of me. She glares at it like she wants to give me detention for breaking some no-food-in-the-conference-room policy. I take a big bite, and she winces.

I whip out my smartphone and text her.

> *Bet you wish you had your detention pad.*

She glances down at her tablet, jabbing at the screen with pale pink fingernails.

> *I'd rather have a samurai sword, zombie.*

I grin. I type.

> *Am I a zombie or Satan? Pick your insult and stick with it.*

> *You deserve ALL the insults.*

> *Bring it. I'm still going to win.*

Over my dead body, she answers.

I type back, *Who's going to be the zombie then?*

I hear her exhale, sharply. I chuckle, though. Point, me.

Dell fires up his laptop, and the screen at the front of the room lights up with his presentation. Interesting. He doesn't have to sell us, we're here. This is for Imani's benefit.

Not sure where Imani lands, but I *know* Nami isn't going to sell to us. But that's the fun part. Finally, a challenge.

I flick a crumb off my lapel and pretend to listen to Dell talk about the amazing Toggle universe, and why Rainforest would be so lucky to have Toggle, when we both know the opposite is true. I feel Nami glaring at me. Burning a hole in my cheek with her eyes, gone solid black with rage. I'd forgotten how it felt to have Namby staring at me. She used to do it every day in calc, in English lit, Honor Society meetings, and tennis practice when she'd whiff on a volley because she'd be hate-glaring at me instead of watching the ball.

I take another bite of croissant and pick up my phone, mischief in mind. Despite me regularly sending her social connection requests, she's rejected every one.

I send her another follow request. Her tablet pings and she glances down at it. Thick, luscious eyelashes downcast. Beautiful shiny lips pursed into a perfect pink bow as she considers.

The frown line between her eyes gets deeper. She hits the tablet screen so hard with her perfect shell-pink nail I swear she breaks it.

I glance at my phone.

Request *denied.*

A little amused chuckle escapes my throat. This makes her glare harder at me.

> You really should've accepted the old ConnectIn
> request a few months ago. Then you would've
> known I moved here to work for Rainforest.
> Maybe you would've seen me coming.

I can almost hear her grinding her molars to dust.

*I think we both know accepting an invite
from the devil means selling one's soul.
My soul isn't for sale. Also, Imani is never
going to go for this buyout. You're wasting
your time.*

I glance at Imani, and see she's watching Dell's presentation intently. She *is* the wild card here, no doubt. But Dell is finishing up his little pitch, and now he's handing me the floor.

Showtime.

I feel a little tingle of nerves, just like the first day of kindergarten. Of course, my first day was worse than most. I showed up speaking almost entirely Korean, where everyone else there spoke English. Or Spanish. Not a single Korean speaker in the bunch.

Dad felt Korean-language preschool was the way to go, since my grandmother, who spoke very little English, was living with us at the time, and happened to be my primary caregiver during the day when both my parents were at work. Nobody bothered to consider what it would be like when I started at the public school, where the only second-language program was Spanish. Maybe it was then when I started second-guessing Dad's edicts from on high. I know better than most that Dad does make mistakes. Like the one that got me stuck in remedial classes in elementary school until I learned English.

I still, sometimes even all these years later, feel a pang of doubt when I speak in front of people. Like I'll open my mouth, and no one will understand me.

I push aside the old fear. I've got this. I'm not five anymore.

I put down my croissant and stand, buttoning my jacket. I send everyone along the conference room table my Disarming Smile. Time for the Amusing Story about my experience with Toggle . . . How I swapped time at my Chicago condo for a week at a beach house in Costa Rica on the app, but instead of a cute one-bedroom hut on a private beach . . . found a straw lean-to without running water and a llama living *inside*. And it was my fault, because I never swiped through all the pictures, and never did my homework or read the fine print. This is the story that brings the house down. It warms the most awkward of cocktail parties. Melts the chilliest of first dates. And, the thing is, I've got dozens of these stories. I love being the center of attention. And I've got a knack for it. Soon, I've got everyone at that table eating out of the palm of my hand.

Everyone except Nami.

She hasn't cracked a smile. Not once. I almost hear her disdainful eye roll from across the table, creaky and loud, as I talk about the llama chasing me into my own rental car. How can she not find that funny? I really want to know.

She sets down her coffee mug and crosses her arms, determined not to be taken in with anything I say. I'm strolling about the room now, making it my own. I add in a tidbit about the genius of Toggle and Imani gives me a head nod. I cross behind Nami, and I can see her back stiffen, and she clutches her hand around her stylus as if she's going to use it as a weapon and try to take out my eye. Does she think I'm going to attack her? Try out a reverse sleeper hold? I pause before I remember where I am in my story. I'm now transitioning to how Rainforest buying Toggle won't change Toggle. We believe in letting innovators innovate, and all that jazz. Blah, blah, blah. It's just what you all want to hear so you can run off with the big cartoon bag of money.

"Rainforest and Toggle have been flirting for a long time, but I'm so glad that we're finally going to prom," I say.

Dell claps, loudly. We all know where he stands. Imani, bless her, grins. I think I'm winning her over. This deal could be done by the end of the week.

"I have a question." Nami. I take my eyes off her for one second and she is coming for me. I should've been watching *her* the whole time. She's still holding her stylus like a dagger.

"Yes?" I flash her a smile. Her face twists in disgust as if I've just eaten a large cockroach.

"You say Toggle will get to 'be Toggle'? How are you going to guarantee that?" Nami clearly hasn't gotten the message that Toggle is in trouble.

"Well, you mean aside from being the most envied couple at prom?" I quip, and some in the room chuckle.

Nami doesn't even crack a smile. Prom, clearly, is a sore spot. Who did she go with again? I'm trying to remember.

"Well, if I were seventeen, I'd be thrilled. But, you know, hashtag adulting." She smiles at the table, a warm, blazing smile that blinds the room and temporarily steals anyone's ability to think clearly. Amazing how she does that. She flicks a cascade of shiny black hair off her bare shoulder, a small gesture that I worry might become a boomerang loop forever in my brain.

A couple of chuckles escape from my people at the table. Mutiny! I glance at them and they all quiet down.

Now, Nami is talking tech. I heard she had a computer science degree and did some pretty mean programming herself out of college before she went to law school. She's talking about how their code is amazing and innovative. She throws around Big Tech Words. And I realize she actually does understand them. Huh. Interesting. I have no idea what she's talking about. I smile, though, like I do. I understand business. High concepts. What sells. I leave the mechanics to others.

Maureen, at the table with me, frowns, concerned, sending me a warning look through her clear glass frames. It's her way of saying, *Watch this one.* Oh, I know.

"If Rainforest does interfere with our programmers, I think it's a real possibility the best and brightest will leave."

"We can find more," Dell says, not knowing what he's talking about. "The coding is irrelevant. Always has been."

"That's not true," Nami protests, offended. "And code aside, I'm also concerned about the true interest of Rainforest in buying us. You have a reputation for . . . not playing fair." She emphasizes the last words a little bit too much; I think she might mean me personally. "What assurances would we have that you'd try to keep staff after the sale?"

"We can add in clauses to the purchasing contract."

"You and I know very well that even those are hard to enforce."

This is the Namby who used to brutalize me in trig. This is absolutely not the Namby who once did the grapevine to Kesha's "Tik Tok" in my backyard.

She taps on her tablet, and I fear she's pulling up blackmail-level information. "And the labor . . . uh, disputes . . . that have been in the news don't paint a rosy picture for your warehouse workers. There's been a lot of bad press about how you treat your employees."

I swallow. True. Word of no bathroom breaks and warehouses without AC or heat have been pretty damaging. Not our proudest moment, even I admit.

"We wouldn't want to let you slash our employees' benefits or time off."

I stare at Nami, and she stares at me. For once, I know it's not empty talk. Namby loves nothing more than to lecture wrongdoers. She volunteered to do it in our high school hallways. It's as annoying now as it was then.

"We're not a perfect company, but we're looking to be better," I say, worried I'm sounding like a serial cheater begging his long-suffering spouse to take him back. "Trust me, we've learned some tough lessons."

"Trust you?" Nami almost snorts her derision. Imani raises an eyebrow. "After Rainforest's takeover of Natural Foods?"

She. Is. Not. Letting. Up.

And it's exactly what I've been looking for. Exactly the spark, the challenge that's been missing from my life for years.

"Toggle isn't Natural Foods." Not yet, anyway.

There are murmurs of agreement around the table. Nami's eyes turn into two solid lumps of coal. Her face gets so pinched, I worry she might lose circulation to her nose.

"And then . . . there's the business about you selling your customers' data."

Well, now things are really getting awkward. We might have settled a lawsuit. Or two.

"Toggle has made a point of being open with our users about data. We don't store it. We don't collect it. How can we be sure that Rainforest plans to change that and just use us as one more tool to mine for more data?"

I'm about to deliver a nondescript, noncommittal response, when Imani jumps in.

"I do get those concerns. Valid points, Nami," Imani begins.

Hell. I am so busy having fun sparring with Namby that I forgot about the real prize in the room: Imani. Brilliant move, Namby. Deflect and distract.

"Listen," Dell says, jumping in. "Maybe we really need to understand what Rainforest can offer us."

Dell nods at me. It's officially time for the cartoon money bags. "Here's what I know," I say, opening my leather-bound legal pad in front of me. "We're looking at a number in this range." I write down two figures on a piece of paper, rip it off the top, fold it, and hand it to Dell.

He opens it and whistles. Then he passes it to Imani. She can't keep the startled look from her face. Then the paper comes to Nami. She opens it. Do her fingers shake? I like to think so.

She glances at the number. I expect surprise, or even the glint of greed. Plenty of do-gooders have been waylaid by one too many zeros. But, to my surprise, Nami glares at the number as if it's personally insulted her entire family.

"You can't put a price on integrity," she says, folding the paper up as if she couldn't care less.

Could her holier-than-thou act be real? Until this moment, it hadn't occurred to me she might actually walk the walk.

I can't help it, I'm impressed.

More than impressed.

I might be a little turned on.

"Really?" Dell asks, skeptical. "That's a fair offer. More than fair." More than he expected. I know this.

"We built this company to be different from the rest, not to sell it to the *very* person—er, corporation—that's going to make it like all the rest." Nami stares at Imani as she says this.

I have to jump in, or I'll lose her.

"Look, I'd be worried if you *weren't* asking tough questions," I start.

Imani glances at me, looking a little relieved. She's not ready to throw her banner behind a side just yet, and I've made it so she doesn't have to. That's me, providing the out.

Easy. Except I glance at Nami, and her dark eyes burst into pure flame.

"How about all three of you come to Rainforest? You can see we're more than our bad press. I'll give you a personal tour, and you can ask me any question you'd like."

Nami's face goes ashen. Apparently, the thought of spending any time at all with me is her worst nightmare. I try not to take it personally.

"Nami? How does that sound?" Imani asks.

"Well . . ." Nami begins.

"She'll do it," Dell barks from the end of the table. "I mean, if you want to be a . . ." Dell stops himself just in time. ". . . a naysayer about it," he manages, correcting himself. Good one, Dell. None of us knew what you were really thinking. "Then let's just take a vote right now."

Nami flicks him a look that would incinerate a smaller man. I'm also not impressed with Dell. Next, he'll be talking about how a woman can't be president because they're emotional. Since, clearly, red-patchy-faced, furious Dell has all his emotions in check. I think if he loses this deal, he might start angry, toddler-tantrum crying, blubbering about his wealth and power being an inalienable right. I've seen it before. Yet, an hour later, he'll still tell you with a straight face only men should have the nuclear launch codes.

Imani shifts uncomfortably. She doesn't want to vote because her back's against the wall. Nami clocks it, too. If there's a vote right now, Nami might . . . I emphasize the *might* . . . lose.

"I'd rather . . . not vote today." Imani looks pained. "Let's go see their office. Okay?" Imani asks Nami this directly, and now she's got no choice.

"Yes, of course," Nami bites out, as if the words are cyanide capsules.

"Great," I say, smiling once more. "Shall we connect on ConnectIn? So we can set up our calendars?"

It's the very app she just rejected me on fifteen minutes ago. I might be gloating. Maybe. She can't turn me down now and she knows it.

Got her.

I glance at her, and her gaze meets mine, and there's no mirth in it. Her brown eyes glitter, like polished granite, and I am absolutely sure she is imagining a million ways to kill me, all of them painful and terribly slow. I just smile brighter. Because for the first time in a long time, I'm not bored.

Finally, a real adversary.

"Yes. Of course," she counters through teeth lightly clenched. She looks down at her tablet and I'm surprised it's not instantly incinerated. I get a little pinging notice on my phone. Well, will you look at that. A connection request from Nami Reid.

And . . . a message as well. What has the gorgeous goddess sent me? An apology, maybe?

Sorry I hate-stared at you all meeting? Or sorry I trashed your company? I do love apologies.

I click open the missive.

It's a single poop emoji.

I swallow a laugh as I click Accept. It feels like we're right back in high school with Nami sticking her tongue out at me from across the chem lab table.

The meeting ends then, and she turns on her heel and stalks out, literal steam flowing from her ears. I know she'll have something terrible in store for retribution, and I kind of can't wait. I watch her angry-walk back to her office, each long, lean stride making her wall of shiny ebony hair bounce hard against her perfect back.

SIX

Nami

Someone moved my office chair to the break room, and THIS IS
NOT OKAY. My office chair is MY OWN PROPERTY, and not to
be used by anyone else BUT ME. My chair is a HANS WEGNER
ORIGINAL!!!

> DELL OURANOS
> PARTNER, CO-OWNER, BUSINESS INFLUENCER AND
> TRENDSETTER
> #ALL-HANDS-ALERT CHANNEL
> TOGGLE INTERNAL CHAT

Who's Hans Wegner?

> ARIE BERGER
> CIO

Master of Danish Furniture Design! Father of the Danish Modernist
Movement. A genius. His furniture is INCREDIBLY expensive. I
bought this chair AT PRIVATE AUCTION. It SHOULD NOT be
touched. EVER.

> DELL OURANOS
> PARTNER, CO-OWNER, BUSINESS INFLUENCER AND
> TRENDSETTER

I watch Jae pal around with Imani and Dell in his glass corner office,
diagonal from mine, trying very, very hard to pretend like I don't
care. The other suits from Rainforest left, but Jae remained behind,
tactically wooing Imani. Dell is right there with her, too. I've been

debating going over there. I need to make sure she hears my argument. But I also know my argument will be more powerful if I can get her alone. I know I can convince her if I can get her out for a coffee, or a quick meal. Just the two of us. But with Dell and Jae there? No way.

Jae is poised to steal us away for a nice chunk of change, which would more than appease the board and investors. But given Rainforest's reputation, it would be terrible for our people. Even if Rainforest's powers that be grant them mercy and keep them, some might walk out on principle. Any way you look at it, Rainforest buying us will destroy everything that makes Toggle, Toggle. I can tell Jae cracks a joke because Imani laughs. I wish she'd told me this was in the works. Why didn't she trust me with this? Did Dell wrap her into this from the start? Or did he go behind both our backs? I have so many questions.

Also, I can't help thinking about the irony of my birthday wish. Artemis (or whomever) couldn't have gotten this more wrong. *Jae Lee* is not my soulmate. He's my hate mate.

Arie and Priya appear at my glass office door as I sit at my desk, trying to spy without looking like I'm spying. Dell is busy showing off his fancy office chair, and Jae is pretending to listen. Danish furniture designer. Blech.

"The news is bad, isn't it?" Priya whispers. Even her blue hair, worn up in two pigtails, seems to vibrate with nervous energy.

"I'm afraid so," I sigh. "They're serious about buying us. Dell wants to sell. Imani's on the fence."

"You?" Arie asks, worried.

"Hard no."

They both visibly relax. Priya exhales as she puts a hand over her heart. "Oh, thank God."

"Did you tell Imani they're data pirates?" Arie asks.

I nod.

"Our users will flip if we get bought by them," Priya says. "They're with us because they trust us not to mine their data!"

"I know." I sigh.

"And, they're probably just going to steal our AI, muscle out our competitors, and then fire us all, best case," Jamal says, wheeling up to us. He stops and taps the arm of his wheelchair anxiously, eyeing Imani and Jae through the glass office walls.

"Or turn us into little Rainforest drones without free will, worst case," Priya predicts. Priya and Jamal exchange an anxious glance.

"Those thoughts have crossed my mind." I glare at Jae, but when Imani catches my eye, I flash her a bright white smile. "Imani says we should go visit with them. See if they're as bad as we think. She thinks they might not be."

"They are." Arie sighs, flicking a nonexistent piece of lint off his brown plaid button-down. "You don't negotiate with the Borg."

"Yeah. I know."

"If they buy us, does this mean we'll all have to wear Depends?" Priya quips. "I hear they work everybody so hard, nobody gets a bathroom break."

I laugh at that, but part of me knows it's true. Rainforest is the company everybody loves to hate, but even I have Rainforest boxes waiting for me to open at home. We had to expect them to come for us. They come for everyone, eventually.

"Why does Rainforest even want us?" Arie asks. "They don't even really do apps."

"Not yet, anyway, but I think that's on their list for world domination," I say.

"But their code is trash," Jamal adds.

"I know. I tried to explain that in the meeting." I absently pick up a pen on my desk and twirl it between two fingers. "But Dell said it's not about code."

"Not about code?" Priya looks stricken. She glances down at her distressed T-shirt with *I code and I know things* in the *Game of Thrones* font. "Everything is code! They just want to steal ours because they can't write their own. Plus, what does Dell know? He wouldn't know Java from coffee beans."

"Did Dell bring these guys in?" Jamal asks, suspicious.

"He's enthusiastic about selling," I say. "That's all I know."

Jamal scowls. "Of course the Grinch wants to sell to Rainforest."

"This can't stand," Priya says, meeting Jamal's gaze.

"You are one hundred percent right," he says.

This might be the first time the two of them have agreed on anything.

"Don't worry. I'm on this," I reassure them all. I won't let Rainforest gobble us up. I won't let Jae lay off everyone who made Toggle great. Or betray our users, the people who supported us from day one. There is such a thing as what's right. Jae never really understood that. He only ever went for What Was Best for Jae. Just like when he and his brothers won the talent show in their boy band routine, both senior and junior years, technically breaking the rules by having pyrotechnics on stage and by bribing the organizers to let them go last. People still talk about their performances. Nobody remembers now that I played Beethoven's Sonata #9 on my violin, which, granted, was solemn and about fifteen minutes too long, and no one appreciated my finger work except my orchestra teacher.

Right then, Jae meets my gaze from across the room. I wish I had heat-ray vision, because then I could melt him from here. He doesn't seem fazed. Per usual. My stomach tightens as he stands and Imani leads him out of the office. I pray they're headed for the elevators. Instead, Imani seems to be leading him right to me.

"All right, back to work." Arie shoos Jamal and Priya back to their desks. "Look alive," Arie cautions me.

Hard not to feel alive when hate is coursing through every vein in my body. I scramble up from my desk and stand with Arie at the doorway, and then mentally kick myself because I look like I've shot to my feet to greet royalty. I should've remained seated. This is my office. Not his. Not yet.

Jae approaches with his perfect suit in his easy, long stride. He's taller than I remember. Maybe he grew in college? That, or he's wearing lifts. I glance at his long legs, his broader torso, and bigger shoulders. No lifts, I think. There's just more ... of him. More than I remember. Imani barely comes to his shoulder and Arie, too, must look up to meet his gaze. When did he get so tall? He flashes an easy smile, all charm, and my stomach flips.

Shit. He's good-looking. My heart starts to pound harder. Jae's always been ... cute. Boy band cute. Classmates crushed on him all the time. But he's a man now. A very seriously handsome man, who looks like he ought to be negotiating with spies in an action movie, or modeling designer men's suits in some commercial. Though there's no way that I can actually *be attracted* to Jae Lee. He's the devil, I remind myself. A really, really well-dressed, tall, and broad and fit, chiseled, clean-shaven devil. Whose bright-white dimpled smile makes my stomach feel weird.

Arie steps closer to me for moral support.

"Nami," Imani says smoothly, giving me an easy smile. "Just wanted to bring Jae by so you two could sync your calendars."

"Sure. No problem." I say this too tightly. I'm going to need to be a better actor than this. Plus, since when do we need to "sync" our electronic calendars face-to-face? That's what calendar invites are for.

"I'm Arie," he says, jumping in between us, holding out a hand, like a dad meeting his daughter's date.

"Jae. Nice to meet you." Jae takes it and the two men nod at each other, firm handshake lasting a beat too long.

"Jae wanted to take a look around our offices, too. Would you mind taking him?" Imani blinks innocently. She has no idea how dangerous this is. Giving Jae any inside information—even something as small as the soda our database folks like to drink—could prove deadly. Hell, for all I know, he's trying to slip a thumb drive into one of our computers *Mission: Impossible* style and steal all our company secrets. Then he could drop this silly pretense of a partnership and maybe back out of the deal.

Or, maybe the three of them cooked up this idea in Imani's office: Jae wanted one-on-one time with me to . . . try and convince me selling is a good idea? Please. He's going to need more than a Gucci blazer and his expensive hair product for that.

Jae flashes a larger-than-usual grin, which makes my stomach bubble.

Maybe I have food poisoning.

I kind of hope I have food poisoning.

"I'd really love a tour," he says, amused.

I bet you would.

"I'd be happy to give you one." Straight out the fire stairwell to the dark, narrow alley where I hope you trip and fall into one of those mystery oily puddles always lurking in the potholes.

Arie steps in front of me, ready to distract the lion so I can escape. "I could tag along and—" he begins, but Imani interrupts.

"Actually, Arie, I wanted to talk to you. I was hoping we could talk about the deliverables for next week? I've got a few questions for you."

Arie sends me an apologetic glance. I can see him warring with himself. Neither he nor I want me to be alone with Jae Lee.

"Arie?" Imani adds, her command unmistakable as she turns back to her office.

"It's okay," I say to him. "Go on and talk with Imani."

Arie reluctantly retreats, tagging after Imani. He sends worried, furtive glances back at me.

"I see you've still got your adoring admirers," Jae says without any hint of irony as he watches Arie slip into Imani's office, his eyes never leaving us.

"What are you talking about?" I snap, more annoyed than I'd intended. He'd better not be trying to insult Arie. "The man adores his wife. He worships her."

Jae just shakes his head. "Never mind." He flashes me another grin. A twinge flutters in my stomach. "So, I'd ask how you've been since high school, but I see you're still seething about being salutatorian."

"I don't care about that." I do. A lot.

Jae smiles wider. My neck hurts looking up at his smug face. When did he get so . . . so intimidating? So damn tall and broad? He used to be a skinny little thing. Not, I realize, anymore. "So, you aren't still sore about losing to me by point two five points?"

"It was point two four five points."

Jae laughs. A big, throaty laugh that I feel in my chest.

"So, you are still sore." He arches an eyebrow and suddenly I feel completely naked, exposed. My stomach still feels weird. Maybe it's food poisoning and not the intelligent glint in Jae's dark eyes.

"I'm sore you cheated." I plaster on a fake smile, because I can feel Imani and Arie watching us from their glass offices. A glance at Arie tells me he's in pain and wants to come rescue me. I almost wish he would.

Jae shakes his head, wagging a finger at me. "Taking summer school isn't cheating."

"Some of us had to work in the summer," I grind out. Jae's parents were upper-middle-class rich: his father, a successful surgeon, his mom, a teacher. He didn't have to work for his clothing allowance, like I did. Or to help save for his college tuition. He had all the time in the world to learn flash dances and boy band songs to woo starry-eyed cheerleaders. I was too busy mopping floors at our local burger joint to pad my GPA with extra courses. If he hadn't had the extra time and money to take extra credits at the community college, I'd have beaten him by a mile, and we both know it.

"It's nice to see that all you've been doing for the last dozen years is think of me."

I snort. "I haven't thought of you at all. I'd prefer never to think of you, and wouldn't, if you'd just kindly take yourself and your greedy Rainforest buddies and go sniffing around someone else's company."

"Careful. Your partners are watching." Jae nods out into the open office plan, by the marketing team. Dell is pretending to talk to Jamal, but he's watching us. Closely. Imani, from her office, is pretending to be absorbed in her computer, but she keeps cutting looks at us.

I laugh a little and flash a brilliant smile. Look charming. Look like you're trying to be nice and welcoming. "I don't care," I say as I fake laugh. "You and your thugs should call off this stupid takeover and then my partners won't care how I talk to you."

Jae just cocks his head at me. "No can do." He extends an arm out toward the floor, inviting me out of my office. "Shall we take that tour now?"

My fake smile suddenly feels brittle. "Of course. I'd absolutely love to show you the exit. Elevators first? Or fire escape? Or I could just open a window? The fact we're ninety floors up makes no difference to me."

Jae laughs again. "Oh, I missed you, Namby," he says, which confuses me momentarily. Miss me? My rebellious stomach tightens again.

"Why? You want someone to trip on your way to the finish line?"

"Why would I bother to trip you when you'll just stumble yourself? You fall rather gracefully, if I remember the district tennis finals."

"The court was uneven," I counter. Match point, I tried to run down a lob, only to face-plant near the baseline. "And unlike *some of us*, I didn't get brand-new sneakers whenever I wanted them." Or ever, actually. I think I wore the same ragged tennis shoes most of the way through high school.

"You think I played well because of my shoes?" Jae looks dumbfounded.

"Or your private lessons," I snap. "It sure wasn't your ability."

Jae laughs and shakes his head. "Sounds like someone is jealous."

"All I can say is none of those fancy pairs ever helped you return my serve in practice. You always missed."

"I was just trying to build your confidence."

I snort. "Is that why you got all red-faced and frustrated? Because you were doing me a solid?"

"You had a good serve," he admits. "But you never technically aced me. And a lot of your serves were out."

"They were on the line."

"So you say."

I lead him down the colorful carpet toward the break room. We follow the orange-and-blue path away from the programmers' desks.

"It's funny you're giving me a tour now, since you also showed me around Evanston Township High School."

I'm struck by the memory then: skinny, short Jae Lee, transfer student, in the second half of sophomore year. Principal Khan asked me to show him around, and I did. I felt sorry for him then. New to school, not a friend in sight, smack dab before spring break, seemingly a little reserved and shy. He barely spoke two words to me the whole tour. I was super friendly then. I really was. I even told him about tennis tryouts and encouraged him to come. Little did I know he'd upend my whole life. That he'd walk on that court and get a spot on varsity after never having played for a school in his life. I'd been practicing extra hard since middle school, and I'd only make varsity senior year. But then, my parents couldn't afford all of the private lessons Jae got for years. If I'd spent thousands on "a tennis tutor" as he called it, maybe I could be on varsity sophomore year, too.

"If I knew then what I know now, I would've definitely opened the closest window and shoved you out."

Jae laughs again. It's unnerving. I'm not joking. Not at all.

"You haven't changed," he tells me.

"You have," I say.

He cocks an eyebrow, glancing down at me. "What do you mean?"

"Are you wearing hidden lifts in your shoes? Or what?" I know I shouldn't ask him, but he's towering over me. My neck hurts trying to look up at him. He's this giant *man* walking next to me, when the last time I saw him, at high school graduation, I was taller than him in my heels. Next time we meet, I vow, I'll be wearing five-inch stilettos, no matter how uncomfortable they might be in the summer.

Other people in the office notice, too. They stare as we pass by their desks, eyeing Jae, head to toe. He probably gets that a lot.

It's not my imagination then. He is attractive. He does have that underwear model vibe.

"I grew five inches freshman year in college," he admits. "And another three before the end of my sophomore year." He shrugs.

Doesn't explain his seemingly muscled shoulders. The way his athletic-cut suit clings to his shoulders, tapered at his narrowed waist.

"The same happened to my brothers. I guess we Lees are late bloomers."

"Your brothers are giants too, now?" I try to remember the Lee brothers: all slim, short, with adorable floppy hair and impeccably trendy and expensive clothes, out of the budget of 80 percent of the kids at my school. They were all fantastically coordinated during their talent show performances. Now, I imagine all the ridiculously handsome, tall, and broad Lee brothers with charming, dimpled smiles, and designer suit jackets, roaming Chicago and leaving broken hearts in their wake. The image is unsettling.

We walk to the break room, where two different database guys are taking the last of the croissants.

"Did you all take steroids or . . ."

"No. But you do seem disappointed. Wishing you could tattle on us like old times?" Jae arches an eyebrow.

"You three always ran in the hallway. There's no running in the halls."

"How else are we supposed to get to class if we're late?" He flashes a charming grin. Or what would be charming—for anyone else.

"Oh, I don't know? Leave on time?"

"I bet you still have your detention pad, too. Under your pillow?"

"Right. And are you still paying people to take the SAT for you?"

Jae glances at me, frowning. "I paid *tutors* to help me study. *I* took the SAT. You always believe every rumor you hear?"

"Only the plausible ones."

He frowns. "So, what have you been up to since high school?" he asks. "I would've bet money you'd be married with kids by now."

Anger rushes up to my throat, and I feel its thick heat, choking me.

"I'd bet money you'd be in jail. For embezzlement. Or that you would've ended the world by now, antichrist," I snap. "This is the break room," I add tightly, throwing up an indifferent arm.

"So . . . you're really not dating anyone?"

For a panicked second I worry he was one of those roadside gawkers to my life. Did he know about Mitch?

"None of your business." I meet his amused gaze. Sure, *he* can be amused. He doesn't have to worry about high-risk geriatric pregnancies, starting at age thirty-five. He—with his flat abs—has a gorgeous influencer on his arm every weekend. He's probably fending off proposals from them, dying to tie him down. It takes all my willpower not to literally shove Jae across the office and into one of the newly opened elevators.

"It's simply not any of your business," I say through a gritted smile. We turn the corner out of view of Imani's office, and I drop the pretense of smiling.

"I'm just making small talk," Jae offers.

"I'd rather you didn't, Satan. My soul is not for sale." I open the nearest door. "Janitor's closet," I tell him, showing him the mops.

"Perhaps you could take me to the developers and programmers. Would love to—"

"Steal all our secrets right now so you don't even have to buy us at all? I bet you would. No way." I've got to keep my head clear. Protect Toggle. From Jae. I point to an open doorway. "But I'd be happy to show you the supply closet," I say, and offer him a look into the reams of copy paper and boxes of staples. He gamely leans into the door, closer to me than I'd like. I get a whiff of something smoky, yet sweet. Hair product, maybe? I like it. And I hate that I like it. Jae's hair should smell like old gym shoes. Or brimstone.

After perusal of the closet, he turns and looks at me for a beat. His irises are the color of dark chocolate. Warm. Rich.

"You should be nicer to the person who's cutting you a check."

"I don't want your money." I spit the words out.

"You might find you change your mind." Jae's so confident, so cocky. I hate it. I also hate that my body feels wired. I'm hyperaware of him next to me, his hand hanging inches from mine. I back away from him, out of the storage closet and into the airy hallway.

"You want to tell me how you got my number in the first place? I want to know about the traitor in my midst."

"Traitor? Strong word. If I tell you, will you put them on trial?"

"I was thinking of starting with just a very stern talk about privacy—something I know Rainforest cares nothing about."

Jae shrugs. "Your mom, actually, handed over your number. Our moms still talk. My mom asked your mom. Your mom was *more* than happy to give it."

I let out a growl. I'm not sure what's more upsetting: that Mom freely gave out my number, or that both moms probably think Jae's going to ask me out.

"You dragged *our moms* into this? That was a foolish move. They're probably planning our wedding right now." The very thought makes my stomach twist into a knot.

Also, why didn't Mom warn me? Whose side is she on?

"It's better than messaging people on the Sarang app," Jae admits.

"What's Sarang?"

"A dating app used by Korean-American parents trying to find matches for their single grown children."

I bark a laugh, surprised. "Need a little help from your *mommy* to find dates?" I tease.

"Says the woman whose mom eagerly gave out her digits to the first bachelor who asked." I want to ask about a million more questions about Jae's dating life. But I don't. I need to focus. Toggle is what I care about. Not what Jae's doing on Saturday nights. "Why are you really here? What does Rainforest want with us?" I ask as we continue our walk down the colorful carpet.

He cocks his head to one side. "Why don't you tell me why you really don't want to sell?"

"I told you already. You'd destroy everything we've built here. You'd eviscerate Toggle."

"You expect me to believe that stuff you said about Rainforest being evil? You honestly think it doesn't have anything to do with the fact *I'm* here?" A slow, triumphant smile crosses his face.

"This has nothing to do with you."

"It doesn't? Because you're sure acting like it does." He stares at me a beat longer and my heart ratchets up a notch. He's prodding me on purpose. He wants me to take the bait. I'm not going to do it.

"Is this how you woo all victims of your hostile takeovers?" I ask, cool. "Insult them and then when their feelings are all hurt, you pull the rug out from under them and snatch up their companies for pennies?" I tsk as I take him deeper into the less important parts of the office, away from our programmers and from the dazzling ninetieth-floor views of the lake. There are the bathrooms, and at the end of the small narrow white hallway, the fire exit door. Maybe, I think, I can show him right out. Sure, the alarm might sound . . . but it would be worth it to lock him out on the other side in a stairwell where he'd have to walk the ninety floors down.

"It's hardly a hostile takeover. Dell wanted this. And Imani will, too."

"Rainforest only ever wants what's good for Rainforest. I'll make sure neither one of them forget that. Dell might not care, but Imani will."

We've stopped in the narrowest part of the hallway, wedged between the white support pillar and the exit door. Too late, I realize my mistake: I've led him to the most secluded part of the office, so now we're bunched together, him with his back to the exit door behind him, me blocking his way to the populated part of the office. Then again, maybe it's not a mistake. Here, I don't have to fake smile. Here, I can take the gloves off.

I look at his smooth, blemish-free face. His cheekbones are even more defined than I remember. His clean-shaven jaw square and strong.

"I'm not going to let you dismantle this company," I press, hedging him farther in the corner. Jae's back is almost against the bright red push panel of the exit door, marked with all kinds of warning signs. One hard shove and he'd be in the stairwell.

"We won't," he replies.

"That's a lie."

Jae grins. "You should help me, actually."

I snort, disdainful.

"I could convince you it's the right thing to do." Jae sounds so cocky, so sure. It's absolutely what I hate about him. His confidence that everything will—and should—go his way. Because it usually does. "Or we could just wrestle Toggle to the ground until it begs for mercy." His eyes spark and his expression is almost playfully evil.

He takes a microstep closer to me. My whole body stiffens.

What if he does wrestle me to the ground? All six feet of him, with that same devious spark in his eye? I slap that thought out of my mind as soon as it appears. What am I doing? Imagining Jae touching me?

"We can do this nicely—or not so nicely—that's your choice." Jae's close to me. Too close.

My heartbeat is in my ears. Hate, I presume, pushing blood through my body. Not the awareness that Jae is . . . sexy. Seriously, magnetically, broad-shouldered, muscled chest, electric. My throat is dry. He's the devil, I remind myself. Don't forget it. He will destroy Toggle.

"You seriously think that I'd ever believe you'd play nice?" I say, proud I keep my voice cool. Collected. Bored, even. He won't know my heart is beating so fast. He won't know about the white-hot heat boiling in my belly. "You never play nice."

His lip curls up now, almost in triumph. "Really?" he challenges. "I've changed a lot since high school."

All I have to do is look at him to know that's true. He's grown, most likely seventy or more pounds heavier than me, and by his flat stomach, I know it's all muscle. He was never this good-looking in high school. Cute, sure, but not . . . like this. I glance at the buttons of his crisp oxford beneath his blazer. Would his chest feel soft . . . or hard . . . if I pushed him into the exit door? Just how much muscle lies beneath that expensive suit jacket?

"Really?" I manage, but this time, I don't sound so cool. So collected. There's a hitch in my voice. A hitch that I want to cut out and murder right here on this brightly colored carpet. I strangle it and try again. "So that means you're not going to cheat, then?"

"I won't cheat," he promises. "I'll play nice."

But in that moment, I realize I don't want him to play nice. That's the very last thing I want. I want a bare-knuckle brawl. I want to draw blood. I'm staring at his mouth now, I realize, as if waiting for another taunt.

Not because he has nice lips. Full, soft. Nice.

I force myself to look him in the eye.

"Don't hold back on my account," I growl.

He laughs a little, flashing even, white teeth. "You sure you're ready for another go at me, Miss Salutatorian?"

Miss Salutatorian? Only he could make the accomplishment sound mocking. White-hot fury floods me. I *should* push him right out of the office. I should . . .

"Nami?" The anxious voice of Arie drifts down the hallway. Priya is standing next to him, also looking worried.

The hate spell, or whatever it is, breaks. I glance at Arie and Priya, relieved. I won't be assaulting a high-ranking Rainforest executive after all. Also, a little bit of disappointment pinches my stomach.

"Oh, hi," I say as Jae steps aside in the narrow corridor, a flicker of annoyance crossing his face. Good, I think. Be annoyed. I have a backup squad. Team: Nami. "Just finished the tour and Jae was just leaving."

"Out the emergency exit door?" Arie asks, concerned, as he fidgets with his ID lanyard.

"That's up to him." I shrug, finally backing away from Jae, the thump of adrenaline still in my temples. "Shall we head back to my office?" Arie glances at him once more and then at me. Then he nods, and Priya moves protectively to my side. It feels like a sheet of armor. I'm glad for them. I need to get away from Jae's broad shoulders, his sparkling eyes, daring me to . . . what? Lose my mind?

"We're supposed to get something on the calendar," Jae calls after us, thrusting his hands into his pants pockets.

"Why don't you send me a calendar invite on ConnectIn? Isn't that what connections are for?" I throw over my shoulder with cold indifference, even as my stomach roils. I'm proud I sound so collected. Inside, I'm shaking.

I hear a low chuckle, but I don't turn around. I can only hope he doesn't know how fast my heart is beating. That I feel confused, and a little sick.

Am I attracted to Jae Lee?

I can't be.

I won't let myself be. Not in a million years.

SEVEN

Jae

Who took my WEGNER SWIVEL CHAIR?
Seriously—IT'S MISSING!!!

> DELL OURANOS
> PARTNER, CO-OWNER, BUSINESS INFLUENCER, AND
> TRENDSETTER
> #ALL-BULLETIN CHANNEL
> TOGGLE INTERNAL CHAT

Your chair is missing?! That's such a shame. ☹

> PRIYA PATEL
> SENIOR SOFTWARE ENGINEER

The thief WILL return my chair IMMEDIATELY.
THIS IS NOT A JOKE.

> DELL OURANOS
> PARTNER, CO-OWNER, BUSINESS INFLUENCER, AND
> TRENDSETTER

It's definitely not a joke.

> JAMAL ROBERTS
> QA DIRECTOR

Namby is full of surprises.

Just when I think I've got her pegged, she backs me into an office corner and . . . I don't know whether she was going to hit me . . .

Or kiss me.

It sounds ridiculous even in my own thoughts, and I've half convinced myself it's all in my head. But . . . the way she was looking at me. I don't know. There was a different kind of tension there.

"Earth to Jae, come in, Jae." My younger brother Sam nudges me with his elbow and I realize I've been zoning out on my parents' backyard patio for Sunday dinner on our quiet, leafy Evanston street. Sam has been trying to hand me a beer, which I take now.

"Sorry, man." We clink bottle necks, just as Dad plops some thinly sliced beef onto the oversized hot plate at the patio table, where he's whipping up his specialty, bulgogi. Sam's twin, Charlie, younger by ten minutes, stands near the hot plate with his boyfriend, Nick, dutifully taking notes of Dad's technique.

"Should we save Nick?" I lean against the deck railing of our parents' wraparound porch. The house we moved to when Dad relocated his medical practice to Evanston during high school was a refurbished two-story yellow Victorian farmhouse, complete with small white picket fence out front. Dad became head of surgery at Evanston Hospital, Mom still taught English language classes at the Korean church near Glenview, and everything worked out.

"Dad is starting to talk about why you have to use his special marinating technique."

Dad hardly ever talks about anything—except food. And, occasionally, traffic. He makes your typical "strong, silent" types look chatty.

"If Nick can handle Charlie's mood swings, he can handle a lecture on Korean barbeque." Sam shrugs. "And, listen, we should just be glad Dad's come around. I mean, would you have believed Dad would be so warm now by the way he acted at first?"

When Charlie came out his second year of med school, it came as a surprise to no one except Dad, who seemed to be completely blindsided. Mom, Sam, and I celebrated Charlie's announcement immediately, but it took a bit of time for Dad to adjust to the idea. Dad had a whole lot of wrong-headed notions at first, like when he blurted out that he thought only white people came out. Now, he'll laugh at his wrong ideas, but it took a lot of intervention, earnest nagging from all of us, and a PFLAG support group to bring him over. Now, Dad's the first one to teach each one of Charlie's boyfriends his cooking techniques, largely because he knows Charlie burns everything he touches. Without GetGrub delivery, my brother would starve.

Nick, who's dated Charlie for nearly two years now, seems more interested in cooking than any of the others. That's a good sign.

"Nick's really paying attention. I think he's taking notes," I point out. "I think this might finally be getting serious."

We watch the three men for a beat.

"By the way, how's Isabella?" I ask, watching Sam's plus-one, his steady girlfriend since college, through the patio screen door, help Mom make potato salad in the kitchen. "Fine."

"*Just* fine? Are you going to get married, or . . ."

"You sound like Mom," Sam teases. "I don't need to be rushed. We're fine as we are."

"You know, one day, Isabella will wake up and get wise. She'll realize she can do better than you."

"That's what I've been trying to tell him," Mom interjects as she bustles out carrying a tray of adobo and rice. Mom, who is half Korean, a quarter Filipino, and a quarter Japanese, was born and raised in Honolulu, though she spent a year after college teaching English in South Korea. She also has bionic hearing, and has probably been eavesdropping from inside the house.

"I got it, Mom," Sam says. "Message received."

"Mom, seriously, let me help you," I say again, trying to take a plate from her busy hands.

"I'm fine," she insists, as she always does, batting me away with a toss of her head as she sets the tray down on the patio table.

Isabella trails out a second later, carrying a plate piled high with corn on the cob and a bowl of Mom's spicy kimchi. The bilingual kindergarten teacher is always the epitome of adorable and doesn't have a mean bone in her body. She's got her long, dark curls up in a high ponytail, and her sleeveless gingham sundress shows off her bronzed shoulders. "What are we talking about?" she asks in her sweet, peppy voice.

"Well, funny you should ask . . ." I start, fully prepared to ask Isabella if she prefers princess- or emerald-cut engagement rings, but Sam quickly interrupts.

"I was asking Jae when he's finally going to bring home a nice girl for Mom and Dad to meet." Sam flashes me an evil smile.

I glare at him. The jerk.

Both Mom and Dad swivel at the same time and look at me. "That's a question we all want the answer to," Mom says, eyeing me with purpose. "You haven't brought *one nice girl* by since you moved back home."

"Yeah, Jae. What's the holdup?" Charlie grins at me, enjoying my discomfort. Dad clams up, focusing intently on the bulgogi. "I know you've been seeing people."

"You all know why." I wave the neck of my beer bottle at them. "I don't want to expose some poor woman to your endless questions. You all are by far the worst."

"Oh, we're not that bad." Charlie grins, knowing full well they all are. The first—and only—time I brought a girlfriend home during college, Dad basically grilled her for an hour about her career aspirations and the number of children she planned to have.

"Oh, don't blame us," Mom says, wagging her finger. "You're the one who's too picky."

Dad remains silent, per usual, flipping meat on the hot plate and frowning at it. There's a Gettysburg Address in that one expression.

"Me?" I echo. "I'm not picky!"

Charlie barks a laugh. Sam and Isabella exchange knowing glances.

"No girl is perfect enough for His Royal Highness," Mom complains.

"I'm not that bad," I protest.

"You should settle down," Dad tells me, piping in for the first time, with an edict that sounds like a command on high. "When I was your age, I was married, owned a house, you were starting preschool, and your brothers were already on the way." He snaps his bamboo tongs at me.

I sigh. "Yes, and you'll also get social security when you retire. Those were different times."

"You are too selfish, Jae-Yeon," Dad says sternly. "You have to put family above yourself."

The rest of the backyard grows silent for a second, and Isabella shifts uncomfortably. Here we go again. I was wondering how long before Dad trotted out the *You're failing us as the oldest son* routine.

"You should be more like Charlie. He's a good surgeon."

Even Charlie looks a tad uncomfortable.

"I'd make a terrible doctor," I protest. "I'm good at what I do. I like it."

"Like!" Dad sniffs, unimpressed. "What about what the family needs, Jae-Yeon."

"Now, now, why is everything so serious? You want to talk serious, let's talk food," Mom pipes in, the rodeo clown for Dad's bull. "Dinner is served. Sit. Eat." Mom shoos us all to the big patio table, and we take our spots. I reach for the plate of corn, grabbing an ear for my plate.

"Speaking of single girls," Mom begins as Sam piles Mom's kimchi on his plate. Sam and I have never been afraid of spice. Charlie, however, eyes the kimchi with worry. Anytime he eats Mom's spicy cabbage, he begins to sweat profusely and can't drink milk fast enough.

"Did you call Nami Reid?"

I nearly drop the plate of corn in Isabella's lap.

"Namby!" Sam declares, thumping his beer on the table. "Why on earth would Jae call Namby!"

"Mom, I told you to keep that between us."

"You asked for her number." Mom stares at me. "I had a whole conversation with her mom about it!"

"You *wanted* Namby's number?" Sam exclaims. Sam and Charlie both stare at me, shocked.

"Who's Namby?" Isabella asks innocently as she takes the plate of corn from me and gently grabs an ear with silver tongs.

"Jae's high school bully," Sam teases.

"She was not," I manage, trying to scrape together my dignity. "I gave as good as I got."

Isabella looks perplexed. Nick, too.

"Nami and Jae always competed for everything," Mom explains. "A little friendly competition, that's all."

"Friendly competition!" Sam huffs, stabbing at the meat on his plate. "She petitioned the school board to have you removed as vale-dictorian. She spoke at their meeting!"

"Well, the system wasn't one hundred percent fair," I manage, holding my chopsticks a little too tightly. "I did rack up credits in summer school. And we were only separated by a quarter of a point." *Technically, point two four five,* I hear Nami's voice in my head.

"She's just a sore loser," Sam tells me, taking a bite of bulgogi.

"It doesn't matter," Mom says, dabbing at her mouth with a paper napkin. "She was good for you. She made you work hard!"

"Hey, I always work hard. Dutiful firstborn Asian son, that's me," I point out.

I feel, rather than see, Dad giving me the side-eye.

"Ha! Like when you blew off your calc final freshman year in college?" Charlie says, mouth full.

"Okay, so I might have had some adjustment problems when I went away to school," I admit. The whole family laughs. It's a story the twins relish to tell—the time I actually messed up.

"What happened?" Isabella asks, glancing around the table.

"He got on academic probation all of his freshman year." Sam smirks at me. The jerk. "He almost got kicked out."

"He didn't have Nami there, pushing him," Mom points out. "See? She was good for you."

I already know Mom's right about this. It's one reason I sought Nami out after all these years. For the challenge.

"Good for him!" Sam spits. "Only if he wants hate notes shoved in his locker."

"That was only one time, and it wasn't a hate note," I point out, wondering why I'm defending Nami. She was never *nice* to me. But I guess I have my pride. I wasn't bullied by her, either. I want to make that clear. I wasn't some sad sack in an after-school special. "She just outlined the reasons she should've been Honors Society president and then kindly asked me to step down."

"Hate note," Sam heckles.

"Personally," Charlie sniffs, "I always thought it was all a little heavy-handed. The hate note. Maybe she had a secret crush on you." He and Nick exchange a glance.

Sam bursts out laughing. "If she was crushing on you, I'd hate to see what she does to her enemies." He shakes his head. "Not that it matters, I heard she had a surprise party where nobody but family came."

"What do you mean?" I ask, interest piqued.

Sam pulls out his phone, digging through his social. "See? Here. Her mom livestreamed it." He shows me an awkward-looking Nami on camera, which pans out to a very small group of people on her mom's patio. Sam's right. Besides her cousins, the party guests skew . . . mid-sixties. Wow, that is kind of sad. And it seems to bother Nami. I can tell. Her too-bright smile fails to disguise her disappointment. I feel just the slightest flicker of . . . pity.

"Oh, she's pretty!" Isabella gushes, because she can't be anything but sweet.

I watch the video, hit once more by how perfect she is: Smoky eyes. Perfect pink lips. How does she get her hair so amazingly glossy? Not a strand out of place. And, as usual, Nami doesn't have a bad angle.

"I would've thought more people would come," I manage. "She always had admirers." Throngs of gooey-eyed, starstruck followers praying she would show them the least bit of attention. She never did. She always left a swath of broken hearts in her wake.

"Fools," Sam declares. "There was no way that ice queen was going to melt for anybody."

I think about the smoldering look in Nami's eyes. Ice is not the word for it. Red-hot, flaming heat. She's a fire queen if there ever was one.

"Why *did* you ask for her number, though?" Charlie isn't going to let it go.

"It's not what any of you think. It's business," I say. "Rainforest might be buying her company." The minute I admit this, I regret it. Everyone at the table stares and blinks at me.

"Seriously?" Mom asks. "You let me get her mom's hopes up for *business*?"

"I *told* you it was business," I remind her. "I told you it wasn't personal."

Dad groans loudly and rolls his eyes, his disapproval palpable.

"Are you just trying to piss her off?" asks Charlie.

"Maybe." I shrug.

"Be nice to Nami. I am friends with her mother," Mom chastises me.

"I'm always nice." I flash a mischievous grin.

"Why buy her company?" Charlie asks.

"Because it's going to be profitable." I flash them all a smile. "And because we can."

"You're an egomaniac." Charlie throws a wadded-up napkin at me. "Seriously, your ego is out of control. I'm kind of hoping Nami wins this one."

"She probably will. No way she sells to this jerk," Sam adds.

"She doesn't have to. Just her two partners and the board."

Sam whistles. "Ouch. There's the Monopoly Magnate, rearing his ugly head." Sam's referring to the debacle that used to be game night in our house, when I always destroyed everyone in the family with a line of hotels down all the orange and red properties. They used to call that part of the board Jae's Carnage Corner.

"You could've bought Illinois Avenue," I point out. "It's not my fault you wasted all your money buying utilities."

"Can I punch him, Mom?" Sam pleads.

"Only if I get to first," Charlie teases. "I remember when you had me leverage Marvin Gardens for a song, you slumlord."

"That reminds me, you owe me back rent," I tease.

"Bite me," Charlie growls, but he's grinning so I know he's not really mad. He slowly shakes his head. "It's official. I am rooting for Nami on this one."

"Me too," Sam chimes in, clinking his beer bottle against Charlie's.

"This is why you both always lost Monopoly. You can't keep your emotions out of business," I tell them.

Charlie and Sam groan. "Get over yourself!" Sam gives me a playful jab with his elbow. "This is why you will never get married. No woman will ever be able to stand that ego."

That's when Charlie clears his throat. "Um. Speaking of getting married." Charlie stands up now, and has his hand gripped around his beer bottle. "I . . . uh, have a little announcement to make." He glances at Nick, who gives him a sturdy nod of encouragement. Charlie's hand shakes a little with nerves. I glance at Sam. Does he know about this? But Sam looks as surprised as I am.

Charlie takes a big breath. "Nick proposed to me last night," he says in a hurried rush. "And I said yes. We're getting married."

"Congratulations!" I burst out, jumping to my feet. "Man, why didn't you tell me?"

"Or me!" Sam exclaims.

"I'm telling you fools now!" Charlie says, breaking into a huge grin.

We both jostle to hug our brother. And hug Nick.

"Congrats, Charlie!" Isabella gives Charlie and Nick a joint hug.

"Nick, are you sure you want to marry this slob?" I clap Charlie on the back.

"You *have* seen his apartment, right?" Sam jokes.

"Move, you two!" Mom wiggles between us. "Nick, welcome to the family." She embraces Nick. "When are you two getting married? Have you set a date?" She's all questions that Charlie has to fend off.

Then Dad, who has been quiet until now, stands.

He glances at me, but I can't read his expression. I rarely can. Then he quietly drops his napkin on the table, turns, and leaves the patio without a word.

I glance at Charlie, whose face falls. Nick squeezes his shoulder.

"What's wrong with Dad?" Sam asks.

"I'll be right back," Mom promises, frowning, as she scurries inside after Dad, leaving the rest of us wondering what the hell just happened.

EIGHT

Nami

Who put these up all over the office? THIS IS NOT FUNNY.
[attached photo of a flyer on the office fridge that has "MISSING"
in thick black letters beneath a photo of the Wegner Swivel Chair].

DELL OURANOS
PARTNER, CO-OWNER, BUSINESS INFLUENCER, AND
TRENDSETTER
#ALL-HANDS-ALERT CHANNEL
TOGGLE INTERNAL CHAT

I tell myself not to think about Jae Lee. Even though two weeks pass since I gave him that tour of the office. I am not, actually, repeatedly checking my ConnectIn profile to see if he's suggested a time to visit Rainforest. Of course, the expected invite doesn't come. He's either busy, has forgotten, or he's just letting me stew. It's probably just all part of the mind games he's playing.

That's fine. This *isn't* high school, and while he might have the advantage of the deep pockets of Rainforest, this isn't tennis tryouts or class elections all over again. I'm wiser, older, and this time, he's not going to win. Not even if he's better-looking now than then. Not even if his bright white, dimpled smile does things to my stomach.

I mean, so does salmonella, technically.

I glance at the team of programmers outside my glass office. Arie,

Priya, Jamal, everybody, really, working so hard. They've been sub-dued since Rainforest visited, and a nervous anxiety seems to run through everything they do. The break room whiteboard has re-mained empty. They're worried. I'm worried for them.

I glance at my *Best Boss* mug. They're counting on me. I can't let any of them down. I've talked to Imani several times, but she's been stubbornly noncommittal each time, telling me I need to think of the practicalities of keeping some jobs rather than losing *all* of them. She also promised that she'd keep looking for other options, but even I felt like she might be placating me.

I think this means I need more ammunition to convince her. I throw myself into research. About Rainforest. About Jae. I'm trying to find an angle—something, anything I can use to dissuade them from buying us. It's only when the janitors come to empty the waste-baskets that I realize it's already nearly seven thirty. I head to the elevators just as the vacuums start up in the far corner of the office. I pass by all the clusters of long-ago-abandoned desks. A lone Frisbee lies in the middle of the carpet in the programmers' section. I've shut down this office every day this week, and Dell's only come in for two of those days. It's like he's already sold the place.

I'm buzzing with anxious energy. Unlike normal Friday nights, when I'm exhausted and head straight home to eat takeout on the couch and promptly fall asleep. I text Sora, wondering if maybe she and Jack are free for dinner, but turns out they're on a double date with Jack's brother, Ian, and his wife, Kylie. Sora says I can tag along, but I don't want to be a fifth wheel. It's times like these I es-pecially miss having a person, when I'm reminded society expects people to come in pairs.

Sora texts me.

> *I think I'm getting somewhere with Mom*
> *and narrowing down the wiggle room. I*

> *actually convinced her that, yes, it's okay if*
> *Jack makes the cake.*

I blink at this.

> *Jack is an award-winning, Golden Chef baker!*
> *Why WOULDN'T she want him to make the*
> *cake?*

> *That's what Grandma Mitsuye said!*

> *Great minds.*

Sora sends me a laughing face.

> *Be strong with Mom. She just thinks she's*
> *helping, but this is your day.*

> *Is it though? Feels more like everyone*
> *else's day.*

I know what she means. Wedding planning sometimes feels like the only time in a woman's life she's allowed to be completely selfish, but there's even limits on this. Lord help you if you care too much about the details. Then you're a bridezilla.

I head out of my building lobby, waving to the night guard at the desk. She nods at me as I shuffle out through the single automatic doors, since the revolving doors have already been locked for the evening. The sun will set in about an hour, and the tall skyscrapers along Michigan Avenue cast long, dark shadows on the sidewalk. Outside, the warm July air washes over me like car exhaust, and I instantly start sweating.

"Nami?"

I freeze then, a familiar male voice beside me. I turn, reluctantly, and see the short, balding former classmate from high school. I inwardly curse Chicago—the biggest small town in the world—where your past never stays in the past because you never know when you're going to bump into it, even randomly on the sidewalk.

"Chris?" I say, hoping my face doesn't convey the horror I feel inside. I haven't seen Chris Debsharte in years. Chris's father is Chicagoland's most shameless injury lawyer, with billboards of him and his visible hair plugs and shiny pinstriped suit plastered all along the tri-state. Of course Chris went to work for him when he graduated law school, and promptly landed Illinois' biggest hand injury settlement. Since he's Christopher Debsharte, Jr., he started calling himself "Deuce." He actually posted a video of himself shortly after, lip-syncing to "I'm So Paid" while rolling around in hundred-dollar bills fanned out on his bed. That pretty much tells you all you need to know about Chris. Oh, and it will come as no surprise that I'm pretty sure he was one of Jae's pals, or at least ran with that group back in high school.

The last time I saw Debsharte, we were both taking the bar exam. Me for the first time, him for the fifth.

"I thought that was you!" He gives me a fake grin, one I know he's practiced in the mirror. "What is *up*, girlfriend?"

I am so, so not his girlfriend. "Uh, just work, I—"

"You still at that tech company or whatever? Toobie?" he interrupts.

"Toggle."

He waves a hand to show he's already forgotten. "I mean, you want the real dough, you should think about becoming a litigator. I just bought my *second* Tesla."

Hand settlement money, I assume. "Oh? Good—"

He interrupts again. "Eh, they're trendy. You know. But gotta keep up with the Joneses."

"Yeah, I—"

"You ever want real dough, you oughtta ditch that corporate gig. I mean, hit snooze, and put me in an early grave." He laughs at his own joke.

"I don't—"

"Litigation boys play too rough for you, huh?" He gives my arm a playful jab like we're shadow boxing. I had truly forgotten how much I can't stand Chris Debsharte. Figures he was one of Jae's old buds. Chris hasn't let me finish a complete sentence since he flagged me down. Do I really need to be here for this conversation? I wonder if I could just keep nodding, looking like I'm listening, as I slowly ease into the back seat of a rideshare. How long would he keep talking to himself on the sidewalk after I'm gone? I wonder.

"Well, actually—"

"I'm here to meet my gal," he interrupts me. "Take her to a swanky dinner. One of these days, if she's good, I *might* pop the question."

Wow. Lucky her.

"Okay—"

"But *only* if she's good." Chris laughs again. Oh, he's a winner. "Anyway, aren't you getting married soon, too?"

I wonder if he's playing an evil prank on me. He follows my social accounts. I know, because every once in a while I get an obnoxious photo of him in my feed, like him lighting a cigar with a twenty-dollar bill, or him lying shirtless on a yacht in Lake Michigan where he's trying to decide between one expensive bourbon or another with the hashtag #OnePercentProblems.

Surely he knows Mitch and I broke up. It's been eighteen months. Granted, I did not invite him to the wedding, so I did not mail him my *Please cancel the date because my fiancé decided to accept a blow job from a stranger in a party bus, and then a buddy took a blurry video for a laugh* notices. Even without that personal touch, surely he saw my social media posts from more than a year ago. Also, he knew Mitch somehow—a friend of a friend or something.

"Mitch and I broke up," I say tightly. And, wow, I can't actually believe he let me finish a sentence. My first.

"You did? When?"

"A year and a half ago."

"No way! I just saw a picture of you together. Last weekend!" He digs into his pocket and pulls out a new smartphone. "See?" He flashes me a photo from Mitch's account. I stare. Long and hard. Mitch, Cubs hat backward on his head, cocky grin on his face, is standing at some Wrigleyville bar, his arm casually draped over the shoulders of an Asian woman.

Who. Is. Not. Me.

I drink in the photo as my mind flies in a hundred different directions. Mitch has a new girlfriend. She's Asian. Like me. But she's shorter than me by at least three inches by the way the top of her head hits well below his armpit. Mitch's companion is also wearing too much eye makeup, and too much lip liner, and her blush amounts to two streaky lines below her cheekbones. Ugh. She looks like she fell face-first into the sample counter at Sephora and then decided it was a good look and went with it.

I have many faults, but too much makeup, nonprofessionally applied? No, not one of them.

"That's not me," I tell him, feeling my temper kick up.

"Yes, it *is*," he insists, tapping the phone so the photo grows larger, so that I can absolutely see Mitch's new girlfriend's highlighter streaks on her face that make her look a little like a mime and . . . is that a bit of a line from her foundation on her chin? A visible line? Why, girl? Why? Have you never heard of a blending sponge? I blink at Chris, realizing that he genuinely does not see any difference between this woman and me.

How? We look nothing alike. I feel the fury of my Scottish dad's temper burning a hole in my belly.

"Look. At. The. Name." I tap his screen, where it clearly reads *Bridget*.

"Oh. Hey. You're right." He shrugs. Then a light goes off in his head. "Hey, you want to grab a drink sometime? I mean, I don't know if I ever told you this, but I always thought you were hot. Some girls from high school? They have *not* aged well, but you. I mean, I've never been with a Chinese girl before—"

"I'm Japanese."

"Huh?"

"Not Chinese."

"Whatever." He shrugs, unconcerned about this little detail derailing his Asian sex fetish.

"Don't 'whatever,'" I snap, interrupting him as I feel adrenaline flow through my body and to my very fingertips. "Why would I ever want to go out with you? You're shallow, egotistical, casually racist, absolutely sexist, and the only reason you're at all successful is because you're piggy-backing on Daddy's sleazy defense firm. I never liked you. I always thought you were a navel-gazing fool who never cared about anything at all except bragging about all the things you have that you don't deserve, and didn't earn. So, please, do not act as if it would be an honor for me to be the woman you choose to cheat on your girlfriend with."

Debsharte blinks, stunned. I turn and walk away from him, only to hear him grumble, softly, under his breath, "Bitch."

I turn, glaring at him. "What did you say?" I challenge.

He cowers. "Nothing," he mumbles, and scurries away from me down the sidewalk, casting a worried glance over his shoulder as if fearing I'll chase him down.

The anger starts to drain out of me, but instead of feeling triumphant, I feel like he'll just go around telling everyone what a bitch I am. And that, without context, they'll all believe him.

I am not exactly sure why I care about that.

An hour later, snug in my Old Town apartment with a plastic container of Thai curry balanced in my lap, I sit curled up on my modern blue couch, phone in hand. I barely notice the floor-to-ceiling windows facing north, showing off my eighth-floor view of the sparkling lighted condo buildings in the distance, and more than a few rooftop patios, decorated with string lights and oversized open striped umbrellas.

Everything in my two-bedroom apartment is a recent purchase, since I left all the old furniture at the condo Mitch and I used to share. Despite the burning vanilla candle on my coffee table, my apartment still faintly smells like new car, and has the look of a staged model unit lacking personal knickknacks for the most part because I'm too busy to go buy them. I don't even have a TV. I keep thinking I'll get around to buying one, but the idea of figuring out how to hook it up exhausts me. Besides, who has time for TV watching, anyway? And if I do, I watch on my tablet in bed.

If you opened my sleek gray cabinets in my super-modern kitchen, you'd find mostly empty cupboards. I have about two pots and a set of four dishes that Mom gave me, a mismatched set of utensils, and one spatula. I don't cook. Not really. I'd been planning on really stocking up with the wedding registry, but since that fell apart, I haven't really had the heart to go back into fancy kitchen places and buy what I'd been hoping would be a gift to Mitch and me. So now my drawers are filled with takeout sporks and packets of soy sauce and ketchup.

I wonder if Mitch is enjoying that one slotted spoon, the old futon that had been following me around since college, and all those plastic Cubs beer cups that he lugged home from Wrigley Field. I pull up his social on my phone. I unfollowed him, of course, but he never really posts anything as private. There's no way this Bridget woman looks like me. Mitch is taking her to all our old haunts, too. Sheffield's bar. Brunch at Ann Sather, where she's actually eating one of those ginormous cinnamon buns bigger than her face.

Mom calls then.

Ugh. I know I should pick up ... but ... I just ... don't actually feel like I'm up for a call with Mom right now. I'll need to be super upbeat and fine. I don't know if I have the energy to carry the burden of both my happiness and hers right at this moment. The last couple of times we talked, she wanted to make *sure* I loved the surprise birthday party, and I think if she keeps asking me about it, I'll just blurt out that I actually hated it and to please never do that again. No one needs that kind of truth bomb.

Besides, I'm still peeved she gave my number to Jae's mom without asking me first. Even if I get it: Jae's mom is one of her oldest friends. It would be like if Fatima called me up and asked me for a favor. I'd do it without thinking. Just like Mom did. I send Mom to voicemail and then listen to her message.

"Nami! It's Mom." She sounds almost too upbeat then. "I thought I'd make an appointment at that dress shop that did your dress for Sora. They were so professional, and they were named Best Bridal again this year in *Chicago Mag*. I just know Sora will find the perfect dress there!"

Sure. For four to five figures, she'll definitely find the perfect dress. I know for a fact Sora doesn't want that. She told me she was thinking about trying to find one off the rack, or at a vintage resale shop. Sora and Jack want a quirky, small, and most importantly not impractically expensive wedding. Mom missed that memo.

I feel a glint of guilt. Maybe I should call Mom back, dissuade her from this course. Then again . . . this is Sora's battle. I get back to scrolling. Because I'm already down a path of self-destruction, I search for Jae Lee.

Oh. Look at that. He's with his gorgeous brothers. I glance at Jae's face and feel that uncomfortable pinch in my stomach again.

Jae sits with his brothers at a fancy restaurant in Fulton Market, one that's nearly impossible to get reservations for, yet, there they are. They're holding up champagne flutes looking . . . far more grown-up than I remember. And, desperately handsome. Dark, tall, bright white grins, dimples all around. Do they all have impossibly thick dark hair? Squared-off chins? Flat stomachs and lean muscles for miles? Jae's the most handsome of them all. My stomach feels weird, so I glance away from him, and to the caption.

Celebrating my brother's engagement! Jae writes, and I see it's Charlie, and his boyfriend Nick, they're toasting in the picture. That's sweet. Jae's brother Sam is tagged with his girlfriend, Isabella. But . . . Jae seems to be solo. What? No Instagram model on his arm?

Huh.

Interesting.

I wonder why.

Jae always has someone.

I dig back a few more posts, poking into the brothers' accounts. The next picture nearly makes me drop my Thai. Is that shirtless beach volleyball at North Avenue Beach? Yes. Yes, it is. I can't stop staring at Jae's perfectly defined abs. My stomach flutters again.

Suddenly, the AC in my apartment doesn't feel so cool anymore. That, or the curry is getting to me.

I cannot be attracted to Jae Lee.

This cannot be.

I need to cure myself of this, and the fastest way to do that is to text him.

Ran into your best friend, Chris Debsharte.

Jae comes back to me almost instantly. His quick response sends a zing of delight down my spine.

Not my best friend. How is Deuce?

Gross. A terrible human. Did he learn that from you?

Do you really think Deuce takes advice from anyone? He literally gave himself a nickname that means poop.

This actually makes me chuckle a little.

He ate lunch at your table in high school. You're telling me you weren't friends?!

Deuce teased me every day sophomore year, always joking that I should go back to China "where I came from" even though I was born in Illinois. My greatest regret is that I kept telling him I'm Korean. I should've just told him I'm American.

I understand exactly what Jae means.

You probably wouldn't have made him think Asians could be Americans, no matter what you said.

That's true. But I would've made him use his two brain cells to think about it.

I send him a laughing emoji. *So why did you let him sit at your table?!* I text.

Keep your friends close, but your enemies closer.

Hmmm. Is that what you're doing with me?

Now you're catching on.

I laugh, more delighted than I should be. I start typing a response.

Tell me the truth: did Deuce's dad sell his soul to you? Deuce and his dad? They must've, to be so rich.

You really think their souls are worth that much? Please. The devil has standards. I said no.

I laugh again.

You're not going to make your brother and his fiancé get married in some weird satanic ritual are you? Pentagrams and goat's blood might frighten the guests.

Hmmm. You know about Charlie. Been stalking me online, Namby?

Shit. Caught. I backpedal.

Just researching the enemy. Preparing for battle. Looking for weaknesses to exploit.

I'll save you the trouble. I have no
weaknesses.

Please. You have at least four: Sunlight. Garlic.
Wooden stakes. Holy water.

Maybe garlic. Only if I'm trying to keep my
breath fresh. And just to be clear: is Satan
a vampire?

In this case, yes. And maybe you're a werewolf,
too. And demon spawn.

So, what are you then?

Van Helsing. Blade. Anyone who will vanquish
you.

How will you do that? With your running
man dance moves? I'll play Kesha. Is Tik
Tok still your favorite song?

I freeze for a full second. I almost forgot about that. Jae's graduation party. My one and only moment of weakness. I don't even know
what I was thinking going to the party. The real shock had come
when Jae had invited me at all. He'd surprised me one day by
my locker on the second-to-last day of school and offered me
an invite. A truce, he'd said. But I'd been so stunned, I just said
yes. I wasn't used to being asked. People didn't invite me to their
parties.

Later, I almost didn't go, fearing Jae planned to drop a bucket of
pig's blood on me in front of the whole class. Turns out, his parents
were out of town, and he just invited everyone at school.

I had the tolerance of a mouse back then. One half red plastic cup of spiked punch and I was done for. My face burns hot.

You will forget about that immediately.

Oh, no. I'll never forget. I only wish I had video. You'll need to show me those moves again.

No way. Never.

Too bad. You'd have the perfect opportunity to show me those dance moves when you all come to Rainforest. How does Monday morning, 11 am sound?

I forgot for a second that there's a point to all this. That I have to save Toggle.

I'm in. I'll bring the holy water and stakes.

And I'll bring the disco ball.

NINE

Jae

Stop trying to make everyone happy. You're not chocolate-chip cookies.

#DAILY INSPIRATION CHANNEL
TOGGLE INTERNAL CHAT

It's 11:02, and I'm pacing my office, worrying that Namby is going to stand me up. I've been looking forward to this all night. I wonder which Namby will show: the hate-glarer in Toggle's conference room, or the playful, hate-flirt in my text messages.

This meeting is a nice way of ignoring the growing crisis in the family since Charlie announced his engagement. Everyone's on board except Dad. Anytime Charlie, Nick, or the engagement is mentioned, he clams up. Or leaves the room. Or stubbornly stares at his phone as if none of us are there.

Mom has told us all repeatedly to give Dad time, which we have all taken to mean she'll work on him. When it comes to Dad, you can never hit him head on. You've got to zig-zag like a fighter jet avoiding a missile.

"I mean, I thought he liked Nick," Charlie moaned to me over brunch yesterday.

"He does. Nick is the only one who listens and takes notes about Dad's recipes. And Mom says it's not about you. Or Nick."

"Then what's the issue?"

"She says she's not sure. Yet. She promises it's not you. Or Nick."

"Then how does she know it's *not* Nick. Or me?" I wish I had a better answer for Charlie. "Ugh. This is med school all over again."

"No. It's not." At least, I hope it's not.

"I tied myself into knots, going pre-med, getting all As, everything Dad wanted . . . because I knew . . . I just knew he wouldn't be okay with me being gay."

"He came around," I say.

"After some hard-core deprogramming of wrong-headed ideas he got as a kid in his home country that still, by the way, hasn't legalized gay marriage," Charlie says. "And how do we know it really took?"

"You should just talk to him," I say.

"Talk? Have you met our family? There's no two-way communication. It's Dad issuing edicts, and us following them. That's it."

I laugh. It's true.

"Still, maybe we could try."

"Dad won't talk about it, anyway. You know he won't. Not until he decides he's ready. No matter what Mom says."

I sigh. Charlie's right. "Don't assume the worst."

"The longer he doesn't talk, the more I won't have a choice," Charlie says, making it all too clear there might be a point of no return for my brother.

Not that I blame him. I should talk to Dad myself, but at the same time, it's not like Dad and I have seen eye-to-eye for a long while. The last person I think he'd ever listen to is me.

I push aside thoughts about Charlie and Dad. That's an unsolvable problem at the moment.

Right now, I've got to worry about Namby.

I pace by my corner window, overlooking an old office building being transformed into a new set of luxury condos. I glance at my smartwatch again and fight the urge to check ConnectIn. She won't stand me up. She can't afford to.

I shove my hands into my pockets and pace. I glance out of my open "office"—just three glass walls. It's an open floor plan awash in light, glass, and overgrown, gigantic houseplants, which hang from the ceiling. Somebody, somewhere thought it all worked: the macramé hammocks and chair pods, the complete lack of blinds, and the giant stairwell in the center, which also doubles as an auditorium for big announcements and Friday Fun games. Two wooden staircases line each side, and in the middle lie large wooden slabs covered in throw pillows—basically the world's most decorative and comfortable bleachers.

We're beyond Ping-Pong tables. Our office contains a half basketball court, a lap pool, and a full tennis court on the roof. Sometimes I'm not sure if we're a tech company or a gym, but somehow it all works. Since half our employees work from home, coming to the office needs to be an event. We lure them in with swim time, and court time, and personal trainer time, and an endless variety of delicious free food. There's also state-of-the-art dog daycare and child daycare on the premises. It seems like we've got everything, but the fact is it's all strategically placed to make our employees spend their entire lives here.

There's almost no need to go home. That's by design.

Just then, Treely, our smart device, pings. "You have guests in the lobby," it announces in a pleasant voice. "Shall I send them up?"

"Yes, Treely. Please."

I move past the trampoline-floor break room and quickly to the main, oversized staircase. I focus on the automatic glass doors. Nami walks through, her two partners trailing after her, but I barely notice them. She's a gorgeous goddess in a white linen sundress, tanned, muscled legs fully on display. Damn, those legs. The hem of her dress skims the top of her knee. I feel a flush coming on. Heat floods my neck.

Mirrored aviators sit on top of her head as she swivels, looking for me. Thick lashes, big brown doe eyes. Perfect heart-shaped face and light pink, full lips pursed in a bow. For a full second, as the sun glints off her impossibly shiny hair, I am rooted to the spot. In my brain, I fear some Disney princess music might be playing. Birds ought to be flying around her head, laying a flowered crown on her. Then she looks at me and glares.

I trot down the stairs to meet them and extend a hand to Nami. She stares at it as if it's a furry spider she'd like to crush. But reluctantly, she shakes it. Her grip is so firm I worry she's trying to break my fingers. The hate-flirt of my text messages is all hate and no flirt.

"Thanks for coming."

I turn to Dell and Imani, shaking their hands in turn, and giving them a brisk nod. I have to remember there's work to be done.

"Shall we go get breakfast and then I'll give you a tour?" I'm almost gleeful as I lead the group to our kitchen. It's twice the size of Toggle's, all gleaming chrome and white tile, and is filled with breakfast staples: a buffet of bacon, sausage, and the like, as well as a toasting station for bagels and croissants. And, because we can: a gourmet chef running an omelet station.

Nami's mouth goes slack in surprise. "Your employees get omelets?"

"Would you like one? He makes them to order."

Nami sighs in defeat. "You do win Breakfast Mondays."

Now that we've all half-eaten a delicious breakfast, and I've given them a tour around our very impressive, if I do say so myself, facilities, we pile into a conference room, featuring reclining chairs and hammocks. Nami perches on the edge of one of the recliners. Dell heaves himself into a hammock, and Imani takes her place in the pod chair in the corner. I take the large leather-back chair at the end of the table, the power position.

"So, as we mentioned earlier, we want Toggle to be Toggle," I begin. "We want to keep you mostly intact."

"Mostly?" Nami cuts in sharply. She's got her tablet out, ready to take notes. She glares at me so hard, her stare feels like a punch.

"There will be a few redundancies, of course, but we don't want you to give up your culture, or your values."

"That's not the impression I get from the other companies you've bought. You've made them all into little Rainforests from what I can tell. Natural Foods. ShoeFactory. ABCkids."

"Many of those we bring into the Rainforest family simply opt to adopt our ways because they like them better," I say, talking point number one. "The omelet station and unlimited vacation time are two great examples of that."

"Unlimited vacation only means that no one actually takes it, if the pressure is on everyone to be at work," Nami points out.

"Not true," I counter, even though more often than not, that is true. "We just had someone spend a month in a yurt in Iceland. We encourage people to take the mental health breaks they need."

"Who cares about vacation? I never take it myself," pipes in Dell, unhelpfully, from the macramé hammock as he strokes his fleshy chin. "Look, let's just get down to brass. Let's stop being pussies about it, and just get to the point."

Classy, Dell.

"I mean, you want to buy us. We're in a tight spot. Let's just have a show of hands right now to see where everybody's leaning?"

Imani shifts uncomfortably.

"Dell, I don't know—"

But he barrels on without me. "All in favor of selling in the range that Jae offered, raise your hand." Dell raises his high.

Imani and Nami keep their hands at their sides. Nami raises a triumphant eyebrow.

"All in favor of *not* selling right now, raise your hand?" Dell continues.

Only Nami raises her hand.

Imani keeps her hands down. I could've told Dell that.

"Okay, so let's steer away from votes," I offer. I turn to Imani. "Since you're the tiebreaker, let's talk about your concerns. For the next however long it takes, I'm all ears." I lean across the table. "But, before we really get into it, anyone want to hear some music?" I hit the remote near me, and the built-in stereo system in the conference room blares out the first bars of "Tik Tok." Dell and Imani look puzzled. Nami's face goes beet red with fury.

"Anybody want to dance? I hear some of you like to dance." I meet Nami's gaze. "Nami?"

"Don't care for it," Nami grounds out, her laser vision searing a heat ray through me.

"Oh? My mistake." I grin at Nami, but she just throws imaginary darts of rage at me with her eyes. I turn down the music. I glance down at my watch, pretending a meeting notice has popped up there. "Actually, we'll need to continue this tomorrow. I've got something that's come up." Classic look-too-busy-to-be-bothered-and-let-them-sweat technique. "We could continue this meeting in the board room tomorrow, but actually, I have an idea. Who here plays tennis?"

TEN

Nami

Not funny, guys. Absolutely not funny.
[Attaches a picture of a ransom note with cut-out magazine letters,
which reads: "We have your Wegner. She will be returned to you
safely if you meet our demands." Demands: 1. Breakfast Mondays
become Breakfast All Week. 2. Do not sell Toggle to Rainforest. 3.
Be nicer. To everyone.]

DELL OURANOS
PARTNER, CO-OWNER, BUSINESS INFLUENCER, AND
TRENDSETTER
#ALL-HANDS-ALERT CHANNEL
TOGGLE INTERNAL CHAT

The blistering August sun hits the blue tennis court on the roof of the Rainforest building, reflecting the Chicago heat up to us. Even my mirrored aviators don't reflect all the light, and I'm beginning to wonder if a little tennis match is really that great an idea, especially as I notice that Jae has the best, new fancy racket with the bright yellow pinstripe, plus some one-of-a-kind blindingly white sneakers. Also, his polo fits stupidly well to his shoulders, and he flashes a too-confident grin as he runs a hand through his thick, nearly black hair.

My stomach feels weird again.

I hope it's because I skipped breakfast and I'm hungry.

I catch Imani looking at me curiously, wearing a bright yellow polo and white shorts, and I wonder if I've been just staring at Jae's chest the whole time as he explains how Rainforest installed this monstrosity of a tennis court on the roof for the employees. Yeah, for the employees. Just another way to sucker them into spending more time at the office. I always felt like people should want to be there because of culture and common purpose. No tennis court changes that.

"Warm-up?" Jae asks, and we all nod.

Jae and Dell naturally head to the far side, as Dell asks Jae about some finer points of tennis court construction, and Imani and I stay nearby.

"Have you made a decision? I mean, you're not letting fancy tennis courts sway you, I hope."

"I haven't made a decision," Imani says, voice devoid of any emotional clues about which way she might be leaning. And that worries me. "Now, let's play."

She nods over to the other side of the court. I glance up and realize Jae is on the other side of the net. He lobs me a ball, casually. Watching the bouncing yellow orb sail to me, I smash it back as hard as I can. He returns it, making it look effortless.

"That's the best you've got?" He lobs me another overhead. I put all my hatred in it, and it bounces straight upward, to the net above the court designed to keep balls from escaping out and falling the six stories into traffic below.

Then Jae sends me a forehand, and I whip it back, hard. Ditto with a backhand. Perspiration drips down my temple. Jae, however, hasn't even broken a sweat. "Should we practice volleys now?"

He moves up to the net, flicking me a short ball. I hit it before it bounces, and pretty soon we're pinging balls back and forth, and I have only one goal: beat Jae. Except he always gets the lucky angle, the lucky bounce, the lucky flick of his racket. He gets two by me. And I only get one.

This is infuriating. I just. Want. To. Win.

"You realize this is a warm-up," Jae jokes. "Do you always try to kill everything in the warm-up?"

"Maybe," I retort, swinging. "You're not used to this at your fancy tennis club?" I say this and regret it, because I realize I've tipped my hand again. A picture of him playing in an exclusive private club last weekend got hundreds of likes on his social media.

"Stalking me again online?" Jae asks, teasing. "Tsk. Tsk. Keep this up and I might think you're interested in me."

"I'm about as interested in you as watching paint dry," I bite out, even as my face feels hot. I turn to head to the back court to pick up a loose ball. Dell, for his part, takes up a position on the other side of the court, with Imani, to warm up. Dell groans and grunts so often, I worry he's going to pop a joint when he runs. Also, every time he reaches for a ball, I am ninety percent sure, he passes gas. I get a whiff of rotten egg drifting over the net from his side of the court every so often.

I wait as Jae sends me a ground stroke and slap a forehand back hard. I forgot how nice it feels to hit a tennis ball as hard as you can. Jae jogs to the corner, and whips it back.

"You know, Coach always said you never had any trouble with the killer instinct."

"I know," I say, hitting a ball hard. Too hard. It flies long.

Not that it matters. This is a warm-up.

We get into a volley so intense, and so hard, that both Imani and Dell stop their own warm-ups to stare at us. I hit it crosscourt. Jae fires back down the line. I run to the net, picking up the ball on approach, and Jae sends it high in the air. I demolish it with an overhead smash, but Jae deflects it up. I smack it again.

This time, Jae's ball goes up and out, to the tall chain-link fence around us.

"Whoa, guys, save some for the match, am I right?" Dell scoffs.

"Are we ready to play?" Imani asks, looking at me with mild concern.

I watch as Dell takes a practice swing with his square Yonex racket as if he's just gotten out of a time machine from 1988, and begins some odd bending stretches that require a lot of exhaling air, which is what he does before every serve, whether he's receiving or not. His SAE baseball cap looks even more bleached out in the sun.

"I sure am! My vintage Yonex and I are ready," Dell says, twirling the unusually small, odd-shaped racket in his hands. "You know, only five of these exist in the world now."

"Because they're so old?" I ask.

"No!" he spits, annoyed. "Because they're so *valuable.* I got this one at private auction."

I sigh. Has he never heard of a mall?

"So, teams, I was thinking . . ." Not with Dell. Or with Jae.

"I'll be on Dell's team," Imani says, and I think she's just being nice, because she knows I can't stand Dell, but doesn't realize I can't stand Jae more.

"Imani knows a talented player when she sees one," Dell brags, taking another deep knee bend as he groans.

"Imani, that's not necessary," I say.

"Oh, I think it is." Imani nods to Jae, and then I realize what she's doing. Some kind of strange, wrong-headed matchmaking that absolutely has nothing to do with the fact my stomach is doing backflips.

"I think that's a *great* idea," Jae declares, which is exactly how I know it's a terrible idea.

Standing behind Jae, getting ready to return Imani's serve, I watch his calf muscles tense, and wish this would all be over soon. I don't like being on the same side of the court as Jae, or the fact that he glances back at me every so often, a cocky smile on his face. I've never been on Jae's team, not once, not in high school debate, not on the tennis court—never. I don't know what to do with myself.

Dell fires a serve at me—where did that power come from? I was too busy staring at Jae's backside, and my return goes wide. Dammit.

"Fifteen–love," Dell calls out the score, a little too braggy.

Jae moves over and holds out his hand for a low five. It's what we'd always do after every play with Coach Howig. She always said we needed to pump each other up, even on the bad plays. Actually, especially on the bad plays. But I hesitate.

"Are you really going to leave me hanging? We're *teammates*." He hangs his hand out. I reluctantly slap it.

"There, that wasn't so bad, was it?"

"Just play, okay?" I grind out.

Dell fires a serve to Jae, who returns it easily. Imani volleys it back, but the ball snags the net, bouncing upward . . . and straight to Jae's racket. There it is: the famous lucky bounce. He fires his return right past Dell. I give him a low five. He nods at me.

"We got this," he cheers. His dark eyes sparkle.

Dell fires another serve, but this one goes long. He serves again and rushes the net. I hit it to Dell's backhand. He connects with it—volleying back, hard down the line, and right out of Jae's reach. He swipes his racket in the air in frustration.

"I think Dell was pretending to be bad in warm-ups," Jae tells me as we walk past each other.

"Why?"

"I don't know, maybe because he's actually hitting the ball now and not whiffing?"

"Maybe he just worked out all that gas," I joke.

"Gas?" Jae asks, confused.

"I'm pretty sure in warm-up he farted every time he hit the ball."

"Well, maybe that's how he's getting his speed," Jae jokes, and I can't help but snicker.

Dell serves, and the return snaps back to him. Dell uses it as an approach shot and now, he's at the net. With both of them there now, a lob might work, or, even better, down the middle.

As if reading my mind, that's exactly where Jae puts it. Both swipe at it, neither connects.

He turns and mouths, *Down the middle* . . .

Solves the riddle, I finish. What Coach always used to tell us. Jae gives me a quick nod. The next point, Jae's on it again: face determined, body agile, and . . . if I'm willing to admit it, damn attractive. He's not even winded when he chases down a lob and fires it down the line for a winner. Powerful muscles. Quick reflexes.

I feel hot, and it's got nothing to do with the August sun. My stomach rumbles its discomfort again.

Pretty soon, we've almost won the game. And Dell isn't happy about it. He fights back with a couple of winners, and then, they're ahead. Dell scowls at me every time I take a swing at the ball, and he actually laughs at me when I miss. He's a terrible sport. I didn't think it was possible to dislike him more, but here we are.

I hit a winner, and Dell misses. He curses, throws down his racket, and glares at me, as if the shot were a personal insult.

"That's out!" he lies.

"That was in, Dell," Imani corrects him. She shakes her head and shrugs.

Dell glowers at me, that insult in his eyes again. He smashes his very next serve into the net because he's too angry to concentrate. The second serve, he manages to get over the net. Jae returns the ball. We lob it back and forth, until an uncharacteristic miss-hit from Jae sends it up in the air. Dell attacks it, slamming the floating ball, and aiming it right at my face.

"Ahh!" I cry, turning, but I can't deflect fast enough. The ball hits me hard, smashing into my right ear. The impact is so hard, my ear temporarily rings. Game to Imani and Dell. Instead of apologizing, Dell just sends me a gloating, triumphantly smug smile.

"Hey! Watch it!" Jae cries in my defense. Imani also shoots Dell a look that tells him he went too far.

"Sorry!" he calls much too late, and far too insincere. I shake off the hit, rubbing my ear, as the sound returns to normal.

"Hey," Jae says, moving toward me. "You okay?"

"Fine," I grumble. All I want to do is fire a serve into Dell's face.

Jae frowns. "He shouldn't have done that." It implies that we both think the same thing: he did it on purpose. "You sure you're okay?"

"I will be if we beat him." I don't think Imani will mind. She's scolding him right now about his tactics.

A slow, wicked smile crosses Jae's face. "Then let's do it." Jae says it like he's going to enjoy serving up a game of whoop-ass. His competitiveness sidles up to mine, and it's like we've always been a perfect match.

Now, it's a new game, and Jae's serve. He whips one hard at Imani, who swings and sends the ball straight up in the air and out. The next one, Dell fires it right at my face again. But this time I'm ready with a defensive volley right back. We get into a back-and-forth, but ultimately, I lob one over Dell's head that he can't reach, and Imani, despite her desperate running, barely gets a racket on it, sending it out, against the fence.

Now it's time to strategize for the next point. "You thinking what I'm thinking?" I ask.

"I hope you're planning on poaching."

I grin. It's what I loved to do in high school. I'd cut off the crosscourt return. I'm surprised Jae remembers.

Jae connects his first serve, taking Imani wide so that she almost certain hits it crosscourt. I step up, bam, poach that return, and hit it right at Dell's feet. He can't move fast enough to even react.

Point, us.

Now I give Jae a real high five. Soon, Jae and I begin playing as if we've always been partners. We're like a machine, demolishing our opponents, cutting off their returns, smashing their lobs. Jae runs down every ball like a man on a mission—even managing to hit one between his legs. I launch every ball like it's a set point, like the entire match is on the line. We both want to win. We've always both hated to lose. Together, we're laser focused on winning.

Soon, we're not even strategizing. We're just improvising. Dominating. Jae and I might never agree on anything, except that there's no such thing as second place. With his lucky bounces and my serve? Well, together, it's almost like we're unstoppable.

Imani might be a formidable player and Dell fights us with all he's got, but it's not enough. I've got Jae's back and he's got mine, and there's no way in hell we're going to lose. By the end of six games, we've demoralized and destroyed them.

Completely. Totally. Viciously.

Imani doesn't take it personally. Dell, however, looks ready to murder someone. Sweat drips down his beet-red face. At match point, Jae blasts a forehand barely over the net. Dell lurches for it, but can't reach it in time. He's so frustrated, he throws his expensive vintage racket clear across the court in a show of petulant rage. The privileged toddler who didn't get his toy.

Jae throws his racket in the air and shouts, like we've just won the doubles match at Wimbledon. Before I know it, he's hugging me, and lifting me up, parading me around the service line like a sports hero. A giggle of pure joy bubbles up in my throat and I let it out. Looking down at his face, I get lost in his dark eyes beaming with pride. "You were amazing," he gushes, and means it.

"So were you." And *I* mean it.

And right then, as he sets me back on the ground, never taking his eyes off me, I feel something in me shift. A new and unfamiliar sensation tickles my throat. It makes me uncomfortable. It makes me anxious. I swallow, trying to push it down, but it's coming anyway. Could Jae and I . . . could we . . . possibly . . . be friends?

I have a flash of us playing mixed doubles in a league, destroying anybody who comes near us, playing match after match . . . Week-ends filled with delicious victories. What would my life be like if we did that? Thrilling. Exhilarating, even.

No.

That can't be right.

My brain feels like a computer that's crashing. Nothing about this computes. Jae Lee and I were enemies. No, still are.

But what if we aren't?

Sunlight washes over Jae, and his jet-black hair gleams, impossibly shiny and thick. The smile on his face fades a little, and something serious, something . . . different, moves between us. It's not hate. Hate, I know. It's something else. A kind of energy I haven't felt before. The entire world falls away and it's just Jae. And me. His dark, knowing eyes, slightly amused, as he raises one tiny-bit-wicked eyebrow. They are telling me something. Something I think I already know.

Deep down, maybe, possibly . . .

"Good game, all of you." Imani breaks the spell.

"Whatever," mumbles Dell, who is still pouting. He doesn't even offer his hand for a shake, instead crossing his arms across his chest like a toddler.

"Good game," I tell Imani. I glance back at Jae, but the look, the moment, is gone. It's just Jae. Ridiculously handsome Jae.

"We should try for a rematch," Dell huffs, wiping his sweaty brow.

"I think we're done with tennis for the day," Imani says, glancing from me to Jae and back again. "And I think at some point, we do need to talk business. Some of the board members will be flying in this week. Some of them are interested in what's developing here."

I shoot Imani a look. This is news to me.

"Right," Jae echoes, but a little less enthusiastically. "We do need to get down to business."

That reminds me why I'm here. Jae is not my friend. We're not going to be tennis partners in some imaginary league. He's the one who's trying to secretly take over the company I helped build. Not just a company; Toggle is—and has been—my everything. He's the one trying to fire all my loyal employees and mine data from unsuspecting users. He's the bad guy here. How could I think that years of him showing me up in high school, of being only out for himself then, would be any different now? I have to remember that. This tennis match is all part of his elaborate scheme. Get me to lower my defenses, so he can attack me when I'm vulnerable. It almost worked.

ELEVEN

Nami

I don't know what's more disconcerting: that I almost fell for Jae's
distractions yesterday, or that Imani has been avoiding my calls. It
makes me worry Jae has gotten to her. That's why I've been watching
her office and the elevators, waiting for her to appear. I glance at my
watch. It's already ten. It's not like Imani to be this late to work without a call. I hope everything's okay at home. I hope she's not sick.

I glance at Arie's desk, and he raises an eyebrow at me as he nods
at Imani's empty office. I shrug. I have no idea where she is.

My phone rings. My heart leaps. Is it Imani? I glance down and see it's Mom. Ugh. She just has the worst timing. I send her to voicemail. I'll call her. Later. When things are calmer. When Toggle isn't on the chopping block and everything I care about is balancing on a knife's edge.

The elevator doors ding then, and Imani walks out, wearing a bright blue suit and matching square glasses.

She makes eye contact with me and gives a faint wave.

Shit. She has been avoiding me. It's not my imagination.

"Imani!" I stand up and wave frantically, already on the move to intercept her on her way to her office.

"Morning, Nami," she says.

"Is everything okay? At home? You're not usually late."

"Everything's fine. I . . ." Imani isn't meeting my gaze. "I just decided to work from home this morning." Still no eye contact as I trail after her into my office. I feel Arie—and the other programmers—stare at us as I gently close the glass door behind us.

"What are you thinking?" I ask her, settling into a brightly striped chair in front of her glass desk.

"About what?" Imani keeps her focus on her laptop as she unfolds it on her desk.

"About Rainforest?"

"I'm not sure." Her hesitation—her uncertainty—unnerves me.

"Not *sure*? You can't seriously be thinking about selling."

"All I can tell you is the investors and the board, they want us to sell. That's why they aren't going for another round of funding."

"You talked to them?"

"Some of them. This morning."

Ah. Now her late arrival makes sense. She took the call at home. I can't help but feel left out. I know she normally works as the liaison to the board, but I wish I'd been there. I could've helped them see how wrong they are to take the very first offer on the table. Especially one that would destroy everything we've built together.

"I wish you'd included me in that call."

Imani glances at me, guilt flickering across her face. "Things are delicate right now. That's all."

"Okay, we need to sell, but do we have to sell to the Borg? There must be another option out there."

Imani exhales a frustrated sigh as she slumps into her chair, pushing up her bright robin's-egg-blue glasses. "I'm working on it. I am. But who would be better than Rainforest? Joust?"

"Maybe." Still, I wrinkle my nose in distaste. Joust also has issues.

"That's my point," Imani says. "There are just a limited number of companies who have the money to take us over. We might be down to the best of a slew of bad choices."

"You can't offer me the Borg or Klingons, and tell me we should be happy about our new overlords."

Imani just shakes her head. "You can't seriously keep answering me with *Star Trek* metaphors."

"Oh, I can. And when I run out of those? There's always *Star Wars*."

I nod to the giant whiteboard in the break room, visible through the glass wall. The polls have returned, and Priya stands before it, scribbling her vote in the latest question: Who would win a game of thumb war: Yoda or Thor?

Imani laughs. "Lord help us." She pauses, studying me through her glasses. Her dark eyes seem sad, but it's the resignation that sends a chill deep down my bones.

"You know, sometimes business is brutal, that's all. But we can—and should—be proud of all we've done so far."

"Yeah, but what if we can do more? We can't just give up." Panic chokes me as I think of my life without Toggle.

She hesitates, and then nods. "Listen, Nami. I don't want to sell any more than you do. I'm also working on options, okay?"

I nod, feeling a bit of relief. Imani hasn't gone over to the dark side completely. Not yet. "Thank you. For not giving up."

"Of course. Just . . ." She pauses. "Just don't tank the Rainforest deal before it's even materialized, okay? For one, we can use it as leverage."

I hadn't thought of that. But she's right.

"And for another reason, if it's the only option on the table, we're going to have to seriously consider it. We've talked about the reasons why."

"Imani, I'd do anything to avoid it. I'd sell you more of my shares if you want. I'd give you majority control moving forward."

Imani pauses. "You'd do that?"

"Anything to save Toggle." I mean it. Imani can have most of my shares if she wants them. If it will change her mind.

"I couldn't take your shares. You put as much blood, sweat, and tears into this company as much as I have."

"I know. But if it tips the scales, I'll do it."

Imani sighs. "It just may not be up to me, is all."

"But if it is, let me know. I'll give you a controlling share. I don't want to think about a world without Toggle in it."

"I know." Imani rubs her chin, considering. "But I can only do so much. We might have to take Rainforest's offer."

I bite my lip. "But not until we've exhausted *all other options*."

Imani nods. "You've got my word."

I keep to myself for the rest of the morning and even turn down Arie, Priya, and Jamal's invite to lunch. I feel terrible about it, but they're just as worried as I am, and I have no answers for them.

I need time to myself, to clear my head, and also deal with the panic that seems to have lodged itself in my throat. I hate feeling so out of control. I hate relying on Imani to find another way out. But this is how we decided to divide responsibilities way back when.

I head down in the elevators and out the door of my office building, barely even noticing the heavy humidity that's hanging in the air, the choking summer hazy heat radiating off the asphalt.

Toggle is my . . . everything. The people there are more than work family, they're just plain family, and I can't imagine what my roadside wreckage of a life this last year would've been without them. Toggle lifted me up when I thought my life was over. Showed me that even if my engagement fell apart, I had a place where I belonged.

Maybe, I realize with a start, it's the only place I've ever really belonged.

Toggle and its people have become such a part of my life that saying goodbye feels like ripping an essential part of me away. Toggle might have begun as my baby, but now it's become something much more than that. It's my reason for getting up in the morning. It's my purpose.

What do I do if I don't have that anymore?

A taxi honks at me as I step into a crosswalk that's just turned red.

I hold up both hands in defense, and jump back on the curb as the angry driver pulls ahead. I sigh. Summer storm clouds suddenly crowd the blue sky, blocking out the sun. The humidity grows even thicker, if possible, and the wind from Lake Michigan stalls flat, and there's a stagnant, weighty feeling in the air.

The first big drop of rain hits the sidewalk in front of me, followed by another. Crap. Knowing my luck today, it'll start to pour. I spy a restaurant on the corner, tucked under the bright yellow L tracks running down Lake Street. A ramen joint, by the look of the small square sign boasting a red outline of a bowl of noodles, sticking off the side of the building like a T-shirt tag. I cross the street as the rain picks up, dotting the sidewalk in front of me. A big silver CTA train rumbles over the tracks above my head as I duck inside.

Inside, there's art graffiti on the walls: giant koi fish, red, gold, and blue, their flowing tails lashing across the walls and ceiling. Thunder rattles the windows of the restaurant, and the sky really opens up, rain pouring down on the concrete. I glance over my shoulder in time to see a man run in through the door, shaking off drops of rain from his jet-black hair, which spray in every direction. My relief from avoiding the rain evaporates as I see Jae Lee straighten, hair glistening and perfect, like he's in a glossy music video. His cotton button-down, now half-drenched, sticks to his chest and leaves almost nothing to the imagination. Of course he'd be trying to get caught in the rain just to flaunt his muscles.

My stomach tightens. This is the man who will take Toggle. Take everything away from me that matters—and gloat while he's doing it.

He meets my gaze, and his lip curls up in a cocky smile.

"Namby! What a surprise." He grins to show me it's not. I realize this meetup is no accident.

"You're stalking me."

"I got caught in the same rainstorm as you." Jae shrugs. "Also, this is my lunch place. So, technically, you're stalking me."

"As if I would ever do that." I frown.

"Really? Because you're already doing the online version. Have you dug up any more details about my tennis club? Or my brother's engagement? Did you see where I ate dinner last night?" Amusement quirks his mouth.

I only pray my face isn't as red as it feels. "I don't care about you. I care about Toggle." The very mention of my pride and joy makes my heart squeeze. I have to remember Jae is the enemy. He's coming for Toggle.

"Is that why you're always texting me at night? Toggle?"

A soft growl escapes my throat. Before I can reply, the Asian man in the white apron behind the counter sees Jae and bellows, "Jae! Back for more abuse?"

"Mark, this is my friend, Nami. Nami, Mark Hashimoto, owner of this place."

"Nice to meet you," I manage.

"You, too." He shakes my hand with a firm grip. "You better watch this one. He's a sneaky sumbitch." Mark laughs to show he's kidding, and for the first time I realize he's got a southern accent.

"Mark came up from Texas to open a ramen place," Jae says.

"Been here near five years and still not used to the damn cold!" Mark grouses. "But y'all think eighty degrees is sweltering, and that's kind of adorable."

Jae flashes another smile, and my stomach feels weird. Jae hangs at my shoulder and I'm overly aware of how close his arm is to mine, how his damp shirt sticks to his well-defined biceps.

"What are you going to get?" he asks me.

"A rideshare? To take me away from you?" I bite out.

"Scared to be in the same room with me?"

"Hardly. It's just the smell of brimstone that's so overwhelming." I angrily cross my arms over my chest.

Mark glances from Jae to me, and back again. "I hate to"—Mark clears his throat—"interrupt, but what will y'all have today?"

I glance up at the menu above the register, noting the build-your-own-ramen option, fantastic for nitpicky eaters like me. I'm mentally building my perfect bowl (shoyu, fish cakes, corn, lava eggs, pepper flakes), when Jae interrupts.

"If you want to make lunch interesting, you should try the Hell Ramen."

Jae nods to the flat-screen video menu hanging above the counter, and sure enough, there's a ramen bowl with red devil horns on it. Flames burning in the upper right corner, daring customers to try the nine levels of Hell Inferno Ramen. Anyone who can finish a bowl of #9 wins a hundred-dollar gift card, and their lunch refunded. "I normally get number three, and let me tell you, it's *spicy*. Mark does not fool around."

"No, sir. I do not." Mark grins.

"Number three?" I scoff. "That only has habaneros and kimchi. Please. Do you have baby taste buds? Want some applesauce, too?"

Jae quirks an eyebrow. "Are you *challenging* me to a ramen-off?"

"I know I can do better than a number three," I tease. "I love spicy. Bring it." I do like things spicy. Mostly. Sometimes. Okay, not really, but who cares? If it's about beating Jae, I'd eat a bowl full of nails.

"Okay. Okay. It's probably an easy win. I bet your spice tolerance is about as bad as your overheads."

"There's nothing wrong with my overheads!" I cry.

"Only that they always go out." Jae grins. "How about the person who finishes the ramen first buys the other lunch?"

I feel like we're right back in geometry, each rushing to finish our quizzes before the other, and slap our papers down on our desks first. I won more than half the time. Only this time, the stakes are far, far higher.

"Deal," I say.

"Okay, what about a number six? I can't even imagine how spicy that's going to be, but it has ghost peppers in it, so I know I'll be crying. Probably begging for my mom."

"Please. As if you don't beg for her every single time you stub your toe."

"Only *bad* stubs." He laughs. So do I. This almost feels . . . fun. Almost.

"Why don't you just give up right now, and pay for my lunch," I counter.

Jae shakes his head slowly. "Never."

"Well, why not just go for broke? Number nine?" I slap the counter.

"Are you hearing this, Mark?" Jae asks as we step up to the register. "My friend wants a number nine Hell Ramen."

"Hey, man, your funeral." Mark's southern accent softens his words. He rolls up one sleeve, revealing a colorful arm tattoo of a koi fish. "Y'all sure you wanna risk your life . . . and possibly your esophagus on this challenge? Or you could just play a nice ol' game of thumb war to settle . . ." He glances between us. ". . . whatever *this* is between you."

"There's nothing between us," I snap, even as I feel the air between Jae's elbow and mine, like a living, breathing thing. Hate, I tell myself. It's not that his hair looks amazing wet. Not that the air is tinted with the smoky, sweet scent of his hair product.

"She's secretly in love with me," Jae tells Mark in an exaggerated whisper.

"I am not!" I shout, even as I feel my face burn red.

"Or hate. I don't know. It's a fine line." Jae shrugs. "She loves to hate-flirt with me."

"I absolutely do *not*."

"And she stalks me online. All day. All night."

"Not true," I grind out. "He's an egomaniac. He thinks everybody is in love with him."

"Sure. Uh-huh." Mark just slowly nods, placing his palms flat on the counter. "Well, if y'all are crazy enough to try this ramen, you're gonna need to sign your lives away first."

"Excuse me?"

"Liability waivers," Mark says, reaching behind the counter and pulling out a legal document that would make your typical phone's user agreement look like a tweet. "Can't have you suing me, because you're damn fools."

I scan the document. "Can't eat number nine if you've got a heart condition, allergies to peppers, pregnant, or chance of being pregnant, over the age of sixty-five . . ." The list is long and extensive in prohibitions.

"You scared now?" Jae whispers.

About fifteen minutes later, Jae and I sit across from each other in small corner table near the window, two steaming white bowls of ramen in front of us.

"Okay," Mark says, as he sets down chopsticks and two white ceramic Asian spoons. "Rules are simple. You have ten minutes. You have to finish the entire bowl."

It's not the biggest bowl of ramen I've ever had, so that's good. There are two slices of pork, one lava egg, and bamboo shoots sitting on top of traditional ramen noodles. I lean forward and inhale, and get the notes of shoyu, and something darkly, deeply spicy. It might scare me. A little.

"What you've got in front of you is the hottest damn ramen you'll ever eat. It's the hottest because it's got a heaping helping of Carolina Reapers. Hottest pepper in the world, according to the *Guinness Book of World Records*." He nods to the bowls.

"How bad are they?" Jae asks.

"Only about eight hundred times hotter than a jalapeno." Mark backs away from the table.

"And then there's the scorpion peppers in there for a nice little added kick. If you're ranking this ramen on the official heat scale, it's about one point eight million Scovilles."

"That doesn't sound good," Jae says.

"Oh, it's not." Mark's face breaks into a devious smile. "And don't forget, the winner gets this lovely piece of merchandise." Mark whips out a T-shirt tucked in the back waist of his apron. He flips it open and on it is a giant ramen bowl engulfed in flames with I SURVIVED THE 9TH CIRCLE OF HELL . . . RAMEN in orange-and-red lettering. Mark turns the shirt over. On the back, it reads HELL RAMEN, HELL YES!

"How many people won that shirt so far?" asks Jae.

Mark grins, mischievous. "Only one, sir. That's me."

"How many people have tried?" I ask, hopeful it's not many.

"Only about two hundred. Give or take."

"This is the moment where you can call it quits, Namby," Jae says.

I feel that old stubbornness in me, like when I was learning to ride a bike on Grandma Mitsuye's driveway. I will do this, no matter how many skinned knees I suffer. I glance up at him, meeting his challenging gaze. "Never."

"Save it for the competition, lovebirds," Mark interrupts, throwing a hand towel over his shoulder. "I'm not a monster, so I've gotten you each milk." He nods to the half-gallon milk carton near each of us. "You've got a glass there if you want to use it, though you might want to just pour the jug all over your face once the heat really kicks in."

I laugh.

"Oh, I'm serious," Mark says, face solemn.

Now I am starting to feel nervous.

"Also, lemon juice here, if you want it." He nods to a small yellow squeeze bottle.

"Oh. Good."

Mark laughs a little. "But let me tell you, none of this will really help you. Not all that much." He backs away from our table. "Don't forget, the bathrooms are right behind you. In case things really go wrong." He chuckles as he pulls out his phone from his pocket.

"Y'all ready for me to start the timer?" he asks.

"You *sure* you want to do this?" Jae asks me. Worry knots his forehead.

"You can back out anytime," I counter, staring at him. A flash of challenge crosses his dark eyes. No way he's going to give in. But neither am I.

"Not going to happen," he promises.

"Good." I want the challenge. I am going to beat Jae at something. I. Just. Want. To. Win.

"*Good*," he echoes, almost mocking. Jae pushes up his wet sleeves, rolling them farther up his muscled elbows. "That shirt is mine."

"No. It's mine." I glare at him and grit my teeth. He glares back. Neither one of us blink.

I'm locked in the tractor beam of Jae's eyes. His eyes are dark, glistening with determination. I won't break the stare first. It feels like giving in.

Jae unsheathes his wooden chopsticks from their paper sleeve without looking at them. I do the same. We are glaring at each other like boxers waiting for the fighting bell.

We stare at each other, not the soup, chopsticks hovering in the steam.

"Ready, set . . ." Mark starts. His finger hovers over the stopwatch of his phone. My chopsticks twitch in my hand. "Go!" he shouts.

I dig into the bowl and snag some noodles. Jae does the same. The noodles drip into the bowl as we glare at each other. I take my first bite. Then another. I'm shoveling it in as fast as I can, because I only have ten minutes. Jae picks up speed, too, one bite after another.

"It takes a second to kick in," Mark says.

Somewhere around bite four, I feel it. The heat blooms on my tongue. Not heat. No, a firestorm of white-hot searing pain. In self-defense, I cough, my throat desperate to keep the peppers out.

"You okay, Namby?" Jae asks me, quirking a concerned eyebrow. I drop my chopsticks.

"Are you?" I ask, wheezing. My eyes instantly start to water.

"Huh. Not as hot as I thought it would be," he says, nonchalant. Then everything about his face changes. "Oh. Wait."

Dawning realization hits his eyes as pure panic. I know that panic because I'm already feeling it. I realize with clarity right in that moment that I've made a terrible mistake.

I can't feel the entire top half of my tongue. It's gone numb. Except the fire is now scorching down my throat. No wonder Mark made us sign so many waivers. I blink back tears. Another hoarse cough escapes my throat.

Yes, I made a mistake. A very, very bad mistake.

Jae takes another bite, and against all my better judgment so do I.

My lips burn now. How are my lips on fire? The heat is running through every part of my body. Even the tips of my fingers tingle.

Jae coughs a little, too. "You're starting to sweat," I tell him.

"So are you," he counters.

He slams the table with his open palm.

"It's getting to you, admit it."

Jae shakes his head. "I just like slapping tables."

"Liar!"

Jae slurps up more. So do I. My heart is racing now. Can you have a heart attack from spice? I wonder.

"Your face is red," Jae says.

"Really? Is it as red as your nose? Because Rudolph would be jealous."

"We can stop anytime." Jae wheezes a cough, and slaps his own chest.

"You mean *you* can quit. If you want."

Jae slowly shakes his head. We take another bite.

"You've got five minutes," Mark tells us.

"I think my throat is closing up." Jae, weepy-looking now, with tears streaming down his face, shouts over to Mark, "You are a terrible person. A terrible, terrible person."

Mark laughs. "Wanna quit?"

"No," Jae bellows. He eats another bite.

So do I.

I nearly gag. My entire throat is on fire. My sinuses burn. I am never going to be okay again. This is a mistake. Maybe the worst mistake of my life. I blink back tears.

"Are you sure this is edible, Mark?"

"Barely." He grins.

"When do most people quit?" I manage to wheeze.

"After the first bite," he says. "Y'all are brave—or foolish—to eat all of that so fast."

"I hate you," Jae murmurs, swiping sweat off his forehead. "I hate you, Mark. We're now mortal enemies."

I'd laugh, except that my entire face is now on fire. I might never be okay again. I glance at Jae.

"Having trouble?" I ask Jae, because the only thing keeping me going is beating Jae.

"No. I just think I've melted my face. Also, how are my ear canals burning, too? How?" He slaps the table again. This time, he reaches for the milk. I do, too. I guzzle it, but it's like trying to put out a forest fire with a squirt gun.

Nothing.

"This might be the worst day of my life," Jae says. He chugs milk. "This isn't helping. Like. At. All."

"God, whose idea was this? It was a terrible idea," I joke.

"Yes, and why did I agree again?"

"You've got a death wish?" I suggest. He dips his head back and glares at the ceiling, slapping the table again.

"Please quit. Like please. If I eat the rest of the bowl, I might die," he begs.

I sniff, grabbing a handful of napkins from the table to stop the steady stream of tears. Even through the pain, the horrible, horrible pain, I see an opportunity.

"I'll quit . . . *if* you call off the Toggle deal."

"What?" Jae seems like he's coming out of a dream. "I can't do that. You know I can't."

"Then we keep going." I blink fast. Is the room spinning a little? "I think I might be hallucinating. The room is getting wavy."

"Oh, that's just the 'vision disruptor' phase of the ramen," I hear Mark say. He sounds like he's talking to me from the end of a tunnel. Are my ears working? I don't know. Can Carolina Reapers make you go blind and deaf?

"Three minutes," Mark adds.

"I hate you. Have we established that? What kind of person serves death in a bowl?" cries Jae.

I agree with him. I hate to admit it, but this ramen is going to kill me. Literally kill me.

"Y'all can quit anytime," Mark teases. "Two minutes."

I've only eaten about a third of the bowl. Jae's a little farther, but not by much.

My face has gone numb. My entire face.

Jae squirts lemon juice in his mouth, coughs. "This isn't working at all. Like, not at all."

Now the heat has built up a lava flow straight to my stomach. It rumbles its discontent.

Mark announces we've got less than two minutes. I don't know how this happened.

"Want to call it quits? I'll quit. For you, Namby. I'll do it for you." Jae is sweaty. And a little bit shaky.

"Less than one minute now." Mark again.

I shake my head.

"Can't stop. Won't stop," I growl.

"Are you quoting Young Gunz to me right now? At a time like this?" Jae's eyes widen. "Are you going to bust out your knee-high white socks and plaid schoolgirl skirt?"

"Only if you wear your throwback NBA jersey."

"Thirty seconds." Mark glances at his phone stopwatch.

I glare at my bowl. I can't feel my tongue, and every kind of liquid: sweat, tears, everything, is running out of my face, but I have to do this. I pick up my bowl and begin slurping. Not to be outdone, Jae grabs his bowl. We're glugging down white-hot ramen as Mark counts down.

"Ten . . . nine . . . eight . . ."

I feel hot and cold all at once, and light-headed. My stomach burns.

Jae slams his bowl down first. Then proceeds to cough for several seconds. "Oh God. I regret that. I do. I wish I hadn't done that." He coughs again.

"Five . . . four . . ."

Tears stream down my face. I can't feel my nose. I glug down the rest of the soup.

"Three, two, one . . . and . . ."

I slam my bowl down.

"Done!"

Mark clicks off the stopwatch and looks at our empty bowls. "Wow. I can't believe it. You *both* won."

I cough, tears pouring down my cheeks. "We can't be tied."

"Yeah, this isn't soccer, Mark," Jae says. "We need a clear champion."

Mark laughs. "Sorry, folks. You both get shirts."

That's when my phone goes off. And so does Jae's.

It's from Imani: *Got important news. Let's convene at Toggle. I've invited Jae. Can you come to the office ASAP?*

Jae sighs. "Imani wants us . . ."

"To meet now at Toggle." I blink back tears. My entire face is burning. My throat feels like it might close up. The idea of even trying to seem like I'm not dying while sitting in a conference room sounds terrible.

"Can we do that?" Jae asks, his eyes red.

"I don't know if we have a choice."

TWELVE

Jae

Okay, kids. Per Dell's request, I'm instituting a "respect others' workspaces" initiative. Please, do not take or move other people's office items.

PAULA HERNANDEZ
HEAD OF HR
#ALL-HANDS-ALERT CHANNEL
TOGGLE INTERNAL CHAT

Paula will begin firing people if my chair is NOT returned. ASAP, you assholes.

DELL OURANOS
PARTNER, CO-OWNER, BUSINESS INFLUENCER, AND
TRENDSETTER

I hate to be a party pooper, but technically, you cannot fire everyone over a chair. Also, I respectfully ask that you refrain from using expletives in the group chat.

PAULA HERNANDEZ
HEAD OF HR

I don't actually know how Nami and I got in the rideshare. I think I blacked out on the sidewalk for a second. Despite drinking a half gallon of milk, my entire mouth still burns, and my voice box feels like someone has taken a cheese grater to it. Don't even get started on my stomach, which feels like an angry volcano about to blow. Nami doesn't look much better, either.

"Would you tell me why we destroyed ourselves for this shirt?" I ask her, weakly holding up my Ramen Champion shirt.

"I don't know. It's not even one hundred percent cotton," Nami croaks, sounding like Linda Blair in *The Exorcist*. She's amazingly adorable when she's near death.

We're slumped together in the back of the rideshare, guards down, because neither one of us have the strength to keep it up. I would gloat about how much pain she's in, except that it's taking all the energy I have in my body not to cry.

"This shirt is worthless." She tosses the shirt onto my lap. Weakly, I stuff hers and mine into my messenger bag for safekeeping, but the small movement makes my heart race.

"I think I'm actually going to have a heart attack. I think my heart rate is like two hundred right now." I put my hand on my chest. "I can't wait to see what my calorie burn is for today."

"I can't feel my face," Nami admits.

"I *wish* I couldn't feel my face. I think I burned all my taste buds off the top of my tongue and all the skin from the roof of my mouth." It's true. It's like I ate an extra-large cheese pizza straight from the oven. The heat still hits me in waves, and I don't know when it's going to end. If ever. "I don't think I'm ever going to get this taste out of my mouth. I think I'm going to die tasting Carolina Reapers."

"The good news is death is probably coming for us sooner, rather than later," Nami says. "My insides are melting."

"If I'm ever foolish enough to eat a Carolina Reaper again, please, punch me in the face," I say.

"Deal," Nami says, and we both chuckle darkly as we clink water bottles together. It's about the only thing I can muster. I'm working on not hurling.

"Maybe we should tell Imani we can't make the meeting," I offer. "Then I could just curl up in the fetal position and pass out."

"Don't tempt me," Nami says. "I'm not even sure I'm alive right now. I think my soul left my body five minutes ago."

"Is it just me, or do I feel like we just went to war?" I ask.

"It's definitely war. Someone dropped weapons of mass destruction on my tongue." Nami smacks her mouth. She takes another swig from the bottle of water Mark gave us. "This doesn't help at all."

"I know. It's like flicking water into a volcano." I inhale. "I didn't realize Mark was such a sadist. I'm sorry I introduced you."

"Not his fault. He tried to warn us with all those liability papers."

"I really think I'm going to die," I admit.

"At least you've been to Paris," she says, sounding envious. "I always wanted to go to Paris."

"Okay, stalker. For your information, that trip to Paris was business. And I was only there for thirty hours, eighteen of which were spent negotiating a deal. The only thing I got to see was the Eiffel Tower, and that was just a quick stop on the way to the airport."

She glances at me. "Really?"

"Yes, really. That photo of me doesn't show my carry-on bag in the cab, or the fact that the cab driver took my picture. You always believe in Insta-lives? You know it's all self-marketing." I shrug. Then another wave of unease rolls through my queasy stomach.

"You don't want to take a picture of us now, dying?"

"No," I cry, desperate. "Seriously. How are we going to survive this meeting?"

Nami swipes sweat from her brow. "I suggest we hit the coffee kiosk in the lobby and get a frozen frappa-whatever they have, and then encourage Imani to make this quick."

I glance over at her sweaty, pale self. "That's actually pretty smart thinking."

"I know. It's why *I* should've been valedictorian."

Nami

I actually do not know how I'm able to walk and talk and function, because the entirety of the inside of my body has disintegrated. Just melted away into nothing. The fact that the only thing I had to eat *before* the Hell Ramen was a single bran muffin this morning is the true tragedy of it all. I don't know how I'm going to sit through a meeting. I know I've done something terrible to my body because I can't even drum up any hatred for Jae Lee.

As we take our seats in the Fishbowl, me angling for the chair nearest the door, and ergo, nearest the bathroom, I glance at Jae's sweaty, semi-clammy self, and all I feel is pity. *Pity*. For Jae Lee! Because I know he's suffering. If he's feeling just half of what I'm feeling, he's a wreck. It's like someone has taken a blowtorch to my small intestine. My throat is still burning, and more than a little hoarse, and I am pretty sure I'm losing my voice. I plan to stay quiet, keep my head down, and head straight to the elevators when this meeting is over.

Imani heads to the conference room, takes one look at me trying to sit very still, and at Jae, who's got his forehead against the conference room table, and frowns.

"What's wrong with you two?" Dell barks from the other end of the table. "You both look . . . sweaty."

It's true that I might be having cold sweats. I'm sure that's totally normal after ingesting a poisonous amount of hot peppers. Jae raises his head and blinks. He does look pale. And sweaty. He rubs his temple, as if trying to massage a headache out.

"It's just rain," I say quickly, even though the storm has long since passed. The sun is even starting to peek out through the clouds outside, a single beam trained on the water of Lake Michigan, many stories below us.

Jae gives a little nod. He winces, though, and pinches the bridge of his nose.

"Are you feeling okay? You sound . . . funny."

I nod. "Allergies," I croak, and then my voice box closes up, packs a weekend bag, and tells me it's leaving to recharge.

Arie walks by, sees me in the Fishbowl with Jae, Imani, and Dell, and sends me a text.

*Everything okay? Borg isn't taking over, is
it? You look like the Walking Dead.*

I text back,

*Not yet, don't think. Ate Carolina Reapers for
lunch. Do we have ice cream in the building?
Tums? A full digestive system transplant?*

Yikes. I'll see what I can do.

"What's the important news?" Jae asks. He also sounds like he's talking through a voice modulator. Jae coughs, politely covering his mouth. I know how much that cough hurts, too. I see him flinch. He takes his frappa-vanilla-ice-cream coffee and sips on it. I'd do the same, except I sucked mine down in nearly one gulp in the elevator. My stomach gurgles as the blended ice coffee and Hell Ramen fight it out for dominance. I hiccup, loudly. Dell glares at me. All I want to do is crawl into a bathtub filled with vanilla ice cream and sleep there.

"Tyler Evans has inquired about us."

I sit up a little straighter in my chair. So does Jae. "Owner of Joust? That Evans?" Dell asks.

Imani the miracle worker, I think. I should never have doubted the Girl Boss of All Girl Bosses.

"I thought he was all obsessed with colonizing space," Jae adds. "Does he want to use Toggle to rent out rooms on his space station?"

Jae probably should've kept that last thought to himself. It's the Carolina Reapers talking, probably.

"Yes, that Evans." Imani ignores the space station comment. "I just want all interested parties here to know there might be another option on the table. Early to say, for sure, but interest is there."

Dell leans back in his chair, pensive.

"Is it a real offer, though?" he asks, voice laced with skepticism.

"I'm sure we'll find out soon enough," I say, happy about the new development, but not at all eager to prolong any of this. "Well, that means that our talks are stalled for the moment. Might as well wrap up?" I glance at Jae. He's gone unusually quiet, frowning at the floor. He rubs both temples.

"Yes, let's definitely wrap up," he mutters, almost to himself. Then he seems to realize he's not alone. "I appreciate the information," Jae says, and stands. "I'll take this back to my people, and we can discuss this further at a later date."

Jae's getting out. Oh, not without me he's not. He doesn't get to go sneak home.

"Let me take you back to Rainforest. I can give you a ride." I'm on my feet. It's my ticket out of here, too. I just want to go home, curl up on my couch, and wait for death.

Imani glances at me, surprised. I sniff, wiping my nose.

"I'd love a ride." Jae nods at me.

Both of us scurry out of the conference room, followed by Imani and Dell's curious stares. We nearly collide into Arie, who has a half box of donuts.

"Thanks, Arie," I cry, grabbing the box. I give him a grateful hug and then pull away, as he glances at me, confused.

"Are you going somewhere?"

"Yes, gotta run!" I cry as I tug Jae to the elevator bank and duck into an open elevator. We do our best to look like functioning, upright adults, until the doors close and we both sag against opposite walls.

"I thought I was going to die in there," Jae admits.

"You? I am one hundred percent sure I passed out right when Imani started talking."

We laugh again. I shift the box of donuts in my hands.

"So, where are you parked?" Jae asks me.

I laugh. "Nowhere. I actually don't have a car here. Dell and Imani are probably remembering that I take the train in right about now."

Jae chuckles, too. I meet his gaze and for a second, I forget that my mouth is still burning. My stomach feels weird, and for once, I don't think it's got anything to do with the Carolina Reapers.

"Rideshare?" Jae asks, pulling out his phone.

The mood of the moment shifts again, thankfully, and I nod, slumping more against the wall. I should probably eat a donut, but my stomach is roiling. I'm also still processing the fact that Toggle might be saved—by Joust of all companies? I should be savoring this moment of triumph over Jae, but he's pale and sweaty and the victory feels all wrong. Besides, nothing's a done deal, yet.

"Your address?"

"I live near North and Wells."

He taps on the phone. "Okay, so a rideshare will arrive in one minute."

I barely register the information. I'm too busy trying to figure out if I can claw out of my own body. The donut box feels suddenly too heavy in my hands.

"Let me make it so you get dropped first," he offers.

"You're Gold Coast. You're on the way. You should get dropped first." It just makes sense. I open the pink lid of the donut box and stare at the meager contents: one powdered donut and two glazed.

Jae glances up at me, amused. "You know where I *live*? And you say you haven't been stalking me."

"I'm not stalking. You just brag too much about your condo in public posts." I meet his gaze.

"Sure. Stalker." Jae grins into his phone as he hits Confirm on our ride.

My stomach sends up a gurgle of protest, and I reach for a stale glazed donut and stuff it into my face.

"Does that help?" Jae sends me a hopeful glance. "I heard sugar is supposed to counteract the spice."

"Not really," I murmur, mouth full of stale pastry. "But sort of."

Jae grabs one himself and eats it, shrugging one shoulder.

"Seriously, how long is my mouth going to be *on fire*? Forever?" I moan to the ceiling of the elevator. "I might need to call my mom. And cry. Are you okay with that?"

"Only if I can cry to her, too." Jae grabs the last stale donut. "Want to split it?" He divides the powdered into two and hands me the larger half, like a gentleman. Surprised, I take it.

The elevator arrives at the lobby, and as we both limp out, I toss the empty donut box into a nearby trash can.

"Should we get another frappa whatever?" Jae asks, nodding to the kiosk. My stomach moans.

"I'll be honest, not sure my stomach can take any more dairy."

The two of us cross the lobby, ambling like the walking wounded. Jae's phone dings in his pocket. "Rideshare's here."

"Oh, thank God. I'm not sure I can stand any more."

"Me either. Also, does your head hurt? Mine is killing me." He pinches his nose.

"Everything hurts," I admit, and Jae chuckles in shared pain as we both head out to the black sedan waiting for us. Jae opens the back door and lets me in first, a small gesture that might earn my eternal gratitude. I fall into the back seat of the car. Jae scoots in then, and without even thinking about it, I lean against his shoulder. It's strong and soft and warm all at once. I shut my eyes. "If I suck on my thumb and ask for my mommy, don't judge me."

"Never," Jae says. "What happens in this rideshare, stays in this rideshare."

Thankfully, our driver is the strong, silent type, and just gives us a nod as we pull out into traffic.

"My body hates me right now. Really hates me."

"Should we leave a pile of flaming dog poop on Mark's stoop?" Jae asks as the city whips by us, a blur of silver buildings and crowded sidewalks.

"You keep some of that handy?"

"Always."

"We might need him, though," I add. "We do need to break this tie at some point." We hit a red light and the car slows to a stop.

Jae groans. "Do we? Really?"

We both laugh a little. I'm going to miss Jae, I realize, after I drop him at his place. I'll have the rest of the ten-minute ride on my own. I wish I didn't have to go that stretch by myself. Talking to Jae distracts me from my uneasy stomach and burning throat.

"How about we just slam our heads really hard against the wall and see who doesn't pass out? It would be less painful," he adds.

"True, but, I mean, why stop there? How about we walk on burning coals next?"

"I hear snake charming is awesome," Jae jokes.

"Bear wrestling?"

"Tiger taming."

"Cliff diving."

"Storm chasing."

We go on like this for I don't know how long. Before I know it, we're pulling onto my block. I sit up, blinking in surprise. "You're seriously letting me off first? You just doubled your trip. It's going to take you at least ten minutes to get back to your place."

"It's only because I know you're weak and can't make it, Namby."

I give him a playful shove. "Please. I'm tougher than you."

"Says the woman who said she wanted to cry and call her mommy just a minute ago." I flash him a wry grin as I reach for the handle of the car door.

"Wait," Jae calls. "Don't forget your shirt of honor." He pulls the garish Hell Ramen shirt out of his messenger bag. "We almost died for this. You now have to protect it with your life."

I laugh. It's true.

I hold one end of the shirt. He holds the other. Our knees are still touching in the back seat. Our eyes meet. For a second, everything else in the world falls away: my burning throat, numb tongue, and angry stomach. Toggle. Joust. Rainforest. They all fade away. I forget right in that moment why I hate Jae so much. I'm just grateful he made sure I got home first. It means a lot, because I know he's dying as much as I am, and it's a real sacrifice. I realize it's probably the nicest thing anyone has done for me in a long time.

And for the first time since I don't know when, Jae actually doesn't look perfect. His hair is mussed. He's pale and sweaty and clearly disheveled. His normally starched shirt is wrinkled after air-drying rain, opened at the collar and half untucked, and he looks like he was in a fight and lost. To top it off, he's got a dribbled stain of ramen on his shirt. He kind of looks defeated and pathetically adorable.

And he's even more defeated because Joust might just elbow their way into Rainforest's deal. Now that he's on the ropes, there's something just . . . irresistible about him.

I'm drawn to him, and his wrinkled, tired self, like he's a black hole that I'm about to tumble into. I move closer, not because I want to, but because I can't help it. I'm locked in. I don't even know what I'm doing until it's done.

I press my lips against his.

And kiss him.

THIRTEEN

Nami

I'll make rational decisions about who I date.

BRAIN

You're so adorable when you think you're in charge.

HEART
#DAILY INSPIRATION CHANNEL
TOGGLE INTERNAL CHAT

Jae's lips are warm. And soft. And taste just faintly of Carolina Reapers. The heat blooms on my own lips, a sizzle of either pepper residue or electric chemistry, I don't know which, but a heat that has nothing to do with Scovilles. Jae, still at first with shock, comes alive, and kisses me back. That might be the most shocking thing of all. Jae's kissing me *back*.

The very idea that he's kissing me back at all makes the world tilt. Like maybe, just maybe, a solid law of physics like gravity no longer applies. Maybe I was wrong about him. About us, this whole time.

Our lips, touching, ignites a heat that runs through my entire body in a way that scorpion peppers never can. My lips feel numb, and I don't know if it's the ramen residue or Jae's talented lips, but everything I thought I knew feels turned upside down. I'm kissing Jae Lee. And I'm not hating it.

I want to. I want to badly. I tell myself I hate it. That I hate Jae's amazing, soft lips. The way they part, just a little, like a gentleman opening a door. The way he lets me lead, the way he tastes a little smoky, a little sweet, and all amazing. The way every nerve ending in my body lights up like a bright, blinding Christmas tree of endorphins.

I hate it.

Except I don't.

I just have to dig deeper. There's got to be something in the man's delicious mouth that I hate. My hands roam to his hair, his perfect, amazing hair, and my entire body feels alive. With hate. No, with . . . want. Shivering, white-hot want. Because I want more of this. More of this . . . More of him. More.

I realize in that second, nothing in the world will ever make sense again.

My eyes flick open as I pull away, and I see an unasked question in Jae's eyes. But I have no answers. I blink fast, feeling like I've just come awake from a deep sleep, like I've been under a spell that's just worn off. There's only one reasonable thing to do: I flee. I open the back door of the rideshare and skitter out, running to my apartment building before Jae can call after me.

I spend most of the night chewing on chalky antacids and trying to convince myself the kiss didn't happen. How could it? In what universe would I kiss my nemesis? Never. No matter how adorably a mess he happened to be right then. Also, sidenote: Is this how I like my men? Maimed and vulnerable?

I don't want to know what that says about me.

My ramen shirt lies crumpled on my leather ottoman, and I'm sitting, knees curled to my chest, on my modern, squared-off couch in my small living room, the new upholstery smell not helping my nausea. I glance out to the view of the rooftop patios, decorated with strings of lights, bright against the darkened sky. Across the street someone is having a barbeque; smoke filters up from a grill on their deck, and I can hear the sound of laughter and music floating into my open window.

The rain cooled off the summer night, and now it's a perfect seventy degrees. The breeze blows in, and I wonder if I should eat something other than Tums.

Imani texts me.

> *Evans will be in town. You free next*
> *Tuesday morning for a meet?*

I'm free whenever you need me, I text back. I need to get my head in the game. Need to do some research on Joust. Figure out if it's even a better option than Rainforest.

Sora video-calls me as I'm debating.

"Nami—help!" she cries. Sora's in her cozy new condo that she shares with Jack. She's curled up on the couch in her living room, with her rescue pit, Larry, taking up nearly all of the sofa behind her. He thumps his massive tail against her cushions.

"What's wrong?"

"Mom made an appointment. At your bridal store. I told her I didn't think that was a good idea—that place is so expensive—but she did it anyway."

I sit up, guilt flickering in my belly. Mom warned me she was going to do this, and I didn't stop her. "Did you tell her to cancel the appointment?"

Sora bites her lip. "No."

"You have to set *clear* boundaries. She thinks she's fixing things. She thinks she's helping." And I probably should've called Mom back and told her it was a bad idea.

"I know. But . . . I'm not good at telling Mom no."

"Do you *want* to spend ten thousand dollars on a wedding dress?"

Sora goes pale. "No, I definitely don't. It's just . . . things with Mom have been better lately, and I don't want to rock the boat."

"Do you want me to talk to her?"

Sora bites her lip. "No. I should do it. You're right." She studies me. "Why do you look so pale? And sweaty? Are you sick?" she asks.

I tell her about the ramen-off.

"You ate a Carolina Reaper? *You?*" Sora looks shocked. "You barely tolerate sriracha. What are you thinking?"

"I like spicy," I protest.

"Pfft," Sora disagrees. "You mean you *want* to like spicy things, but really, you just want to slather mayo on everything. Also, you can't even eat mildly hot chili without dumping in half a container of sour cream."

She's not wrong.

"I just wanted to beat Jae Lee at something, okay?"

"This isn't high school." Sora rolls her eyes.

"No. It isn't. Also, I might have. Kind of . . . kissed him," I admit.

Sora stares at me a whole minute. And then she bursts out laughing.

"Why are you laughing?"

"Only because you've been hate-crushing on him since high school," Sora says as her laugh dies out. She lays this out as if it's gospel truth. But this is news to me.

"What. Are. You. Talking. About." My stomach twitches again.

"I mean, you've always hated on him a little hard," Sora says, almost apologetically. "Mom and I always thought . . ."

"Oh, no. Do not do that. Stop *ganging up on me!*" That's Mom and Sora, always heads together, judging my life from afar, like when they both secretly agreed they hated Mitch but failed to tell me.

"It's not bad. I promise. It's just . . ."

"I never liked Jae Lee."

"Okay." She throws up one hand in surrender. "Okay. You never liked him."

"I never did. Ever. He's the worst." Except the more I say it, the more I start to doubt even myself.

Sora nods slowly, but says nothing. I don't think I've convinced her, and even worse, the more I deny it, the more I'm starting to doubt myself. Do I secretly like Jae Lee?

"Look, all I'm saying is the opposite of hate isn't love. It's indifference," Sora says. "At least, that's what my friend Stella says. That hate and love have a lot in common. There's a lot of passion there."

"You think I feel *passionately* about Jae Lee?"

"Well, you've never felt indifferent about him," Sora points out.

Dammit.

"I can't like Jae Lee," I argue. "He's . . . full of himself. An egomaniac."

"Yeah. Okay." Sora sighs and sits up a little straighter. "Do you need my hot take?"

"Am I going to like it?"

Sora shrugs. "You kissed Jae. After a hard day where you both acted a little bit like fools. You've both got this weird history and you've always had this super-competitive vibe. So, you kissed him. For whatever reason. Maybe you wanted to hate–make out."

"Hate–make out?"

"Like having hate sex, but PG-rated."

The thought of hate sex with Jae Lee makes me feel woozy. "Never mention hate sex to me again."

"Okay. Well, do you remember Mara and her ex-boyfriend?"

Mara is our cousin, Dad's niece, the freckled redhead who lives in San Francisco, a vegan environmentalist who runs a net-zero-carbon vegan purse company. "Which boyfriend?"

"The cattle lobbyist from Houston? They met on a flight to Washington, DC, instantly hated each other, but also ended up having hate sex in the lavatory at fifteen thousand feet before the plane landed. I'm just saying that sometimes, we're attracted to people we hate."

"Oh God." Nothing seems right anymore. Everything is upside down. "This is terrible."

"It was just a kiss. You can pretend it never happened."

"What if I can't pretend it didn't happen?"

Sora lets out a frustrated sigh. "Maybe you need to call Mom. Ask her what she thinks."

That would be easier if I wasn't avoiding Mom's calls these days.

"Speaking of Mom, she said she called you but you haven't called back." Sora has that pinched, disapproving look on her face, the one she always gave me when I talked back to Mom or Dad when we were little.

I avoid Sora's gaze, glancing down at my lap, suddenly intent on a piece of lint there. "I've been busy."

"What's going on with you and Mom anyway?"

"Nothing." How do I tell Sora that I only really feel like I can talk to Mom when I'm happy and everything in my life is perfect? "She did give my number to Jae's mom, which started this whole mess."

"No. Seriously? This is a *Mom setup*?"

"No. It's not a Mom setup. I hate Jae."

"Okay. Okay. I mean, Mom's been friends with his mom for years. I've got no doubt the two of them have been plotting to get you together for decades."

"That's why you're not going to mention *anything* about what I just said."

"My lips are sealed," Sora promises. "But you should call Mom anyway."

"Okay, says the sister who won't tell Mom she doesn't want to buy a wedding dress that costs as much as a used car."

Sora looks decidedly guilty. "Touché."

"Look, I can talk to Mom. Or you can ask Grandma Mitsuye for advice."

"I already did. She told me just to go buy my own dress. Then Mom can't keep making appointments for me."

"Not bad advice."

Behind Sora, Larry jumps off the couch. The one-eyed rescue pit wanders over to her for a head scratch, but misses and seems to be begging for one from Sora's ottoman. Sora glances down. "Oh, Lar needs to go outside. I'll call you back, okay?"

"Okay."

The second Sora hangs up, my phone dings with an incoming text. It's Jae.

> *I'm just checking in.*

Ugh. Checking on . . . the kiss? Please don't mention it. Please don't . . .

> *You still feeling the burn? It's been two hours, and I think I might have actually done permanent damage to myself.*

I'm relieved. Ignoring The kiss. Thank God. I think about typing a reply, but . . . all I can think of are my lips against Jae's. About how I liked it.

He pings me again.

> *If it still hurts to swallow after five hours, is an urgent care visit in order? Asking for a friend.*

I want to reply.

> *Are you okay, Namby? Do I need to call an ambulance? Also, do ambulances make two stops?*

Now I have to respond.

*Hanging in. Do you know if a person can
overdose on antacids? If I got blood drawn right
now, I think it would be citrus-flavored powdered
chalk.*

He sends me a laughing emoji. I smile with relief. Maybe the kiss doesn't have to be awkward. Maybe we can both just ignore it and go back to hating on each other. I feel immense relief.

*Also, heads up. Tyler Evans is coming to
town next week.*

Imani just texted me about this. How does Jae even know?

How do you know?

Ha. I didn't. Thanks for confirming.

Dammit. Another text pops up.

You can't trust him, FYI.

Why not?

My phone rings then. Oh God. Jae is calling. I answer, tentative. "Hello?"

"Don't sound so scared, Namby. It's just me." His voice, deep, self-assured, rumbles through me. He sounds a little raspy from the Reapers.

"I thought you butt-dialed me."

"No, this is a deliberate finger dial."

"Why not just text me?" I'm wary. Who calls anyone?

"Because I wanted to hear your voice. Proof of life."

"Funny."

"You looked pretty bad in the cab, that's all I'm saying."

"You didn't look too good yourself." I press the phone against my ear and stand, wandering to the window in my living room, my legs suddenly tingling with nervous energy. Below, the streetlights are flicking on as dusk settles on my street.

"So why can't I trust Evans?" I pace, wandering across the geometric patterns of my living room rug.

"I could tell you, but then you'd have a strategic advantage."

"I already have a strategic advantage. I've seen you cry-eating Hell Ramen."

"You were *also* crying," he points out, amusement in his voice.

"Tears of pure competitive joy. Tell me, or I'm going to challenge you to another spicy-food-off."

"No way my colon can take it. Fine, fine, you win. I'll tell you." Jae inhales. "I don't know, because I haven't talked to anyone at Joust, but it doesn't make sense for them to dominate the vacation space."

I feel my heart sink. "Why not?"

"My gut tells me it's not what they're after."

"Your gut? *That's* what you want me to believe?"

"My *gut* is why I'm the highest-paid and youngest VP of acquisitions ever at one of the world's largest companies," he adds in a way that's completely egotistical, and sadly, also true.

"If you're done with your not-so-humble brag, can you get to the point? I mean, maybe you're just jealous because Joust is better than Rainforest."

"Please! You think *Joust* is better than us? We're not trying to turn your grandparents into radicalized domestic terrorists. You tell me that Thanksgiving in America is better with Joust and their social media platforms and then I'll believe Joust is better than Rainforest."

I pause in my pacing, hating that he has a point.

"Joust says they're working on that." My protest is weak.

"Right. When their model is to get eyeballs, no matter what it costs society," Jae points out. "Ask all the depressed ten-year-olds out there with body-image issues. Joust is even more ruthless than us when it comes to the bottom line. Trust me on that."

Could he be right? I don't want to think he is. And yet . . .

"Maybe you're just trying to rattle me." I don't want to think that Toggle's one great hope is also evil.

"Look at the deal, Namby," he says. "Why would they want you when they have Vacay?"

He has a point. I sink into the ottoman at the end of my couch, ignoring that it's new and stiff and scratchy.

"Then why pretend?"

"Maybe just to mess with Rainforest."

"Why get our hopes up?"

"Trust me when I tell you that Evans doesn't care about anyone's hopes. He's trying to launch himself into space every other week-end. All he cares about is himself. And winning."

I both admire and hate that Jae's so damn cunning. I should've seen that angle. Jae saw it first.

"Okay, so you could be right." Even though I don't want him to be.

"I know I'm right." He sounds so smug.

I sigh. "Why do you have to be so good at your job?" It's more of a complaint than a compliment, but Jae laughs.

"Tell that to my father. He thinks I'm the biggest disappointment of all time."

"What? Why?" I can't imagine any parent not bursting with pride.

"If you're not a doctor or a lawyer, you're a nobody to Yong-Jae Lee." Jae says this matter-of-factly.

"He can't be serious. You're head of acquisitions at *Rainforest*. They employ like a million people. They're huge. You probably make a bazillion dollars."

"Actually, it's a *gazillion*, thank you very much." Jae sniffs. "Dad doesn't have a lot of respect for business. Thinks it's not good for supporting a family. He doesn't think it's respectable."

"Huh." I'm stumped. "Your dad really gives you a hard time?"

"Do you not know about Korean dads?" Jae jokes.

"I guess I don't?"

"Well, they're a whole other breed."

I feel bad for Jae. And now I feel like it's my turn to share. There's something about a phone call, his voice in my ear, that just feels surprisingly intimate.

"Well, ever since my dad died, my relationship with my mom has gotten weird and strained, and I've been avoiding her calls because I think she's relying on me to be happy in order to be happy, and it's all just too much pressure. Plus, she failed to tell me she hated my ex-fiancé."

"You were engaged?" Surprise laces Jae's voice.

"Don't sound so shocked. I'm almost offended."

"No. It's not that I don't think you get proposals every week. I am sure you do." He doesn't actually sound facetious. Interesting. "I just wondered what happened?"

"You didn't see it on my social? You might be the only one who didn't."

"You mean all the accounts you refuse to let me follow you on?" he points out.

Oh, right. That's true. "I'll tell you, but you can't tease me about it."

"Then I will definitely tease you about it," Jae says.

"Jae." My voice is a warning.

"I'm just kidding. I'm not going to kick you when you're down. What fun is that?"

"Promise?" I tug my legs under me on the ottoman.

"On my Rainforest stock options."

"Okay." I swallow. Why am I telling Jae this? I don't know. Because all my other friends got tired of me complaining about it? Or is it because, actually, as it turns out, I don't have friends? "He cheated on me the week of the wedding. Got a blow job from someone he met at his bachelor party in his neon party bus."

I brace myself for the mocking laughter. I opened up to Jae, showed him a scar, so surely there will be pointing and laughing, stock options or no. But he doesn't laugh.

"What a phenomenal asshole." Jae seems genuinely indignant on my behalf. I'm . . . relieved. "I hope you kicked his ass."

"Well, it was partially my fault."

"How on *earth* was that your fault?" He sounds astounded.

In so many ways: I ignored all the warning signs, like he never wanted to really talk about his feelings, which I took to mean that he was in complete agreement with mine. Like he wasn't all that excited to get married, but I pressured him to do it anyway, because I thought that's what all happily married women did: drag their men to the altar.

"Because I pressured him to get married."

"You pressured him? What? Did you put him in an interrogation room and keep him locked there until he agreed to put a ring on your finger?"

"No."

"Then he's a big boy, and he can take responsibility for his decisions."

"But I'm very persuasive," I protest.

"I know, Namby." I can almost feel Jae rolling his eyes. "But you're taking blame for what he did. He made the choice to cheat."

"The worst part is that he said it would be rude to tell her no . . ." I sigh. "Actually, that's not the worst part. The worst part was he told me it was my fault. That I spent too much time at work. That I . . . neglected him."

I've never told anyone this.

Not Sora. Not Mom. Not even Fatima, who was very pregnant then and had just moved out to the burbs, but still let me complain for hours on the phone. Because part of me worried it was true. Because I did spend more time at Toggle than with him.

Why am I telling Jae this? My enemy?

I don't know. Maybe it's because of all the people in the world, I think he might really understand. He probably spends as much time or more in the office than I do.

"That's complete bullshit." Jae really sounds hot now. "If he was a real partner, then he would've understood what you're trying to build with Toggle. What did he do for a living?"

"Well, aside from getting fired from a lot of jobs and flunking out of a couple of colleges? He worked for his uncle. And he played video games. A lot."

Jae exhales. Slowly. Clearly trying to keep his temper in check. "How did you decide to marry this guy, again?"

"He asked?" I joke.

"Namby." Jae sounds almost disappointed in me.

What else can I say about Mitch? He fit the bill: tallish, decent-looking in pictures, passable at dinner parties, and he never yelled. He never even raised his voice to me. Not once. And he was agreeable, going along with whatever I wanted.

Until he didn't.

"I don't know. He just . . . seemed to check all the boxes."

"An Xbox addict who can't hold down a job except one given to him by a relative checks all the boxes?"

"He was a good plus-one."

"So, you're saying he had a pulse." Jae sighs. "Namby, Namby, *Namby*."

"I know!" I moan. "But I did neglect him. I did work all the time."

"No. Uh-uh." Jae clears his throat. "I want you to listen to me, okay?"

"Okay."

"Your ex was a lazy, entitled guy who was jealous of your accomplishments, because he could never achieve anything close to what you've been able to achieve," Jae says. "And he punished you for making him feel little by cheating on you. You could've showered him with attention, spent every waking moment with him, and it would've changed nothing. He still would've cheated. Because he knew you were too good for him, and he couldn't stand it."

Sora and Mom both said something similar about Mitch. Yet Jae's words hit me harder. Jae is telling me the unvarnished truth as he sees it. He wouldn't soften the edges for me, or lie to make me feel better. He has no reason to do that. In fact, the opposite is true. If I'd been to blame, he'd be the first one to point it out. I realize I've been holding on to some guilt when I should've let that go a long time ago.

"You're right," I admit.

"Of course I am. I'm always right." The note of gloating in his voice is unmistakable.

I bark a laugh. "You are an egotistical maniac. Has anyone ever told you that?"

"Once or twice." He pauses for a beat. "Maybe we should send your ex some Hell Ramen."

"We definitely should." The idea of his esophagus melting makes me happier than it should.

"Give me his address. I'll send him my hundred-dollar gift card, but I'll tell Mark that it can only be used for Hell Ramen number nine."

I can't help but laugh. He can take his new girlfriend there. That's a social media post I'd be dying to see. My laugh pitters out and silence settles on the line. Jae breaks it.

"By the way, the other reason I called was I've been meaning to invite you . . . and Imani and Dell, board members, and whoever else you want from Toggle, to Brew Fest next Friday."

"What's Brew Fest?"

"It's only this huge beer garden that Rainforest does every year. All the local indie brewers, live bands, carnival rides, raffle drawings with vacations and cars as giveaways, the whole shebang. Free to all Rainforest employees . . . and their guests. We're not all Evil Empire, you know."

"I thought you were more Borg, but that's just me."

"Borg? Please. Don't insult me. We're Dark Side all day."

I laugh. Then I'm suddenly suspicious. "Why are you inviting us? You don't have to invite us."

"I'm being nice."

"Why?"

"I'm always nice." He laces his words with mock indignation.

I snort. "You are not. So, fess up. What's your ulterior motive? You haven't insulted me in at least five minutes."

"I was wondering if you'd notice."

"Seriously. What's up with you?" Now I'm really on guard.

"Well, to be honest, I like you, Namby."

I burst out laughing, thinking he's joking. The silence on the other end of the line tells me he's not kidding.

"You're serious." I still can't believe it.

"I'm as surprised as you are," he admits.

"What do you like about me, then?"

"You're smart. You're witty. You're ambitious. You're driven to win. You're good to your employees, and not just when other people are watching. You're annoyingly hard-lined about following rules, but I think that's because you actually really believe in doing what's right." He ticks off these traits quickly, easily, as if he's been thinking about them awhile. Each word lights a little wick of warmth inside me. "You make a damn good tennis partner. And . . . you're kind of gorgeous, but I think you already knew that."

No, I didn't know that. Inside me, somewhere, there's still the girl who wore bottle-thick glasses and headgear in ninth grade and who was never asked to prom.

"If you like me, you have a funny way of showing it." Like taunting me, or trying to buy my business out from under me.

Jae just chuckles a little. "And if you still hate me," he begins, voice low and deep, "you have a funny way of showing *that*."

"I don't know what you mean," I lie.

The kiss. He means the kiss.

"Sure you don't." Advantage, Jae.

Then, suddenly, I'm right back in the back seat of that car, my lips pressed against his, a white-hot flame running through me. I feel my entire body flush red. From the roots of my hair to the tips of my toes. I tell myself I'm embarrassed, but what if it's not embarrassment that's making my face flush so hot?

At least I know now that he isn't going to ignore it. That the kiss might have changed everything.

"Don't worry. Your secret is safe with me."

"What secret?" I ask, even as I know I'm falling right into his snare.

"That you like me, too."

FOURTEEN

Nami

Jamal, I KNOW you took my chair. It had to be you, okay? Just stop with all the games.

DELL OURANOS
PARTNER, CO-OWNER, BUSINESS INFLUENCER, AND
TRENDSETTER
#ALL-HANDS-ALERT CHANNEL
TOGGLE INTERNAL CHAT

Why would I take your chair?

[attached: photo of Jamal in his wheelchair]

I'm going to let you walk that back, Dell. Nice and slow.

JAMAL ROBERTS
QA DIRECTOR

Maybe I like Jae.
   Maybe.

I tell myself that there are worse things than changing one's mind about a nemesis. Maybe I have been too hard on Jae. Honestly, I can afford to be magnanimous now that I'm sitting across the conference table in the Fishbowl from Evans, the CEO of Joust, who's regaling Imani, Dell, and me about his latest trip to space.

"Seeing that big blue marble from three hundred and fifty thousand feet, let me tell you, it puts things into perspective." Evans stretches, and I try not to be distracted by his vibe, which feels like Divorced Dad Trying Too Hard. The fifty-five-year-old with the silver goatee is wearing the same now-iconic gray T-shirt he wears to everything: from the Met Gala to the White House. The most distracting element of his outfit, though, is the neon green straw cowboy hat perched on his head. Seems like an odd choice for a business meeting, but, just as I think that, a programmer walks by the Fishbowl wearing plaid pajama bottoms and orange fuzzy slides. I guess . . . people in glass houses. Evans is Toggle's last and best hope, and yet I can't shake the feeling that he is a bit of a blowhard, and I'm not sure I trust him to look after my baby, either.

"I tell you, once I landed back on Earth, I knew what my purpose was."

To flight climate change? Help the poor?

"Get every single person on planet Earth on one of Joust's platforms. Get all the eyeballs. Double Joust's profits in five years. Put Rainforest out of business. Make enough money so I can build my own space station and look at that blue marble any time I want!"

He laughs at this, sounding like a Bond villain. Next he'll be deciding he wants to drill to the center of the Earth. Dell heartily joins in. Imani and I just blink at each other. Is Joust better than Rainforest? On paper they are. In person . . . not so sure.

I glance at the window as Priya walks by, looking hopeful. She's dyed the tips of her blue hair orange in honor of Joust's orange logo. Jamal, from his desk, is busy running some kind of statistical analysis of the odds of Joust versus Rainforest buying us. They both like Joust better because Joust at least acknowledges that data piracy is bad and they admit they have flaws in their own systems. They admit that social media needs reform, and pay lip service to trying to deliver that change. They revere coders, too. The developers and programmers are in such hopeful spirits that they've even covered the whiteboard in the break room with a new monthly debate: Which is faster—warp speed or hyperdrive?

Even from here I can see the makeshift drawings of the *Millennium Falcon* heading up one list, and the *Star Trek Enterprise* on top of the other. Someone has even put some actual mathematical equations up on the board. As if you can calculate theorical propulsion systems.

"Mr. Evans, how would you see Toggle working as part of the Joust family?" Imani asks, politely steering the conversation away from world domination.

Evans tips his cowboy hat back and grins at Imani. "Well, I think you know what you're doing, and there's no way I want to interfere with that. I want you to do what you do. Ask any of the companies I've bought. I keep the management largely in place. I let them do them. Why would I buy you if I want to change you? You're the golden goose."

Imani glances at me across the table. It sounds good. It does.

"What about user data?" I ask. "Our users are very particular about that."

Evans grins. "The world is changing. You either change with it, or you go the way of the dinosaurs. I respect that."

"So, you'd respect data privacy?"

He laces his fingers together on our glass table. "There are other ways to be profitable. We don't have to be assholes."

Of course, I note, that's not exactly an answer. *You can't trust Evans,* I remember Jae texting me. Imani, however, looks ever hopeful across the table.

"Right. Yes. One more question," I continue. "You do have Vacay. Why buy us?"

Evans grins at me. "Vacay has issues," he admits. "I'm sure you've heard about the background check scandal. I'm not sure Vacay is the right model in this space."

I glance over at Dell, vindicated.

"That's where Toggle comes in," Evans says.

"I see." This is better than I hoped. And Jae was wrong. Of course he was. He wouldn't be thinking that someone would be concerned about a bad product if it still made money. Evans, for all his idiosyncrasies, does. That's where Joust and Rainforest might just be different. I glance at Imani.

"We believe, like you do, in being good, not evil." Evans smiles.

It almost seems too good to be true. Jae said I can't trust him, but Jae might just have planted that seed of doubt on purpose. It's what I'd do if my back was against the wall.

"Joust is a respectable company, no doubt. And we'd be a good fit," I finally admit, batting down a feeling of disappointment. Part of me just doesn't want to sell Toggle, no matter how good an offer. Evans might be the best solution, but part of me will never be okay handing Toggle over to anyone else.

Evans slaps his knees. "Good, I'm so glad to hear that. How about I get my people to work up some numbers?"

Imani meets my gaze across the conference room table. "That would be great. Really great," Imani says.

"Why aren't you happier?" Imani asks as we huddle together in the pop-up beer garden in the parking lot of Rainforest during Brew Fest Friday evening. A giant, fully air-conditioned white tent shields three different bars, all stocked with top-shelf liquor and rare craft brews, and waiters wander through the crowd offering up appetizers and glasses of specialty beer. A local band plays on the sound stage on the far west side of the lot, filling the air with atmospheric rock. My white linen pants and white tank top feel a little too polished for the event, which is dominated by cargo shorts and T-shirts. "This means we can play hardball with Rainforest. You don't have to be absorbed by the Borg."

"I know Rocket Man is the best option, but . . ."

I sigh and glance at the open bar, where Jamal and Priya, as well as a couple of other developers, are getting another round of beer.

Imani raises an eyebrow.

"You still don't really want to sell."

"Toggle is my family," I say defensively, and my chest tightens with the idea of letting it go. Who will make sure Maria has her extra leave? Or that the whiteboard *doesn't* get erased?

I overhear Jamal and Priya debating who would win a battle between the Ewoks and the Hobbits. They're my family. Not perfect, or even anywhere close to perfect, but mine.

"I know how much you love them." Imani looks at me with pity. Even though she's the Girl Boss, she also has an amazing knack not to take things personally. She could move on from this and form a dozen more businesses without losing a night of sleep. Me? I might as well be a teary-eyed mom at the preschool classroom door, sobbing about my baby being all grown up.

"I love them, too, you know," Imani adds.

"I know you do. You are the reason we even exist." Without her wizardry at raising money, Toggle wouldn't be possible.

I sip at my Belgian something or other with a floating slice of orange. I don't normally like beer. Again, that was Mitch's territory, but when in a beer garden . . . Imani, who's wearing a bright red sleeveless blazer and matching red square glasses, has a beer stein filled with a hazy IPA. Other than Toggle people, I know no one at this gathering, which must be two hundred strong, and I'm hugging the corner of this tent like it's my happy place.

I keep glancing around the room, and I tell myself it's not because I'm scanning the crowd for Jae.

"I know it's hard to let go, but it'll be better for them if more of them get to keep their jobs," Imani points out.

"I know."

"And I think the Evans offer will be solid."

"Yeah, I do, too," I admit.

"Of course, if Joust buys us, and it looks like they will, then no more Jae."

I scoff. "Why would that bother me?"

Imani studies me, her sharp eyes missing nothing. "You two just seem . . . I don't know. Something."

"We went to high school together. That's all."

Imani raises both eyebrows, skeptical. "Is that why you lit up like a Christmas tree when you played doubles with him on the tennis court?"

I feel a blush creeping up my neck. "I don't think I did." I take a sip of my fruit beer.

"Or why you offered him a ride in a car you didn't have at work?"

I laugh uneasily. "Funny story, that. I—" But just as I'm starting to tell it, I see Jae, walking into the beer garden tent, arriving like a movie star on the red carpet. He's instantly mobbed by fans. He's wearing a black polo, which fits his muscled chest almost too tightly, showing off the time he must spend at the gym. His jet-black hair is perfectly mussed, his flat-front khakis tight to his trim waist. I thought that maybe seeing him in person might disabuse me of the notion that he's attractive. That the kiss in the rideshare was simply a byproduct of pity: of me feeling sorry for his ruffled, hot-pepper-stricken self. But now, seeing him here in his full charismatic glory, my stomach begins buzzing again, and it occurs to me that I might also be attracted to Jae's put-together perfect self, and that the kiss in the rideshare had nothing to do with pity. The realization makes me feel slightly dizzy.

Jae meets my gaze then from across the crowd, and I feel like he's sucked all the air out of the room. That's when I realize it's just me, forgetting to breathe. He shakes off an admirer and heads straight for me. My stomach lurches.

"Well, that's my cue," Imani says, excusing herself.

"Wait. He's coming over here!" I clutch at her arm.

Imani sends me a wry smile. "He's not coming here to talk to me," she adds, and then disappears into the crowd before I can stop her.

"Well, hello, Namby." The deep voice comes over my left shoulder, causing me to nearly leap out of my skin. I take my eyes off Jae for one second and he's already snuck up on me.

I feel my heartbeat tick up. It's in my throat. I turn and crane my neck to look up at his perfectly coifed self. He's clean-shaven, and dangerously good-looking. He's holding a dark stout in a tulip glass, and I want to knock it out of his hands. I don't know if this is hate-hate energy or hate–make out energy.

You like me. The words seem to glint in his eyes as he flashes me a cocky smile.

"So, how did the big meeting with Evans go?"

"Please. As if I'd tell you."

"Maybe I already know." A smug half smile tugs at the corner of Jae's mouth.

"Oh, no." I shake my head. "I'm not falling for that again. You can't trick me into giving away corporate secrets."

"Namby, you should know by now I'm always three steps ahead of you." Jae takes a slow sip of his beer, eyes never leaving mine. For a second, I wonder. Is he? Then I shake off the doubt.

"Really? Is that why you're fishing so hard for details about the meeting with Evans?"

"Okay, okay." Jae raises his hand in seeming surrender. "How about we steer clear of business then?"

"Whatever would we talk about?"

"Well, I'd love tips on how to do the running man." Jae nods to the dance floor.

"Oh, no. I'm far too sober for that."

"Well, we can fix that." He flags down a waiter carrying a tray of dark beers in tulip glasses. His polo is so tight I can see the clear outline of his pectorals. I try to look away, but there's something mesmerizing about his fit, well-defined chest.

"What are those?" I eye the dark beer with distrust.

"Barrel-aged stouts. Why? Are you scared?"

I laugh. "Are you *daring* me to drink one?"

"Well, I mean, I'm sure we can find a beer with a lime in it, if sangria is more your speed . . ." He nods, mocking, toward my glass with the orange slice in it.

I've grabbed one of the dark beers off the tray, and handed the waiter my empty glass. I'm already gulping down a big drink before Jae can take one. It's smoother than I thought, with a slight hint of soy sauce at the finish. Actually, though, good.

"Careful, Namby. That's a dangerous beer. It's fourteen percent ABV."

I wave him off. "I can handle it."

A worried look crosses Jae's face. "Just . . . take it slow." I take another big gulp just to spite him. It fizzes on my tongue, and down my throat. "A few of those, and you'll probably end up proposing to me."

"I will not!"

"I might need a bodyguard." Jae glances around the room. "Security!" he fake calls.

"I won't attack you," I grumble, but actually, he does look good enough to devour. I send a sidelong glance to the developers, now sitting at the edge of the open bar, loudly and boisterously debating who's more of a narcissist: Bender from *Futurama* or Rick from *Rick and Morty*.

"Promise?"

"Please, it's the last thing I want to do."

"Are you sure? Because you've been mentally undressing me with your eyes since I got here. Eyes up here, Namby."

"Please," I huff, but I know I'm caught. "It's just that you're so tall. That's all. My neck hurts looking at you."

Jae turns and grabs an empty stool nearby, and then he scoots it near me and plops down on it. "Better?"

As I'm staring into his chocolate-brown eyes, I realize, no, it's not better. My stomach feels weird again.

"You're ridiculous."

"Am I? I'm not the one who finished that high-ABV beer in less than five minutes."

I glance, startled, at my glass, to realize I have actually finished it. "Well, I guess I'm celebrating."

The beer is buzzing in my brain now, a jovial hive of bees, and I forget that I'm talking to the enemy.

Jae quirks an eyebrow. "And what are you celebrating?"

"Joust's offer seems like it's real. We don't have figures yet, but it's all looking . . . good." I can't help but gloat.

Jae even looks miserable about the idea. He glances at his beer.

"What? Sad you've lost?"

"Something like that." Jae downs the dregs in his glass. He glances at me intently, as if he's got something serious to tell me.

"What?" I ask.

Jae blinks. "Nothing. I was just going to say . . . we'd better toast to you and Toggle."

I'm kind of shocked Jae is giving in so easily. "You're admitting defeat?"

"I wouldn't say that." Jae grins. The waiter comes by with a tray full of more beers. Jae takes one and hands it to me. He grabs another and we gently clink glasses. "I'm just curious about how many of these you need before you're on that dance floor."

"You don't have enough beer in here to get me out there," I promise.

FIFTEEN

Jae

You can dance.

BARREL-AGED BEER
#ALL-HANDS-ALERT CHANNEL
TOGGLE INTERNAL CHAT

It only takes two more beers, and then Namby is flailing around on the dance floor. Look, I tried to warn her about the ABV. Is it *my* fault, she's stubborn and doesn't listen? Or that her tolerance still isn't that much better than high school? I note this, watching her gorgeous cheeks flush pink as she kicks up her knees with a look of pure concentration that absolutely, positively might be the best thing I've seen this month. Or even this year. It's only half past nine, but already some of the Rainforest employees are beginning to make their exit, either to feed dogs or pay babysitters, and those who remain are the serious partiers. Imani and Dell left at least an hour ago, and I would've sworn Nami would go with them, but she's stayed. Either because I dared her, or because the barrel-aged beer has unleashed her inner party animal.

Jamal, Priya, and Arie have joined our group, and despite the fact that Arie likes to talk about crypto *way* too much and I think wears the exact same dad sandals that my own dad does, they're a fun group. It sounds like he and a few others got in on crypto early.

I make a mental note to circle back to him about that. If he got in on DigCoin in the early 2010s but got out before the big crash, as he said, then he might be a whole lot more successful than I thought. He'll probably also be the first one out the door when Rainforest takes over.

Because despite what Nami might want to believe, the Evans deal is far from a sure thing.

I tell my business brain to take a hike. Tonight, it's pure pleasure.

Initially, Jamal, Priya and Arie are wary of me, but I win them over by giving them access to the top-shelf open bar, available only to executives, and with a promise to get them all access to employee Rainforest discounts, even if the deal doesn't go through. Grudgingly, and with the help of premium vodka and whiskey, they come to like me. Because that's how I roll. I can be charming when I want to be.

The local band makes their exit, and a pink-haired DJ takes their place. I may never have had as much fun as this, as some electronica pop blares from the speakers and Nami gamely does her best robot. I knock my elbow against hers, robot style, and she laughs, a full-throated laugh. Tipsy Namby is my favorite Namby of all time.

Okay, not my favorite. My favorite Namby was the one in the back of the cab who surprised me with that kiss, opening up an entire universe of amazing possibility.

"You look ridiculous," she cries, pointing.

"Says the woman doing *the running man* in public." I have to laugh. "You know you can't dance."

"Agreed, Nami. You can't," Jamal adds, breaking between us in his wheelchair, doing the robot with his arms.

"Definitely can't," Priya agrees as she fastens her blue-and-orange hair back into a ponytail with a rubber hair tie.

"I dance like a TV dad, and I dance better than you," Arie says, continuing his side-to-side, awkwardly out of rhythm step-clap dance.

"I *can* dance," Nami proclaims, the beer bringing color to her cheeks. I kind of love it. Everyone, in fact, has loosened up a bit with a few rounds of drinks. I can see why Nami likes her Toggle coworkers so much.

"Really?" I ask as she flails her arms and spins, doing her best impression of a drowning swimmer. "I mean, are you dancing now? Are you sure?"

She just laughs and gives me a playful shove. Her eyes are bright, just like the Namby who came to my graduation party. "Let's see if you can do better."

"You are not seriously challenging me to a dance-off." I clear my throat.

"You scared?" she dares me.

"I'm scared of that move you just did with your leg," I say, pointing to her wobbling knee. "Was that move on purpose? Or was it involuntary?"

She just laughs and twirls, completely unfazed. "As if you can do better."

"You definitely can do better," Priya stage-whispers.

"Well . . . if you're daring me." I bust out some of my old-school N'Sync, classic boy band slide, spin, tap, sway. Boom.

Priya and Jamal stare at me in shock. Arie freezes.

"He's not playing," Jamal says, impressed.

"Those are some nice moves," Priya reluctantly admits.

"You are so dead," Arie tells Nami.

Nami frowns. "I am not," she declares, overconfident in a way that only a high ABV beer can make a person. "But what about this?" She does something that looks part Macarena, part accidental electrocution.

Arie, Priya, and Jamal burst out laughing.

"I'd rather do . . . this." Side-to-side, heel tap, quick reverse spin, elbow out and in, head nod. BTS should call me.

"How did you do that?" Priya asks, in awe. "Show me!"

I show her the move.

"Yeah, yeah." Nami won't be sidelined. "But why do that, when you can do . . . the sprinkler!" she declares, throwing out one arm and doing her best impression of watering a lawn. I bark a laugh.

Jamal and Priya move away from us as if bad moves are contagious.

"Is the sprinkler what you pulled out on the prom dance floor?"

She laughs, throwing her head back so her thick dark hair cascades down one bare shoulder. "I didn't go to prom."

"Was it because you realized you couldn't dance?" I tease.

She shakes her head. "Nobody asked me!" she shouts in my ear, her breath warm against my face.

"Nobody asked you?" I echo, not believing. "That can't be true. You always had an army of crushes following you around everywhere."

"No, I didn't." She looks indignant. "And even if that were true, which it's not, none of them asked me."

"Cowards," I growl. I suddenly have an image of all those lovestruck fans, all of them too scared to ask Nami out. I just . . . I wish I'd known that then.

"In fact," she adds, "nobody ever even invited me to a party except you."

I stare at Nami. Can this be true? Just then, the next song cues up. A slow one. Nami stops bouncing.

"Can't robot slow dance," Jamal says, rolling off the dance floor.

"Okay, folks. It's TV Dad's bedtime," Arie declares as he pulls up a rideshare app on his phone. "My wife is wondering where the heck I am!"

"You're leaving already?" Priya follows him off the dance floor, which leaves Nami and me alone.

Nami turns to leave but I catch her by the wrist. "Wanna dance?" I ask her.

"You want to slow dance with me?"

"I mean, if what you do you call *dancing*. Yes."

Nami snorts, and sticks out her tongue. Her cheeks glow with her recently demolished stout.

"Fine," she says, and moves closer to me. Her hair smells fruity and delicious, like something you'd serve in a glass with a paper umbrella. And, miracle of miracles, she's actually letting me lead.

"You're serious about never being invited to a party?"

"Yeah. I mean, it's not surprising."

"Why not?"

"Because everyone hated me in high school," she says, as if this is obvious. "I mean, don't you remember when I ran against you for class president? You got one thousand two hundred and nine votes. I got eight votes, including one from myself."

"Was it that lopsided?"

"Still is. I don't think—outside of Toggle—I have any friends anymore. And, technically, I'm the boss at Toggle, so go ahead and make fun of me. My only friends are people I pay."

"That can't be true." Though, I think it might be. I remember the video from her birthday party, and only relatives showing up. I spin her out, and then spin her back to my chest, folding into me like she belongs in my arms. Conversation dries up then, and I'm hyperaware of how soft Nami's hands are in mine, our palms pressed together, how her head fits nearly perfectly below my own chin. She leans into me, sighing, and all I want to do is keep her right here against my chest, forever. I meant what I said about liking this woman. Maybe more than like. I can't help thinking maybe Mom was right. When I'm around Nami, the world is a little brighter, and everything's a little bit sharper. The insults. The jokes. The way she pushes me to . . . be more. I wonder what it would be like if she didn't hate me. If maybe, just maybe . . .

"You're not so bad at this," Nami admits into my chest. "Maybe you should lose out on more corporate deals. You're kind of nice when you do. Are you going to get in trouble? If you lose this deal to Joust?"

"I'm not going to lose the deal to Joust," I tell her hair and then abruptly shut up. I'm saying too much as it is. Next thing you know, I'll blurt out the truth: Evans came to see me right after he went to Toggle. He wants to talk about us backing off a battery company we've been threatening to buy, which would put a small dent in his monopoly on that market. He's using Toggle as a bargaining chip, just like I thought. End of story.

In the end, Rainforest will be the only legitimate offer on the table, and we'll take over, and dismantle it. This is the way of the world. This is the wolf coming to dinner.

I told her not to trust him. Now, I can't say anything more about it because I'm bound by a watertight NDA. Even hinting that the Joust deal is far from done might get me in trouble.

Nami pulls her head away from my chest and meets my gaze, our bodies mere inches apart.

"You are *totally* going to lose to Evans. All he has to do is get in the ballpark, which I think he will."

"You're that confident?" I tease, but I feel uneasy. This time, the playful competition doesn't feel so great. I never thought I'd dread winning so much in my life.

"You're against the ropes," she gleefully tells me, as I spin her out, her hair fanning out. I pull her back to me, closer this time, my hand resting gently on her lower back.

"Why do you care if I'm in trouble or not?"

"I don't know if they fire you or knock your pay if you lose," she says, swaying with me to the slow beat of the music. "Or do they just take away your one bathroom break of the day?"

"Very funny."

"You know," she tells me, cocking her head to one side. "You don't have to be evil."

"I'm not evil."

"You're not *good,* either," she points out.

"I'm *successful.* That's not good or evil."

"The fact that you don't even ask yourself if you're good or evil means you're evil," she says. "You have to actively ask yourself: Am I making the world a better place? Or am I making the world a worse place? If you don't ask these questions, if you tell yourself they don't matter, then chances are you're making the world a worse place."

I slow our movement until we've almost stopped, barely hearing the music anymore. She might have a point, though I don't want to admit it. There it is, that patented Namby Nudge.

"Maybe I'm trying to make Rainforest better from the inside."

"How's that going for you?" Nami asks, eyebrow arched.

The song fades away, and then it's just the two of us, staring into each other's eyes in the middle of a mostly empty dance floor.

And, for the first time in a long time, I don't feel great about being the wolf.

"Tag, you're it," Nami declares, slapping my arm and then skipping away from me, across the empty dance floor.

"You won't get away from me that easily," I promise as I follow her to the tent exit, down the small corridor leading to the Rainforest building. She's surprisingly fast, and she dodges my reach as we jog through the sliding glass doors in the empty lobby. She runs into a dead end between a macramé hanging chair and an oversized plant in the corner, and she spins to avoid me, but my reach is long, and I have her, in my arms.

"Tag," I say, but she doesn't try to escape. She's staring at me, dark eyes wide, lips slightly parted. I realize too late this is exactly where she wants me.

I stare at her mouth, her perfect lips, because I know exactly what they taste like: everything I ever wanted.

"Nami?" The single word holds a million questions. Can I?

But she reaches her hands up, wrapping her fingers around the nape of my neck, and she's pulling me down to meet her mouth. Our lips touch, and my brain explodes in a million amazing pixels. Everything gets very slow and very fast all at once as I pull her into my chest. She's soft and amazing and perfect, and I want to melt into her. Maybe I am melting. She's devouring me with her mouth as her hands run up the inside of my shirt, nails skimming my bare back. I'm lit up everywhere, all at once. She's the match and I'm all gasoline. Everything in me feels white hot. She pulls me deeper into the corner, tugging me, and my hands are in her hair, her thick, soft hair. Her scent, her familiar, amazing scent, hangs all around me. This is where I want to live.

She pulls away from me, dark eyes glittering dangerously. "You're not too bad at that," she pants, taking her fingers out of my hair that feels as dazed as I know I must look.

"You're not so bad yourself." Understatement of the century. My entire world has tilted. It might never be righted again. I don't know if I even want it to be.

"Maybe we should see if we can do better," I offer.

"Yes," she growls. "More." And her mouth is on mine again, and the whirling vortex of need has swallowed me, and her tongue lashes me in ways I want to tuck away in the corner of my memory forever. Everything in me thrums with energy. I break the kiss, seizing upon her delicate neck, soft, perfect. She lets out a little sigh that might be my new favorite sound of all time as a shudder rolls down her body. I want to know what other sounds she can make. I want to hear them all.

Giggling voices suddenly put us both on high alert. She stiffens, and I freeze, breaking my connection with her skin. We duck behind the hanging chair basket, and go very, very still. Partygoers headed to the bathroom down the hallway pass us seemingly without seeing.

Distantly, we hear the music cut off. A faint call through the speakers reaches us:

"All right, you all, this is official last call!" the DJ announces. "The bar closes in ten minutes!"

Nami's mouth drops open. "Come on!" she cries, grabbing my

hand and pulling me out of the corner. I'm too stunned to do more than follow. She moves as if nothing has happened, as if she hasn't just turned my world completely upside down. "I need another one of those stouts!"

"Careful with those, they're . . ." But Nami hits the bar, ordering two more for us. Then she makes it four. I'm terrified, and a little in love with her, right at that moment.

"I don't want to go home yet, do you?"

"No." I grin. "Let's find a place to show off our dance moves. Someone, somewhere needs to see you do the sprinkler. Maybe you'll go viral."

"Yes!" she cries, pumping a fist in the air.

Four hours later, Nami is still trying to do the sprinkler in the back seat of our rideshare van, singing the wrong lyrics to her seemingly endless variety of boy band hits from the early 2000s. She's off-key and adorably drunk, and I'm on a mission to make sure she gets back to her apartment in one piece. Jamal and Priya agreed to get dropped off first, because Jamal—like Nami—had kept drinking well into the night, and Priya wanted to see him safely to his condo, which was across the street from hers. Still, Priya only exited the rideshare after she took a picture of my driver's license and promised me all kinds of horrible retribution if anything bad happened to Nami.

"Trust me, you'd have to get in line behind my mom. She'd kill me if anything bad happened to Nami," I reassure them both.

Everyone is concerned for Nami's safety when they really should be worried about my ears. Turns out, Nami can't sing any better than she can dance.

"Go shorty . . . !" she's shouting, even though 50 Cent is *not* playing in the car. In fact, no music is playing. The rideshare driver glances back at us and then his pristine upholstery with concern. When we pull up to Nami's brand-new apartment building on

North Avenue, a sleek glass-and-steel box that reaches ten stories high, I can see into the square lobby of exposed brick, with its modern, armless gray chairs and the large circular desk for her doorperson. The last time I dropped her off, someone was there, but now the desk is empty.

She throws open the rideshare door and stumbles onto the sidewalk. I hop out, offering my arm. She takes it without complaint. My goal is to get her inside her apartment, safe and sound. I know she can handle herself, but at the same time, I've seen enough episodes of *Dateline* to know better than to just leave her drunk and to her own devices at two in the morning.

"We gon party . . ."

"Okay, Fiddy." I wrap my arm around her lower back, easing her to her door. We make it to the sliding glass doors, and she fumbles in her small clutch for the door card, and with one swipe, we're in the lobby. We stumble inside the large open space, and the automatic door slides shut behind us. We make our way across the gray carpet.

"You smell good," she tells me as we limp to the bank of elevators. I jab the call button.

"Uh . . . thank you?" The elevator door opens, and we move in. She swipes at the number for her floor.

"I mean it. What do you use in your hair? It smells. . . . Niiice." She sighs, leaning against me. Nami, guard down, wriggles her way through my defenses. Then I hear her snoring against my shoulder.

"Namby!" I shake her awake as the elevator arrives on her floor.

"That's meeeee," she moans.

"Okay. Let's get you to your room in one piece, okay?" Nami's legs, so full of enthusiastic if awkward vigor a mere half hour ago, seem to have lost all energy. She slumps against me, and I'm basically holding her up like a marionette as we walk down her neatly carpeted hallway. When we get to her door, she has a hard time getting her key into the lock, and I have to help her turn it.

"Home!" she announces, suddenly energetic, as she throws open her arms, and then nose-dives into her sofa. She almost immediately starts snoring.

It's kind of awesome. I manage to get her sandals off, and her feet up on the couch. I ponder whether it's safer for her to be on her side or her stomach, and then after a bit, figure side sleeping would be best. I scoot the kitchen trash can closer to her, just in case things get worse in the middle of the night.

I watch her sleep for a beat, her pink lips slightly open, her thick lashes against her cheeks. I glance around her obscenely neat apartment, wondering who keeps a place this pristine? No dishes in the sink. Trash emptied. Floor shiny without a single dust bunny anywhere. The hint of new car smell everywhere, like she doesn't even spend much time in this shrink-wrapped apartment. There's not much in the way of personal knickknacks, but what I do find are a picture of her and Sora on a roller coaster, probably when they were in middle school, or late elementary school. They're mid-dip but they clearly have ridden the ride enough to know where the cameras are, because while they're hair is flattened backward by the velocity, they are making goofy, silly faces, one making a peace sign, and the other, a heart with her hands, as if the coaster doesn't bother them at all.

There's another picture of her family, an even older one, tucked away behind the first. I pick it up to take a closer look and see Nami and her dad on Christmas morning, her dad holding a coffee mug while sitting on the couch, watching Nami tear into a present. I squint. I think it's a Furby. I laugh, but then look a little closer. No, wait. Not a Furby. A knockoff. A Fooby. Huh. I remember Christmas in 1998, my brothers and I, we all got Furbys in different colors. That was *the* toy of Christmas then. Come to think of it, my brothers and I, we mostly got what we wanted for Christmas. Game systems. Hot toys. It was the only time Dad believed in spoiling us. Christmas was always huge in our house.

Still, despite the knockoff toy, Nami's young face is bright and joyful as she opens it. It's then that I realize her living room is different from what I imagined. Smaller, older furniture, sparsely decorated Christmas tree, much smaller than the one my parents always got in December. I never really thought I grew up rich, especially not since there were actually millionaires going to our school on the North Shore, but I also never really gave much thought to how Nami grew up, either. Her dad is wearing a workman's shirt with his name stitched on the front. Electrician? Plumber? Someone who was likely called out that very Christmas morning to work. Or late Christmas Eve, by the look of the dark circles under his eyes.

Huh. Nami's complaints of my getting to do summer school hit home more now that I've seen this picture.

Nami groans in her sleep, and I put down the framed photograph, and turn. Her arm has fallen off the sofa, and I softly head back to put it right again. I watch her sleep, wondering how many Christmases she opened knockoff toys. How many birthdays, too.

Okay, I've trespassed long enough, I think, feeling as if I discovered a secret Nami wouldn't want me to know. I stuff my hands in my pockets and turn to go. It's then, as I'm standing at her front door, that I realize there's no way for me to lock this up from the outside without her key. I'd need to take the key to secure the door, and what if she wakes in the middle of the night and needs it? It seems weird to take her keys. She moans in her sleep and turns, flopping onto her back. I position her on her side again, bracing her with pillows. Her eyes flicker open, and she grabs my wrist.

"I'm cold!" she announces, and pulls me down to the couch. "Come!" she beckons sleepily, and before I know it, I'm lying down on the sectional with her, and she's spooning against my back, her defenses completely down as she snuggles into me and begins lightly snoring.

I freeze, hyperaware of her soft body against mine, and her hair that's fallen across my neck. Pretty soon, her breathing becomes even more rhythmic. It's time for me to sneak out, but she's got a vise grip around my waist. The more I struggle, the tighter she holds. There's really barely room for the two of us on this couch. But I don't dare move. I don't dare breathe.

I'm certain I'll never fall asleep, but then, I close my eyes, and I'm out.

SIXTEEN

Nami

How do I know one of you jerks hasn't sold my Wegner Swivel?

DELL OURANOS
PARTNER, CO-OWNER, BUSINESS INFLUENCER, AND
TRENDSETTER
#ALL-HANDS-ALERT CHANNEL
TOGGLE INTERNAL CHAT

Proof of life.

[attached picture of Wegner Swivel Chair with today's *Chicago Sun-Times* newspaper on the seat]

CHAIR LIBERATOR

I wake up in a cocoon of warmth, cozy and perfect, until I open my eyes and realize that I'm spooning Jae Lee. White-hot embarrassment floods my entire body from head to toe. The only thing preventing me from dying of humiliation right now is that we're fully clothed. I'm still wearing my very wrinkled linen pants from the night before.

What the hell happened? Why is he here, half falling off my sofa, one leg completely on the ground, and an arm about to follow? Is it his fault . . . or mine? I struggle to remember. Somehow, I know, *know* it's mine, even though I can't remember much of anything after the last beer. Gray morning light filters in through my open blinds, and the clock on the microwave in the kitchen tells me it's nearly seven. The hint of a headache is blooming behind my eyes.

I try to disentangle myself from Jae, but I'm pinned between his massive body and my couch pillows, and there's no choice but to gently shake him awake.

He groans and comes to, blinking.

"What happened last night?" My voice sounds rough, like the answer to my question is that I smoked a carton of cigarettes.

"We eloped to Vegas. We were married by a trio of Elvis impersonators," Jae moans as he sits up and stretches. His hair is sticking up in all directions and he looks perfectly rumpled.

"I'm serious." I give him a playful shove.

"You kidnapped me. I should probably call the police." He smooths down his rumpled hair. I suddenly have the urge to put my fingers in it and mess it up once more. I like him better with mussed hair.

"*Jae.*"

"Fine. You drank too much. I tried to leave but you wanted me to stay." He glances at me, and he looks as tired as I feel.

"How much did I drink?" I moan, covering my face with both hands.

"Enough to want to cuddle." Jae's mouth quirks up in a knowing grin. "Are you always such a savage when you drink?"

I laugh, and then moan, pain thumping in my temples. My mouth feels like I licked wallpaper glue all night long. I gently nudge Jae out of the way, and stand, heading to the kitchen. Jae yawns once more.

"Want coffee?" I ask, yawning myself, having caught his.

"Can I get it in an IV?" Jae moans, stretching out his neck and rubbing it and looking sore. "I think my neck is permanently misaligned."

"Aw. Poor you," I tsk as I fire up my single-serve coffee machine, dropping one of only three pods of coffee left into the slot. "Milk? Sugar?" I open my cupboard and remember again that I barely have any dishes. There are only three mismatched souvenir mugs in there, and one has a cracked handle. I take the two intact ones, and begin to fill them.

"No. Just as is. Thanks."

"Really?" I'm surprised. I would've thought Jae was a loaded coffee kind of person. I am a load-my-coffee-up sort. Milk, sugar, syrup, pumpkin flavor, vanilla, whatever you've got.

"Trying to cut down on the sugars." Jae pats his hard, flat stomach. It never occurred to me he really worked at his beach-volleyball body. I just assumed Jae had everything handed to him, including washboard abs.

He watches me carb-load my coffee. "Are you going to leave any room for coffee in that?"

"I always go for milk with just a *hint* of coffee," I say, defensive.

"You should just have a glass of chocolate milk. It probably has more caffeine in it," he jokes. I hand him his dark brew. "Wisconsin *Dells*?" He reads the logo on his mug aloud, sounding astonished.

I shrug. "We went there once when I was a kid. It was a big trip for us. We usually didn't get to get away much." Not with Dad's working schedule, and the fact that paying basic bills was an elaborate game of monthly Jenga. The Wisconsin Dells isn't Disney, but it was in driving distance, and affordable. That mug actually used to belong to Dad. I took it when Mom was cleaning out her cabinets a couple of years ago. "You can't actually have an issue with the waterpark capital of the world."

"You mean the foot fungus wonderland of the Midwest? No, thank you. Waterparks are gross."

"You don't like waterparks?" I'm shocked.

"I don't like anywhere where we're all supposed to run around barefoot on wet ground and share the same pool water that at least fifty percent of the kids and thirty percent of the adults peed in. No, thanks." Jae wrinkles his nose in disgust.

"You just don't know how to have fun."

"I prefer dry land. That's all. And . . . I think you do, too. Since you spent much of last night doing this." Jae holds up his phone to show me a video of me doing the actual worm. On the ground. Oh no. Absolutely not. I abandon my coffee and lunge for the phone.

"Give me that!" I cry as I swipe at his phone, but he keeps it just out of reach. He nearly spills his coffee as he puts it down on the breakfast bar.

"No way. This is mine. Forever." He looks decidedly pleased about this.

"Jae! You have to delete that."

Jae grins down at me as I hop up, grabbing at air. He scoots back, but his calves hit my stiff ottoman, and suddenly he falls backward on it. I'm too intent on the phone, and I tumble after him, falling smack dab on his chest.

"Are you okay?" he asks me, concerned, warm dark eyes searching mine. Suddenly, the embarrassing video is the last thing on my mind. Now it's just Jae and me, this urgent, but silent, unanswered question between us, the same one he asked in the lobby of Rainforest last night. I remember now making the first move. Pulling his head down so my mouth could devour his. The memory lights a warmth low in my belly.

I nod, my throat closing up, because I know if I say something right now, it'll come out as a squeak. I feel like I'm in that tractor beam again, and I'm moving closer to him without even realizing it. Soon, our noses are nearly touching. Jae freezes, so it's me still moving, but I don't want to stop. My eyes flicker closed as I kiss him.

I kiss him like I mean it. I kiss him like I mean to. I kiss him with my whole mouth. His hands run up into my hair, but I'm consuming him like I need him to breathe. A monster of desire comes alive in me, a monster I'd been keeping chained for so long. And it's hungry. So, so, very hungry. Jae flips me over, and now he's on top, his muscled weight a delicious pressure against my chest. He tastes like dark, rich coffee, and something else that's just him. Just perfect. Just everything.

The hungry monster in me wants Jae. All of Jae. Right now. It's a monster I didn't even know I'd been kept chained until Jae's mouth met mine. Now I realize how long I'd been pulling back, telling myself *no*, tightening those chains. All these business meetings. All the stalking him online, all the times I told myself I couldn't care less. When I do care. I care too much.

Jae pulls back then, up on his elbows, panting.

"What are we doing?" he asks me.

"What do you *think* we're doing?" I challenge him back, the morning light reflecting off his shiny hair, making his almost black eyes look a lighter, clear brown. "We're picking up where we left off last night."

"This could be a bad idea," he murmurs.

"Terrible," I agree.

"Rainforest is—" Jae begins, but I shush him with a finger to his lips.

"Don't," I murmur, and then I kiss him again, and suddenly it's a full-fledged hate–make out party. His hands roving down my body, mine up under his shirt. His back is smooth and hard, and then I'm tugging up his polo, impatient to feel more of his skin. Our mouths wrestle for control, while my palms trail up his smooth, perfect chest muscles, which ripple as he holds some of his weight away from me. He tastes so good, so very good. When he breaks away, cool air rushes across my lips and the monster of desire in me roars.

And then he breaks free.

"Are we . . . ?" he asks, and I can feel his weight, and even more, his want, pressed against me. I'm suddenly acutely aware that it's been weeks—no, months—since I've had a man in my apartment. Since I've even thought about the possibility of sex. I'm not prepared. I don't think I even shaved my legs up past the knee. But

186 | CARA TANAMACHI

those distant alarm bells fade. The monster stomps them out. "Do you have . . . a condom?" Jae pants.

"You don't have one?" I ask, shocked.

"I don't carry them in my wallet like a teenage boy, no." He grins sheepishly. "And having them on me sort of feels like a supposition . . . Even though you did attack me in a rideshare."

"I didn't attack you, and I *might* have one," I moan, and then I'm pushing him off and stalking to the bathroom. I open the first drawer and dig out makeup and makeup brushes, and then the big drawer beneath that one, tugging out a box of tampons and a bottle of lotion. I'm trying to remember the last time I bought them, and I can't, because my love life has been dead on arrival for longer than I'd like to think about.

"Want help looking?" he calls from my bedroom.

"No!" I shout, panicked now as my bathroom countertops are covered with tampons, eyelash glue, and teeth-whitening strips. At the very back of the final drawer, I find a crumpled box, with one single condom in it, probably from the prepandemic era, but still functional. "Found one!" I cry, running out of the bathroom like I've got a winning lotto ticket.

Jae, nearly naked, clad only in his briefs, lounges on my bed, looking like the most delicious underwear model I've ever seen. "*Just* one?" he asks, shaking his head in disapproval. "Well, we'll have to make the most of it."

SEVENTEEN

Jae

Nami Reid wants me. She steps out of her linen pants, revealing a delicate lace thong, and crawls onto the bed like a lioness who plans to have me for dinner. I've never been so happy to be the prey. I reach out and touch her, pull her to me, and her skin is softer than I even imagined it would be. How can anyone's skin be this soft?

I want to prove to her that I won't waste this opportunity. I reach for her, helping her out of her tank top, revealing a lace bra. She's frozen, eyeing me, hunger in her eyes. I can't believe this is really happening. I have only one goal right now: give her the best damn orgasm she's ever had in her life.

I loop a finger into the side of her lacy thong and tug it downward, slowly, inch by inch, still feeling like the luckiest man on earth. Because I am, and I know it. She watches me, frozen, dark eyes studying my every move. I like that she doesn't know what I'll do next, that her breath is coming slow and shallow. I'm painfully hard at the moment as I set her silky underwear aside.

"You're so damn sexy," I tell her, because she is. She blinks fast.

"You too," she murmurs, a little shy now. It's adorable. I bend down and kiss her inner thigh, as I stroke the other one with my hand. Delicately. Deliberately.

She lets out a little murmur of want, a little shiver running down her leg. Good. She likes this touch, I think, and I continue the caress.

I want to show her how I won't take her for granted. How her body is a gift that I won't squander. I trail delicate, deliberate kisses up the side of her leg. She trembles again. I glance up and meet her gaze. Watchful. Hungry. I stroke her gently, tracing a line up her inner thigh. She shivers and moans a little, and her body becomes an instrument I feel like I'm born to play. She's so vulnerable, so completely an open book. I can read her easily, see how she leans into my touch or moves away from it. She moans a little, her head dropping back, as I gently lay a trail of kisses along her inner thigh. Her chest rises and falls, quickly, with sharp intakes of breath, as I move slowly, ever slowly upward.

"What do you like?" I ask her, touching her there, delicately. "This?"

"Yes," she breathes.

I flick my tongue against her lower belly. "This?" I ask.

"Y-yes," she murmurs, gasping. How I love that sound.

I gently, ever gently, explore her with my fingers. She's so willing. So open. So amazing. So wet.

"And this?"

"God, yes," she manages, arching her back.

"I'm going to give you the best orgasm of your life," I promise.

"A little full of yourself, aren't you?" she teases.

"No. It's not ego if it's true. Plus, I just like to win. I think we've been over this."

"My orgasm is a *win* for you." Nami's mouth quirks up in a smile.

"It's a *win-win*, technically." I dip into her hot, molten center with a gentle, relaxed tongue. Soon, she's arching her back; every muscle in her body stiffens as she cries out, a beautiful sexy cry of climax.

Her breath comes ragged as she puts a steadying hand on my chest. "Wow," she murmurs, followed by a sheepish giggle.

Wow, indeed.

"So?" I ask, eyebrow raised.

"Good. Not the best." She flashes a devilish grin.

"Well, then, looks like we'll have to keep trying."

She giggles then, because she doesn't know I'm serious. She'll find out.

Hours later, we lay panting together, collapsed on top of each other, naked, sweaty, the room filled with the earthy smells of sweat and sex. We should audition for Cirque du Soleil: Sex Edition, because I have never actually gone through that many positions in that short a time, not since I played drunk Twister in college. It's actually amazing. Anyone who assumed Nami is cold in bed was dead wrong. She's an apex predator, relentless in her stalking, determined to get what she wants at all costs; it's like drunk Namby meets ruthless boardroom Nami. It's other level in a way I don't think I've ever experienced in my whole life. I used to think mind-blowing was just a saying, something polite and made-up people said about sex, but consider my mind . . . blown.

A pang of guilt pricks me. The Evans deal. In the heat of the moment, I'd actually forgotten about it. Completely. That's what Nami does to me. Makes me forget business entirely.

Would she be this open to me if she knew the truth? I tackle that thought and lock it away deep in my brain. There's nothing I can do about it. I can't tell her the truth without violating the NDA, and it's not likely Nami would keep the secret. She would feel obligated to warn everyone. And me getting fired won't help Toggle.

Because I'm Toggle's last line of defense, if we're all being honest here. I wonder, for the first time, what would happen if I didn't give

Evans what he wanted. What if . . . I didn't back away from the battery company. What if I called his bluff and he had to buy Toggle?

That would be better for Nami. Even if Rainforest took a strategic hit.

I internally shake myself. Am I really thinking about throwing the race? Tanking this easy win? For Nami?

"What are you thinking about?" Nami asks me, lifting her head from my chest and studying my face.

"Nothing," I lie. Everything. You. Me. How part of me worries you'll never believe I want what's best for you. That part of me has always wanted that. That I might throw this deal, and every last one, if there's a chance it makes you happy.

"Nothing, huh?" Nami doesn't believe me. I'm usually an amazing liar, but she sees right through me.

"I was thinking that you've blown my mind," I say.

"There wasn't much there to blow, zombie," she teases.

"Ouch. I guess I find zombie killers sexy. I have a death wish."

She laughs, laying her head back on my chest. I want her here, curled up next to me, forever.

"It's too bad we only had the one condom. There might be one position in the *Kama Sutra* we haven't tried."

"Should we insta-deliver more?" she asks, raising her head, a naughty sparkle in her eye. This Namby with her hair down might be my favorite person of all time.

"Yes," I say, completely serious. She pulls up her phone and peruses the menu.

"A fifty pack?"

"Yes." I nod solemnly.

"You don't think that's too many?" She quirks an eyebrow.

"Do they have a hundred pack?" I counter.

Nami glances at me over her bare shoulder, her hair cascading down her naked back. "Cocky, much?"

"Or maybe I'm just one giant cock."

Nami laughs, a full-throated laugh. "Actually. You kind of are." She bites her lip. "Okay. Condoms in the cart. Anything else?"

"Can we insta-order breakfast?"

Nami's eyes light up in delight. "That's not a bad idea."

"That's why *I* was valedictorian."

Nami gives me a playful slap across my tricep. "Ow," I protest. "What was that for?"

"You know what it was for, cocky."

Nami

The thing about Jae Lee is that he kind of just slides perfectly into my life as if he's meant to be there. We hibernate for the whole weekend, ordering takeout, talking about everything, and laughing about it all. That's when we aren't letting our bodies do the talking all on their own, which works as easily, as seamlessly, as if we were built for each other. There's something so amazingly honest and authentic about being with Jae. I don't mind telling him when he's being a jerk, i.e., when his Thai takeout order is a little bit too high-maintenance ("You seriously asked for curry *on the side*? Are you a monster?") and he doesn't mind teasing me relentlessly about how I have alphabetized my hair products on the bathroom shelf.

We barely even mention Rainforest or Toggle. Even though I still worry about it. Every day. But neither of us brings it up. It's like we've both agreed to just avoid an argument.

Turns out, even without business, we have an amazing amount in common, and we never seem to run out of things to talk about. We can turn a debate about the merits of '80s hair bands versus emo industrial music one second, and whether or not *Alien vs. Predator* or *Aliens* could be considered *Alien* canon, since they weren't directed by Ridley Scott. He pokes fun at my Janeway Pop Vinyl figure standing at the edge of the kitchen sink, and then, at his place, I parade around in his One Direction concert tee, which he swears he only got as a joke to wear ironically at a throwback party.

A week passes, and then another, and we've spent every night together. Sometimes at my place, sometimes at his. He's a slob, and now I know that any pristine pictures of his overpriced condo with the stunning lake views are strategically staged, because there are dust bunnies roving around the corners of his condo the size of dinosaurs. Also, I discover that he loves clothes more than me: his closet is twice the size of mine, and he's filled it. He also has more shoes than I do, but he claims some of them are rare collectible sneakers that he'll never wear, so I guess they don't count?

Every new detail, every new bit of information, from the brand of toothpaste he prefers to the way he folds up an open bag of chips, is information I suddenly crave, and I file every new revelation away, like a precious family recipe. Jae is better than an onion, he's like a Russian nesting doll. Every time I open one, I find another, more interesting doll beneath.

"You're saying I'm like a hollow, egg-shaped doll?" Jae says when I announce this, as we're cuddled together on my couch, binge-watching a true crime series on a Sunday afternoon, that neither one of us is truly watching.

"Yes, but man-shaped." I reach for some popcorn in a big bowl on Jae's lap, happily munching on the buttery goodness.

"You're saying I'm deep. And interesting. And . . . like no one you've ever met."

"You're also an egomaniac—your least appealing quality."

"That only makes me *more* interesting."

I pull away from him a bit and see he's teasing me, his dark eyes sparkling and playful. I toss a piece of popcorn at his chin. He makes an elaborate move of trying to catch it but it hits his face and bounces off.

"It's no wonder you're full of yourself. You always had everything handed to you."

"Handed to me?" Jae scoffs. "I did *not*." He stretches his legs out to the ottoman. I curl my feet under me.

"Really? Big house. Rich parents. College paid for. Amazing abs." I tick off all of his advantages on my fingers. "You were like the poster boy of privilege."

"First of all, I work *hard* for these abs." He lifts up his shirt and shows me a delicious glimpse of one ripple. "And for another, my parents weren't rich. They are *middle class*. And you forget, I have a Korean dad. Who makes questionable decisions. Like not bother to teach me English before kindergarten."

I straighten up. "Wait. You spoke only Korean when you started school?" This is news to me.

"I showed up on the first day of kindergarten mostly only speaking Korean, so my teacher didn't understand me," Jae says, frowning. "I still sometimes have nightmares about it. The teacher asking me to do something, but I didn't know what. I remember her confusion, then her frustration, and eventual anger. I remember the other kids laughing at me. It wasn't a great start to my education. It took me years to catch up."

"But . . . your mom was born here. And your dad . . ."

"Yes, they both speak perfect English. But my grandmother lived with us when I was little, and looked after me, and she only spoke Korean. Dad also felt like Korean preschool was better than English preschool. And he also felt it was more important for me to learn Korean than English, because . . . who knows why. One of several of his decisions that I question to this day."

"Oh. I . . . didn't know." I bite my lip, suddenly imagining how difficult it must have been for Jae. "How did I not know this?"

"Because I don't talk about it. Like ever. To anyone."

There it is: another delicious secret about Jae. I've cracked open one painted wooden doll to reveal a new one inside.

"So, wait," I say, connecting the dots. "You started school not speaking English, and you became valedictorian?"

"Yeah, well, you might have noticed, I like to win."

I laugh. "I might have noticed."

Jae leans in then and kisses me and all conversation ends in the most delicious way.

EIGHTEEN

Nami

Give back my chair. NOW. Or there WILL be consequences.

DELL OURANOS
PARTNER, CO-OWNER, BUSINESS INFLUENCER, AND
TRENDSETTER
#ALL-HANDS-ALERT CHANNEL
TOGGLE INTERNAL CHAT

She actually likes it here. I think she's developing Stockholm
syndrome.

That's especially awkward for her since she's Danish.

CHAIR LIBERATOR

Hello? Nami?" Imani's voice reaches through my cloud nine fog. I blink fast, realizing that I've been sitting in the Fishbowl at a special Toggle leadership meeting with Imani, Dell, Paula, and Arie, dreaming about Jae's amazingly muscled torso instead of focusing on Toggle business.

And the Evans offer we just officially received.

"Oh, I'm sorry. Right." I try to get my bearings. Where were we in this meeting? I glance at Arie, and he gives a nearly imperceptible nod to Evans's offer up on the projection screen.

"As, uh . . . Imani was saying—" At least, I hope she was saying, since I've only been half listening. "It's a strong offer from Evans."

"There are a lot of zeros," Dell says, stating the obvious. "That's all I care about."

"Duly noted," Imani says. "But Nami, what do you think? Should we ask for more?"

"It's more than a fair offer." Of course, it would be. They're one of the biggest, most profitable tech companies that exist. Some could say they invented social media—for better or worse. "I don't know if Evans will go for more."

Dell leans in. "So . . . any sky-is-falling premonitions on this one, Chicken Little?"

"Dell," Imani admonishes, crossing her arms across her flamingo-pink jacket and matching square glasses.

"We need to refrain from name-calling," Paula adds, pushing up her tortoiseshell glasses and giving Dell a warning glance.

"I'd like to rephrase that question," Arie pipes in, eager to defend me, as he straightens his Toggle lanyard that's flipped backward on his sweater vest. "How bad are they? Are they Borg bad? Dark Side bad? What are we looking at?"

I swallow. "Well . . ." I glance around the room. Every face (but Dell's) is looking at me with the same apprehension I have. "As we all know, they've not had the best track record when it comes to regulating their own content."

"They were called before Congress at least twice," Arie adds.

"Yes, but after the last hearing, they have made strides to correct themselves, and they've made a pledge to give more users the ability to protect their data."

I scan my laptop, desperately looking for the report I slapped together earlier this week. I can feel Dell's judging, skeptical eyes on me. Ugh. I hate looking flustered in front of Dell, of all people. I find the presentation deck, and jump from my seat. "Paula, mind if I . . . ?"

Paula nods, unplugs her laptop, and plugs mine into the projector.

I flip to a slide that outlines Joust's new data protection program. I do feel a little uneasy, I must admit, on Joust's efforts to self-regulate. But what options do we have? Rainforest isn't even trying to reform itself. All my old panic starts flowing in. I don't want to trust Joust. But they are the lesser of two evils.

Arie leans forward, studying my slide intently. I can feel eyes peering into the conference room from outside the Fishbowl, as well. Priya and Jamal have shifted away from their desks, and are sipping coffee while staring right at the projection screen.

"But . . ." Arie clears his throat. "While they're getting better at data protection, if they buy us, there's still a chance our users lose control of their data."

"If they don't opt out, yes," I admit. Evans isn't a perfect savior.

"And do we know if this *is* a serious offer?" Arie asks.

You can't trust Evans. Jae's words pop into my brain.

"Imani?" I ask, glancing at her.

"All signs point to yes," she says, quoting the Magic Eight Ball. Arie nods.

"Well, I think . . . for our users' sakes, we should ensure some kind of firewall for their data."

Dell lets out a groan. "Everybody's a Girl Scout," he mutters beneath his breath.

"Duly noted," Imani says. Then she gathers up her tablet and coffee mug. "If that's all, then, we'll be bringing the board this offer, and get an idea where they all stand on it."

We all nod. "Then we're adjourned—"

"One more thing." Dell clears his throat. "I need some support from all of you to find whatever degenerate stole my Wegner."

Arie groans.

"The chair?" I ask him.

"Not just *any* chair. *My Wegner.*" He glares at each of us in turn. "I want assurances from *all of you* that you will do what you can to find it. This has gone on long enough."

"The bigger a fuss you make about it, the more you encourage this prank to continue, and—" Paula says.

"It's not a prank," Dell interrupts. "It's a *crime,* and I'll treat it as such. You all need to grill your people and find out who did this."

"Grill our people?" Arie raises a skeptical eyebrow as he taps his pen on the table.

"Don't take that tone with me. I'm sure it's one of *your* degenerates—"

Arie's eyes flash with a warning.

"Please. No name-calling," Paula says, holding up both hands in a show of peace. "How about we all promise to talk to our direct reports about the chair?"

Arie glares at Dell. "Fine. I'll ask my *talented and essential programming staff.*" He emphasizes each word.

Dell frowns. Arie frowns back.

"If we're all done then, we're adjourned," Imani says, banging an imaginary gavel.

I'm barely out of the conference room doors when my phone rings. It's Jae. Every bit of worry about Toggle and Evans fades to the background as I press the phone to my ear.

"Hello?"

"Hello, sexy." Jae's voice rumbles in my chest. I feel a tingle all the way down to my toes.

"Is that how you talk at work?" I say as I pick up my pace, heading for my office where I can close the door.

"Speaking of, how's the day going?"

"Evans offer came in." I almost feel bad telling him. Guilty, even.

"Oh. I see." Jae goes quiet for a moment and then I regret even mentioning it. It is like pouring salt in the wound, after all. "Uh, Nami. About Joust . . ."

I pause, waiting.

"Yes?"

Jae lets out a long breath. "Just . . . just . . . be careful."

"Is this another one of your cryptic warnings? I thought we were beyond mind games, Jae." I'm only half teasing.

"We are. Of course." Jae clears his throat. "Enough about work. Uh, I'm calling for a different reason. What are you doing Sunday?"

"I was planning to rearrange my sock drawer. Sort them by color. It's a very important task. I know you probably can't compete with that."

"High bar, Namby. But if you can tear yourself away from your socks, my family's getting together for a barbecue at my parents' house." He pauses. "Do you want to come?"

"Are you inviting me home *to meet your parents*?" I ask with shocked exaggeration. I sink into my office chair and spin it around in time to see a Frisbee fly by my office door. Priya runs to get it, and offers a friendly wave.

"You've already met my parents," Jae points out. "And my brothers will be there." He makes it sound casual, like no big deal.

"I don't think I've seen any of them since high school graduation." This is a tantalizing offer. I wonder how many more nesting dolls I'll discover in the one dinner alone. There's no way I'll say no. "But, yes, I'd love to."

"You sure? My family is a little much," he says, and he almost sounds a little concerned.

"I wondered where you got it from," I tease.

Jae seems uncharacteristically nervous on the drive to his parents' house. He also insisted we stop by a farmers' market on the way and pick up fresh cherries—his dad's favorite. He's also told me I should be the one to give them to him.

"Why? Do I need to butter him up? Are you having second thoughts about me coming along?" I ask him. He's driving his sleek

Audi, weaving around slower traffic on Lake Shore Drive. High-rises dot the left and the blue waves of Lake Michigan roll to our right. His hand is warm over mine near the gearshift as I balance the small brown paper bag filled with cherries. I've thrown on a sundress and whipped my hair up in a hasty high ponytail.

"No," he says. He glances over at me. He gently raises my hand to his mouth and kisses it. "My parents . . . they have weird ideas."

"Like what?"

"Like anyone I bring around, I plan to marry."

I feel a little twitch in my stomach. A hopeful, anxious twitch.

"Are they right?" I tease.

Jae's eyes flick to mine. "Are you fishing for a proposal? After not quite a month of dating?"

"No. Sounds like *you're* the one trying to hem me in by taking me to the Family Betrothal Barbeque after not quite a month of dating." I send him a side-eye glance. "Was this your plan? Spring it on me at the last minute so I have to go?"

Jae grins at me. "It's probably not going to be that bad," he says, but he doesn't sound very convincing.

"Now I'm intrigued. Does your mom have a hope chest? Am I going to do Pre-Cana?"

"No—we're not Catholic." Jae sighs. "It's hard to explain." He glances at me across the gearshift. "You'll see when you get there. By the way, I didn't tell them you were coming."

"Why not?"

"You don't want to give them time to come up with more embarrassing questions."

"So, I'm just going to arrive unannounced?"

"It's the best way."

I'm not so sure about that.

The very second we walk into his parents' backyard on a bright, sunny late Sunday afternoon, with a cool breeze rustling the treetops, holding hands because it's become as easy and as expected as breathing in the last couple of weeks, everyone freezes, conversation stops, and six sets of eyes stare at me as if I'm a flying unicorn. His younger brother Charlie's mouth slides open in shock. Charlie's twin, Sam, literally does an actual cartoon double take. Charlie's fiancé and Sam's girlfriend look equally surprised. His mom almost loses a bowl of salad on her way to the patio table, fumbling for it and saving it in the nick of time, and his father, at the hot plate, literally drops his bamboo tongs on the hardwood deck. They land with a surprisingly loud plink.

His mother recovers first.

"Nami!" she gushes, wiping her hands on her daisy apron. "Oh my goodness, how good, how wonderful . . . amazing it is to see you!" Mrs. Lee rushes over and envelops me in a tight hug as if I've just told her she and her whole family have won the lottery. "Jae, shame on you, you didn't tell us you were bringing . . . a date!"

"Sorry, Mom. I meant to let you know." He glances at me. "It was kind of last minute."

I remain silent. Jae's father, still stock-still, gazes at me as if he's worried I'm a mirage that might disappear in the desert. I get the impression that there's a lot of backstory here I don't know. Has he been talking about me? About Toggle? I glance at Jae, but his expression is unreadable. Then again, we have been enemies for more than a decade. I wonder what would happen if I casually dropped Jae into a dinner with Mom and Sora. Their reactions would likely be the same.

Jae's mom releases me.

"Welcome, Nami," says Charlie's fiancé, Nick. "So nice to meet you." He extends a hand. I shake it, grateful for the normalcy. He nudges Charlie, who seems to recover from the shock.

"It's been a long time." Charlie also offers me his hand. "You look great, Namb— Er." He stops himself before he says the dreaded nickname. "Nami. Been doing well?"

"Yes. Thank you. And I hear congratulations are in order to you and Nick! So glad for both of you."

The tension in Charlie's face seems to relax a bit. "Thank you," Nick says genuinely. He reaches out for Charlie's hand, and he takes it. I reflexively glance at Mr. Lee, as Jae mentioned tension in the family about the wedding announcement, but I don't detect any. In fact, when we walked in, he, Charlie, and Nick had been gathered around the hot plate, seemingly in good spirits. Now, Jae's dad has bent down to retrieve his bamboo tongs from the deck.

"Hi, Nami. I'm Isabella. So nice to meet you." It's Sam's girlfriend, and I recognize her from the cyber stalking. She gives me a welcoming hug, even as her boyfriend hangs back.

"Nami. How long have you . . . two . . . ?" Sam manages.

"A few weeks," Jae says.

"Huh." Sam still doesn't seem to process what's happening.

"And this is all none of our business," Charlie says, much to my relief. "All I hope is that you're giving this egomaniac a hard time." Charlie nudges Jae.

"Hey," Jae protests.

"Don't worry." I lace my arm through Jae's. "I *live* to give this egomaniac a hard time."

Everyone laughs then, and the shock and weirdness of the moment subsides, though they are kind of crowded around us as if we're the guests of honor. Then they part, and Jae's dad comes through.

He bows slightly. He doesn't say anything for a whole second. Then he speaks. "Nami, good to see you again."

"Good to see you too, Mr. Lee. You look well. These are for you." I give him the cherries. He takes them, and gives me another nod.

"Thank you," he says. "Please, come. Would you like to learn how I make my bulgogi?"

"Yes. Of course."

He smiles, a genuine smile. "Good. Come."

Jae

Just when I worry I've made the biggest mistake of my life inviting Nami to Sunday dinner, she waltzes in and charms the pants off my entire family. Because . . . she's perfect. I know she's perfect, and now they know, too. She even gets stoic old Dad to *laugh*. Really laugh. Mom buzzes around her like she's the new favorite, and even my brothers seem to grudgingly let her in. Except Sam, of course. He's always been a little more protective.

"You want to tell me what the hell is going on?" Sam asks, nudging me as he hands me a tall boy from the cooler. "What the hell happened? Nami *Reid*?"

"It was unexpected," I say and shrug, twisting off the cap.

"Yeah, I see that."

"You can't talk about this without me," Charlie declares, coming in for a beer and staying for the gossip. "Also, I called this. Somebody owes me twenty bucks."

"You did not call this," I declare.

"I told you she was secretly into you and that her hater persona was just a cover." Charlie studies his fingernails. "It's a curse being right *all* the time."

"Oh, please," Sam counters, and rolls his eyes. "You did not see *this* coming."

"Didn't I, though?" Charlie wiggles his eyebrows.

"I didn't see this coming, so I know you didn't," I add.

"Well, it's got to be serious," Charlie says. "Or you wouldn't have brought her to meet Mom and Dad."

"Unless this is all an elaborate revenge scheme," Sam adds, taking a swig of beer. "Get their hopes up just to dash them?"

"I'm not evil," I say, defensive.

"Really, Monopoly Magnate?" Charlie raises both eyebrows.

I laugh, but I feel a twinge of guilt as I glance at Nami. The Evans shoe has yet to drop, and I'm dreading when it does. I want to find a way to tell her the truth, but I can't. Not if I don't want to be fired. Then sued. Then blacklisted. There's no way I can tell Rainforest's corporate lawyers that I violated my NDA just because I happen to be falling in love.

Love.

God, I do have it bad.

"It just felt right for her to be here." I shrug. The idea of parting with her after spending almost all of our free time together kind of felt like peeling off my own skin. I don't, however, admit this to my brothers. I don't know if they'd understand.

Charlie and Sam stare at me for a long time. "What?"

Charlie shakes his head. "Never thought I'd see the day."

"What?"

"You're in deep," Sam tells me, and gives me a playful punch on the arm.

"What are you talking about?" Is it that obvious?

Charlie and Sam exchange a glance.

"Is she as serious about you?" Sam asks.

"What's *not* to be serious about?" I joke, and grin at them both.

"You are *so* full of yourself, man." Charlie gives me a shove.

We watch Nami as she and Nick listen intently to Dad's philosophy on marinating pork.

"Dad and Nick are getting along. That's good," I tell Charlie.

"Yeah." Charlie takes a sip of his beer. "Dad took us both to dinner to apologize."

"He did?" I'm shocked. "Since when does Dad admit he's wrong?"

Charlie shrugged. "He said he was happy for us, loves Nick, and wants to help us pay for the wedding. Nick and I getting married isn't what's under his skin."

"Hey, man, that's great. I'm so glad for you."

I feel relief flood through me. I'd been meaning to call Dad to try to get to the root of his unacceptable behavior with Charlie recently, but I just worried I'd make it all worse somehow.

"Yeah, but I think you should talk to Dad." Charlie seems somber now.

"What have I done now?"

"Just talk to Dad."

"Food is ready!" Mom calls, interrupting as she bustles by us with steaming hot rice. "Let's eat!"

Charlie clams up, and I make a mental note to check in with him about that conversation later. But for now, all I see is Nami, and her brilliant smile as she glances up and meets my gaze, and for a second, it feels like this moment could last forever.

Or maybe I just want it to.

Nami

Jae slips into the car for the drive home, and revs up his Audi. I click my seat belt as we wave to his parents on the stoop, who have both filled my arms with leftovers, now sitting in color-coded Tupperware in bags at my feet. His mom and dad both grin at us from the porch as Jae backs out and heads to the highway.

"So, when *are* we getting married? Your dad wants to know," I tease him.

Jae groans. "I'm sorry about that. My parents—I tried to warn you . . ." He sends me a sidelong, worried glance.

"I think it's cute. Adorable, actually. Your dad has definite ideas about what we should name our firstborn." The sun dips below the horizon, turning the sky vibrant shades of violet. We're inching down the Magnificent Mile, past some of the city's ritziest hotels and shops, headed to Jae's condo.

Jae slows to a stop at a light and gently knocks his head against the steering wheel. "I tried to warn you about Korean dads."

I laugh. "I know."

"Now's the time when you can tell me things are moving too fast, and you need to go sleep at your place?" Jae actually looks fearful about this.

I shake my head. "No. Now's the time I want to talk to you about that ring your mom mentioned. From your maternal grandmother in California?"

Jae groans again and glances at the ceiling. "It's a one-two punch with my parents. They're really doing their best to make sure I die single."

"Oh, I don't know. They might just want Isabella and me to fight for the ring in Matrimonial Thunderdome. Two daughters-in-law enter, only one leaves." I giggle at the image of me wrestling a kindergarten teacher.

"You'd absolutely win. You're scrappy."

"Isabella's just too nice to play dirty."

We laugh and gaze at each other over the gearshift so long, the car behind us honks to let us know the light has changed.

"You're going to cause an accident," Jae says.

"How?"

"By existing." He casually holds my hand across the center console and his touch feels warm and reassuring. More than that. Feels like an extension of my own arm.

"So . . . how does this all play out?" I ask, and then immediately regret it. Jae stiffens beside me.

"What do you mean?" He sounds guarded. But I'm not the one who brought me home to dine with the family weeks after we fell into bed together. Not sure why asking about where we really are going is an issue. I want to ask: *With us. How does it play out with us? What happens when you lose the Toggle deal?* But I don't want to ask that question of him or myself. I've been deliberately avoiding thinking about what my life will be like after Toggle.

"Joust buys Toggle. I'm jobless. You sure your parents will think I'm a good match then?"

Jae laughs uneasily. "When you sell Toggle, you'll be rich. You can do whatever you want. I don't think they'll have an issue with it."

Somehow, the idea of me being rudderless without my people

with a few more zeros in my bank account doesn't make me feel at all better.

"Maybe I could stay on. In some capacity?"

"Why would you do that?" Jae's voice is sharp as he cuts me a glance.

"Because I love Toggle. I love the people. I can't imagine *not* going into work every day."

He exhales, slowly. "It won't be the same."

"Evans is promising to be hands-off."

Jae falls uncharacteristically silent. He keeps his eyes focused on the road, but he seems distant now. Checked out. Not quite so . . . present. Not sure what I'm picking up on, but it's something. Unease.

I feel a flicker of distrust. What is Jae not telling me?

"Are we moving too fast?" The last time I felt this kind of weirdness in a relationship, a week later my fiancé cheated on me in the back of a party bus. So, call me wary.

Jae glances at me. "No. Not at all," he says, and I believe he means it.

"Then why are you being weird?"

"I'm not being weird," Jae says in a way that makes me think he is definitely being weird.

"You are."

"I'm not." But there's something he's not saying.

"Are we spending too much time together?" I ask. Jae withdraws his hand from mine and sends me a sharp look.

"Do *you* think we're spending too much time together?"

"No." Though, we have been spending every waking moment together when we're not at work. Is that healthy? I'm not sure. It just feels easy. Like I don't think about it. But maybe I should. "No time is enough with you, Namby. When I'm not with you, I want to be."

A white-hot heat rushes from the top of my head to the bottom of my feet.

"And, no, we're not spending too much time together. I plan to take you to your sister's wedding."

"Really? Because that's a, like, six-month commitment."

"I'd wait years to see some of your dance moves again."

I give him a playful slap on the arm, and he just laughs.

NINETEEN

Nami

Dance like there's no one watching. Unless you plan to dance the
Macarena. Then . . . just please don't.

#DAILY INSPIRATION CHANNEL
TOGGLE INTERNAL CHAT

The next sleepy Saturday morning, I wake to Jae's arm around me,
snug, sound. My phone blares, waking us both up.

"Is that ringtone 50 Cent?" he asks, sleepy.

"Maybe," I say as I fumble for it, seeing my sister's number.

"Nami—help!" she cries, breathless.

"What's wrong?" I'm fully alert now. I sit up in bed, the morning
light from Jae's blinds streaming into his penthouse condo on the
Gold Coast.

"I'm cornered in the dressing room of Vogue Bridal." Sora's voice
is low, urgent.

I blink. "I thought you told Mom to cancel that appointment!"

"Well, I, uh . . . meant to. But . . ."

I smack my forehead. "But you didn't."

So much for clear boundaries.

"Can you come? Please. I don't have the proper credit limit for
any of these dresses, and Mom is threatening to dip into her retirement savings to help."

I groan. "I'll be there in twenty minutes."

"Everything okay?" Jae asks me, rubbing his eyes.

"No," I say, and sigh. "Family emergency."

"Need my help?" he asks, hopeful.

"I wish. I could probably use some of your Rainforest instincts today. But it's at a bridal shop. It's a Mom-Sister thing." I suddenly don't want to leave the bed, though, as Jae pulls me even tighter against his chest. "I wish we could just stay here and hibernate."

Jae tugs me in closer. "How about you deal with the emergency, and I figure out something awesome to cook us tonight for dinner?"

"You cook?" Here's another tantalizing new bit of information about Jae.

"Um, of course I do."

I laugh and he nuzzles my neck. "You do what you need to do, and take the time you need. I'll have wine chilling for you when you get back."

That thought keeps me going as I tumble out of my rideshare in front of the roman columns of Vogue Bridal. I swallow down the rise of annoyance in my throat at the loopy insignia of the shop, the same one on the black shroud in my closet. Mom is busy chatting up the saleswoman, who is refilling Mom's glass of champagne— complimentary, of course, paid for by the 150 percent markup of all tulle in the place. The two-story white-wedding extravaganza inside blinds me temporarily. I'm in yoga pants and one of Jae's oversized T-shirts, hardly the proper attire for a place like this. And the bridal saleswoman with the severe blond bob, wearing a Chanel suit, watches me uneasily. I remember her name now: Angelique. She casually inches closer to the panic button near the front register.

"Nami! What are you doing here?" Mom looks surprised, and then dismayed, when she sees my outfit.

"Sora called me." I glance at Angelique. "I'm the sister of the bride."

"Oh!" Angelique claps her hands. She definitely doesn't remember me. "Would you like to look at bridesmaids' dresses? We *just* got in the latest from Vera Wang. We have all the lovely shades of burgundy."

"Burgundy?" Sora hates burgundy. She once went on a rant about how they should just call it *maroon* and stop trying to make a color sound like a vineyard in France. Also, she hates all red tones. If anything, she loves cool colors like blue or lavender.

I glance at Mom, who shrugs one shoulder. Mom's favorite color is burgundy. I see how already the wedding planning has spiraled out of control. Mom's "helping" has already begun to translate into Mom "deciding" things. And Sora's always been such a pushover. It's a recipe for disaster.

"I'd like to talk to Sora first." I look at Mom.

"She's right back here." Angelique moves to show me the way, but I already know this bridal shop inside and out. We head back to the room full of mirrors, and the dressing rooms the size of small bedrooms. Only one is occupied, and I see the bare feet of Sora, toes painted blue, beneath the door.

"Sora?"

At the sound of my voice, she unlocks the door and pulls me in. "Nami, thank God," she whispers. She's wearing a lavender sports bra and matching bike shorts, and has full-on panic eyes.

"Do you need another size, darling?" Angelique asks.

"No! I'm fine!" Sora yells.

"Well, we're all waiting to see that final dress one more time. We have to make sure it's 'the one' before you put down that deposit!"

We both wait silently as we listen to Angelique's heels click away on the shiny wooden floor. The A-line she speaks of is hanging on a satin hanger, with a price tag on it that has five figures. I whistle.

"*This* is the dress you picked?" I ask, surprised. First of all, it's enormously poofy, with enough tulle to circle the Earth at least once. It also has a sleeveless bodice made entirely of sequins—or diamonds, given the price. It kind of has Barbie Dream Wedding stamped all over it. Not at all Sora's quirky, thrift store vibe.

"No!" Sora whispers urgently. "It's Mom's and Angelique's. How do I get out of here? I thought about faking a heart attack. That's how desperate I am."

"Okay, deep breaths."

Sora, her dark hair in a messy bun, has rings of mascara beneath her eyes and gives off the vibe of a trapped animal. "I swear to God, I'm going to elope. I can't take this stress."

"You just have to tell Mom you don't want this dress."

"She'll just bring me another one."

"Tell her you don't want any of them."

"Right." Sora scoffs. "Like *you* told Mom you didn't want a surprise party."

"Technically, I wasn't supposed to know about the surprise party."

"Right. As if you *didn't* know. Mom is terrible at keeping secrets." Sora heaves a sigh. "Anyway, you know that sad, droopy look Mom gets, the expression she wears when we turn down her help."

I know this look well. It's a whole How to Guilt Your Child in a million ways in a single expression.

"And since Dad passed, you know it's even harder to disappoint her."

"I know." I do. Really. Mom's world fell apart after Dad died. Dad might have been a tad bit controlling, and had a temper we all felt, but without him making all the decisions, she was a little lost. Then, amazingly, one summer she found her stride. More than found her stride. She emerged even more determined to be a fixer, happier than ever to volunteer to solve problems.

"But this is your wedding. It can't be Mom's wedding. I mean . . ." I pause. "Burgundy?"

"I know!" Sora moans, sinking her face into her hands. "It's the worst! And now, I'm here—look at this ten-thousand-dollar wedding dress, it's more than I want to spend on the whole wedding, Nami. And Mom loves it, and wants to dip into savings, that she totally absolutely cannot afford. And she's trying to get me to rent out the Four Seasons ballroom, which I do not want to do."

"Four Seasons?" I echo. That's where I'd planned to have my reception. And it was also Mom's idea.

"And . . . and . . . I swear, Jack and I might just go to Vegas."

"You really want to go to Vegas?" I can't imagine either Sora or Jack at an Elvis chapel.

"No. Actually, what I really want to do is rent out the old high school gym and have a prom wedding."

"Prom wedding?" This sounds vaguely familiar, like some idea Sora might have come up with in middle school.

"Yes! Remember? I always had this idea that I could have a big prom, instead of a wedding. All the guests would wear their old prom dresses—or new ones. We'd have a dance in the gym. It would be cheap, and it would be fun, and kind of hilarious. With spiked punch and cupcakes. And it would be low-key, and everyone could have a good time."

"You're serious. About the prom wedding." At first, the idea seems ridiculous, but the more I think about it, the more it seems perfectly Sora. Quirky, fun, irreverent.

I feel a tiny little pang. A little one. Prom, and not being asked to it, was a small bit of a sore spot for me.

"But I can't wear *that* dress." Sora points to the one-of-a-kind designer sample dress. "To a prom wedding."

"You have to tell Mom this."

"Mom doesn't like the idea. Mom says the Honolulu and California cousins wouldn't want to fly in for prom."

"The Honolulu and California cousins will come because of *you*, not because of the Four Seasons. And it's not Mom's wedding," I remind her.

"I know." Sora presses her hands against both sides of her face, as if she can squeeze the problem out. "It's just that I told her that my first wedding—to Marley—"

"At the courthouse."

Sora nods. "I didn't want that kind of wedding this time around. I wanted something special. But also something fun. Not stuffy or fussy. Mom took it to mean I wanted a big over-the-top traditional wedding, but I don't want that either."

"Tell her!"

"How?"

We hear footsteps on the hard wooden floor, and we both fall silent.

"Sora? Nami? What's taking so long?" It's Mom.

Sora's eyes grow wide with panic.

Just tell her, I mouth.

Mom knocks on the door. "Need help?" she asks.

I unlock the door. Mom stares at Sora, in her spandex and not the wedding dress, and frowns. "Does Angelique need to help you with the zipper?"

"No, Mom." Sora glances at me. I nod, trying to give her courage. She opens her mouth. Then closes it.

Just. Tell. Her. Already.

I am blinking so furiously it has to be Morse code.

"I . . . I . . ." Sora begins.

"Yes?" Mom asks.

"I . . . just think . . ."

I hold my breath. Go. On.

". . . Maybe I want to look at veils. That could go with this dress."

What. Is. She. Doing.

I stare open-mouthed at Sora. She gives me a half shrug of defeat.

Mom brightens. "Yes! I can have Angelique get a few!"

"Wait. Mom." I have to intervene. "What Sora *means* to say is that this dress is too expensive."

"Oh, that's fine. I'll just dip into savings and . . ."

"Mom. You're not hearing me." I feel a spark of temper rise in my gut. Sora looks at me uneasily. "Sora doesn't like this dress."

"Of course she does. It makes her look like a princess!" Sora looks deeply uncomfortable. But she is not saying anything. Why isn't she saying anything?

"She doesn't want to be a princess. She wants to be a prom queen."

"Oh! That prom thing again. Forget it!" Mom waves a dismissive hand. "That's a silly idea. We already dismissed it."

"I think *you* dismissed it. Sora still wants to do it."

"What? That can't be. Sora?"

Mom and I both look at Sora. Now is her time to say what she wants. I've opened the door. She just has to walk through.

"Well . . ." Sora begins. Here it is. She's finally going to tell Mom what's on her mind.

"But we worked so hard on the Four Seasons! And in getting an appointment here, and you heard what Angelique said, this dress, there's only one of them in the world!" Mom gives Sora her hopeful, my-future-happiness-rides-on-this look. It's potent.

"And I know your father would just want to see you have the *very* best on your wedding day. He was so disappointed when you opted for the courthouse the first time round. He always told me if you get married again, he'd go full-out. He always called you his little princess, you know. You were *both* his little princesses."

Well, shit. Now she's brought Dad into it. A nice, whitewashed version of Dad, but still, Dad.

"Sora wants the prom wedding, Mom," I offer. "That's it."

"Nami," Mom scolds, "let Sora speak for herself." She glances at Sora.

"Well . . ." Sora hedges.

"Sora." I glare at her. "This is *your* wedding. You have to do what *you* want." Also, don't make me be the bad guy, the hall monitor everyone hates.

"Nami, this is *Sora's* decision."

"I know," I snap, annoyed.

"And this *is* what she wants," Mom says. "Isn't it?"

"Uh . . . maybe?" Sora is absolutely caving. And I hate it. I'm transported to a half a dozen times growing up, my temper clashing with Dad's notorious one, standing up for Sora—for us, about one of his too-strict rules about 9 P.M. curfews, or finishing homework before being able to have dessert, or any of the other things I'd challenge, on Sora's behalf, because I could bring a Category 5, and she could barely muster a rainstorm.

But I was always the one sticking my neck out. I was the loudest. And I always got grounded first. Shouting at Dad was never fun. I might be Category 5, but he was always a once-in-a-century storm, every single day.

"Now, Nami. I know this is hard for you, because you also got your wedding dress here, but you are going to have to just let that go, and let Sora have what she wants."

I stare at Sora, but she won't meet my gaze. Is she really going to let Mom think it's all about some weird envy on my part? Because it isn't. "Sora?"

But she doesn't say anything, and I feel, right in this moment, the betrayal—Sora leaving me, once more, out in the open, alone. Just like when I'd stand up to Dad and one of his tempers, and Sora would hide in her room.

"Need help back here?" Angelique asks, popping in.

"Oh, yes. Sora would like to see veils with the dress," Mom says, gleeful.

"She's going to just have to fight this battle on her own," Jae tells me, later that night, after I've poured out the day's frustration. We've retreated to the couch after finishing his amazing meal of salmon and fingerling potatoes, paired with the most delicious crisp white wine. Turns out, he can cook. Amazingly well. Just like his dad.

"But she *won't*," I protest.

"Then she'll have to have a wedding she hates," Jae says, hugging me tighter as we snuggle together, sharing a post-dinner glass of wine.

"Also, why doesn't she . . . I mean, she never stands up with me. She always lets me do the dirty work. And after all I go out on a limb . . . she just . . . runs away."

"Maybe you're just braver than she is," Jae says.

"Or just more clueless. Because I always walk right into it."

"You're not clueless." Jae holds me tighter. "And it's just the bane of siblings. They never appreciate the help. But she'll come around. She's just scared of upsetting your mom."

"So she lets me do it? This isn't even my wedding."

"I know." Jae kisses the top of my head. I'm grateful for the support, for having someone, at least, in my corner. "I know this is killing you because you want to fix this. And as much as you want to hall monitor the shit out of everything and everyone, you actually can't do that. No one really can."

I laugh, rueful. "You better believe I'm going to hall monitor the *shit* out of everything. I'm going to keep trying, even if it's a lost cause."

Jae tosses a bit of popcorn at me. "Oh, I know. Do you *know* how many detentions you caused me?"

"Not enough, clearly, because you were always late," I tease.

"I was always late because I had to take my two brothers to school, *and* drop off two cousins at elementary school across town."

"Wait. You did?" I pull away from him. I guess I never thought of the boy with the brand-new Jeep having any issues at all. I never thought he had chores and responsibilities.

Jae nods. "Yeah, I wasn't just rolling through Starbucks. I had 'firstborn' responsibilities. Ask my dad."

"Oh. Well, now I feel shitty for giving you all those detentions."

"No you don't."

I flash a rueful smile. "Okay, well, maybe not that much."

"Hall monitor from hell!" Jae growls, but he tugs me closer and tickles me until I can't breathe.

As we slip deeper into September, the weather shifts ever so slightly. The oppressive heat gives way to a cool breeze off the lake, just the barest of hint of the arctic tundra that awaits come January. This is perfect sweater weather, the short time of year in Chicagoland when we can wear cute little jackets, and stiletto boots, and not worry about freezing to death or sliding off an icy sidewalk and into an urgent care.

Autumn.

The Toggle board has given us their blessing for the Evans deal. Now it's all about the countdown to signing papers. In the meantime, distracting myself with Jae feels right. What else can I do while I wait? Plot how I can somehow stay on at Toggle even after a deal is made? Part of me knows that's selfish. It's better if I'm out of a job, but it saves everyone else's.

The sun has set, an oversized autumn moon hangs in the sky, and Jae and I are headed to dinner, having just left his condo. As we're crossing the Madison Street Bridge across the Chicago River, a couple of other people hurry by us on the bridge, eager to get to their commuter trains. Cars also rumble by, hitting the metal grates on the bridge, creating a rhythmic thump of their spinning tires.

Jae holds my hand, his palm warm against the cool September night air. He glances down at me.

"Wait a second." Jae slows his gait. "Stop right there. I want to get your picture."

"My picture?" My hand instantly flies to my hair. "Why? Blackmail?"

"No. Posterity."

I lean against the red, ornate iron railing, a cool fall breeze ruffling my hair. He snaps my picture, and then gazes at it.

"See?" He tilts the screen to me. "You're beautiful."

I'm half laughing, a bit self-conscious by the attention, the moon large in the sky behind me and reflected in the dark waters of the Chicago River. The Lyric Opera House arches into the starry night. It's not my best picture—my hair is ruffled by the wind and the angle is slightly off—but my eyes are shining. I can't remember the last time I looked so . . . happy.

"My hair is windblown," I say, protesting the flyaways.

"Your hair is perfect."

"You should delete that immediately."

"I am absolutely never deleting this. I'm making it my new wallpaper," Jae threatens, though part of me loves the idea of him carrying me around on his phone. "Or I could use this one." He shows me a terrible picture of me dancing at the Brew Fest.

"Absolutely *not*."

"Every picture of you is perfect, Nami." Jae grows serious. "Because you're perfect."

For a second, time stops. The people bustling by on their way to the train station. He stares at me. I stare at him. Something feels heavy and weighty in the moment. Something feels . . . monumental. I look up at Jae and meet his gaze. And then I see it: adoration eyes.

For a whole second, I can't breathe. I know this look. It's how Jack looks at Sora. It's how . . . I'm looking in that picture he just took of me.

Jae pulls me close then. He kisses me softly, deliberately, and I feel my whole body open up to his. We break apart and gaze at each other. "When we've been married for fifty years, I'll be sure to use this photo at our silver wedding anniversary."

I feel a little electric surge at the prospect.

"Fifty years? Aren't you getting ahead of yourself? Don't we have to get married first?" I ask.

"That's the easy part. Please."

"You think I'm going to marry you."

Jae studies me, suddenly serious. "I know you will."

Right at that moment, I don't mind Jae's ego. I kind of love it. And part of me wonders: Could it be possible that at long last, I've found my soulmate? Did that stupid wish on my cake all those weeks ago actually came true?

A giggle bubbles up in me.

"What's so funny?" Jae asks.

"It's . . . nothing. A stupid birthday-cake wish."

"There's no such thing as a stupid birthday-cake wish," Jae says.

"Well, it's just that . . ."

Jae shushes me with a finger. "You absolutely can't tell me that. Then it won't come true. Artemis is listening."

I cock my head to one side. "You know about Artemis?"

"Greek mythology minor," he admits.

"You're a business major and a Greek mythology minor?" I ask, astounded, as he grabs my hand and we continue walking.

"I'm a Renaissance man," he says.

My phone buzzes with an incoming call. I almost ignore it, but something tells me not to.

It's Sora. Odd. It's nearly ten on a Saturday, late for her normal chats. I wonder if it's another wedding planning emergency. I'm tempted to let it go to voicemail. I'm still miffed at her for letting me take the fall in front of Mom.

"Hello?" I answer, guarded.

"Nami." The tone of her voice tells me something is wrong. Very wrong. Beyond expensive wedding dresses wrong. I press a finger to my ear to blot out the rumbling traffic nearby so I can hear.

"What's happened?" I'm right back years ago when Sora made a different call. About our dad collapsing at the top of the stairs. I feel light-headed.

"It's Grandma Mitsuye." My stomach drops. No, no, no. Sora continues in an urgent torrid of words. "She fell. She was on a ladder, trying to change a lightbulb. By herself! Anyway, she's being rushed to the ER. Mom, Jack, and I are following her there. We think she broke her hip, but she might have also hit her head."

Sora sounds scared. Really scared. I feel like I'm going to throw up. "Which hospital?" I say. I remember Grandma's soft hugs. Her jasmine perfume. I've got to get there. I've got to see that she's okay.

I feel Jae watching me.

"Northside Medical."

I know it. Of course. It's the same hospital Dad went to. Fear squeezes my throat.

"I'm going there now. I'll meet you there."

"Okay." Tears make Sora's voice sound thick. I know she doesn't want to go back there any more than I do. But we have to. For Grandma. And Mom. I don't know how she'll be, either. The last time she went to Northside, her entire world collapsed.

"What's wrong?" Jae says, concerned.

"It's my . . . grandma. She fell. Broke her hip and maybe hurt her head. I've got to go. To the hospital. You don't have to come . . ." I feel as if I'm in shock. Like I'm trapped inside a glass jar, with everything around me muted. "I can . . . get a rideshare."

Jae stares at me as if I've lost my mind. "I'm taking you there. My car isn't far."

"Okay, but you don't have to stay." I want to make it clear that just because we've spent some time together doesn't mean he's obligated. Also, it's all lovely to joke about getting married, but it's another thing when we're suddenly back in the real world, where there are obligations.

But soon we're in the car, and Jae is all business.

"Put in the address," he says, nodding to my phone. The tires squeal as he takes the next sharp turn. I grab the handle near the ceiling, but Jae manuevers the car impeccably, weaving deftly around slower-moving cars and one bus. He's deliberate and calm as he presses the clutch and kicks the car into a higher gear. Amazingly, cars seem to magically part for him. All the lights turn green at just the right time. I wonder if this is what it's like to have Jae's kind of luck.

Then Jae takes a left when I think he should go right.

"Wait, isn't it . . ."

"Shortcut," he tells me, winking. "Don't worry. I know what I'm doing."

The engine roars as he kicks it up to get through a single yellow light, and I'm doubtful. Until we pull into the hospital parking lot a mere seven minutes later. Jae pulls into an open, front-row ER parking spot, because he's lucky, and things like amazing parking just open up for this man. Just like all the green lights, and the slower cars moving out of his way. Maybe having things come easy might not always be a bad thing.

Jae hops out of the car.

"Thanks, but you don't have to—" I'm not sure why I'm fighting him so hard. Maybe I don't want to answer questions about Jae. Maybe I don't want him to see me fall apart. Maybe I'm just frazzled, overwhelmed.

"I'm coming in." Jae's voice leaves no room for argument.

I'm too dazed to argue. When he offers his elbow, I take it. My knees still feel weak. I glance up at the big, red, glowing letters of the emergency room sign, and feel a freak-out moving up in my throat.

The last time I walked through those doors, I lost my father.

"Whatever happens, I'm here," Jae says, voice low. I'm stupidly grateful for his arm right then. I clutch his elbow as we walk in.

TWENTY

Jae

Inside the gray-and-mauve waiting room of the emergency room, Nami's family sits huddled together in the far corner, hands clasped and heads bowed in what looks like a silent prayer. Nami breaks free of my arm then and runs to them. Her mother, wet-eyed, envelops her in a hug. Sora's next. A tall, lumbering tree of a man is the last to hug her. It's no relation that I ever met.

"Jae!" Her mom recognizes me with surprise, blinking back her own tears. She gives me a hug, too, but then pulls back. "What are you doing here?" She glances at Nami with confusion.

"We were . . . just grabbing dinner," I offer.

"He gave me a ride," Nami cuts in quickly.

I glance at her. *A ride?* That's all? Surely I rank higher in her life than a rideshare driver. I tell myself not to be offended. Sora looks pleasantly surprised, or mildly amused, it's hard to tell.

"Well, isn't that nice of him." Sora smiles at me. "Thanks, Jae," she says, giving me a quick hug. "I remember you from the tennis team."

"Yeah." I remember Sora, too. Nami's older sister, who would watch our matches when she was home from college. Always smiling, always cordial.

"I'm Jack," the lumberjack tells me, offering a massive paw. There aren't too many men I have to look up to, but he's at least two inches taller than me. "Sora's fiancé."

I notice Sora's diamond flashing under the hospital lights and feel relieved. "Nice to meet you," I say, shaking his paw.

"I'm okay now, Jae," Nami sniffs, wiping another tear from her eye. "You really don't have to stay."

Why is she acting like I should leave? She can't be embarrassed of me. That does not compute.

"I want to. Just to make sure you're okay." Because the color still hasn't come back to her cheeks. For all I know, she'll faint, and then she'll need a doctor's exam herself.

Out of the corner of my eye, I see Sora and Jack exchange a glance.

"How is Grandma?" I ask Nami's mom.

"We don't know yet," she responds. "We know her hip is fractured, and she will likely need surgery, but they're doing a CT scan for her head. They're worried about a concussion, or at her age, something worse."

"What was she doing on a ladder?" Nami asks, exasperated. I can feel her frustration.

"You know Grandma," Sora says. "You can't tell her not to keep busy."

"I'm so glad she had her phone nearby. She called me, and I called the ambulance first, and then Sora and Jack."

Nami frowns, ever so slightly. Her mom sinks down into a nearby chair. "I never wanted to be back here again."

Again? I wonder, but decide to keep my mouth shut. Sora moves to her mom and sits near her. Jack takes up the seat next to Sora. And that's the whole empty row here at the end. No other seats. Nami hugs herself.

My phone pings. A message from Evans.

You ready to do this?

By "this," he means Rainforest backing off the battery company so he can swoop in. The last thing I want to do right now is talk business. Nami needs me. At the same time, who will protect Toggle if I don't? Nami needs me to do that, too.

What if we're not interested? What if we let you have Toggle?

Evans's reply is swift and brutal.

That would be foolish. We'd just roll them into Vacay. You'd lose your toehold in this space, and we'd be right back to square one.

I know what "roll them into" means. It means lay off the entire Toggle staff and slap a Toggle logo on Vacay code. I think I always knew Evans wouldn't be a savior.

I swallow. That means Rainforest—and me—really are Toggle's only hope.

I'll finalize paperwork next week, I text Evans. I stash my phone in my back pocket and glance at Nami, who is staring at her shoes. I want to tell her all of this. But I can't.

"Hey, let's go get a drink from the vending machine," I offer, spying a row of them across the waiting room. She blinks at me, as if coming out of a trance.

"Yeah." She nods.

"Do you all need anything?" I ask the trio. But they all mutely shake their heads. Nami walks silently beside me, eyes dull with worry. When we arrive at the vending machine, she turns and looks back at her family. Jack is whispering something in Sora's ear, and he's got a firm double-grip on her hand, love clear in his face. Nami frowns. For a second, I wonder if she's jealous.

"They're crazy for each other, aren't they?" I say softly, nodding at them. Nami blinks at me, her frown deepening.

"Yeah, they are. And he's great for her." She sighs.

"I feel a 'but' coming on . . ."

"But I don't know. It's hard to be single when your sister has found her soulmate." Her voice sounds lonely and wistful.

"But you're not," I point out. "Single, that is. Not if you don't want to be."

I stare at her. She stares at me.

"I'm not single?" she asks, actually confused.

I wonder if her not mentioning me to her family was actually, seriously deliberate.

"Well, Namby, I guess that's up to you. Do you really want me to be the only one planning our silver wedding anniversary?"

She laughs a little.

"I know this isn't the best time to have this discussion," I say, "but I don't want to date anyone else but you. I thought I made that obvious with all the wedding references, but just in case not . . ."

She blinks, fast. "We're having the 'exclusive' talk by the vending machines in the emergency room?"

"I thought about bringing it up at the intake desk, but decided it was best to wait." I flash her a wry grin.

A smile blooms on her face. "You're ridiculous," she scolds.

"So are you." We giggle, that easiness between us once more. "Look, I realize since you haven't mentioned me to your family, you're keeping me in the casual-and-discard category, but I just wanted you to know, that's not me."

"Casual-and-discard category? Is that better or worse than friends with benefits?"

"Probably worse? Are you really going to make me sweat this out? Because I'm starting to get nervous."

She raises an eyebrow. "Are you *worried*? Is *Jae Lee* worried?"

"Never." That's a lie. I'm really more worried that the news of the Evans deal falling through tanks everything. Even though I'm already making plans in my head to keep Toggle however Nami wants it. If I can. Would Rainforest's CEO even be on board with that? How much trouble would I get in? Part of me worries I'd just be fired and replaced with a different wolf.

She reaches up on her tiptoes and kisses me, slow and deep, lighting up every reward center in my brain. When she pulls back, the light is back in her eyes. "You're not in the casual-and-discard file. I don't want to date anybody else but you, either."

I feel immense relief.

"Are *you* sure you want to be exclusive? After just a month." She raises a skeptical eyebrow.

"A half hour ago, I was talking about our fiftieth wedding anniversary," I point out. "And yes. I want to put a label on this. I want you to be my G-word." I might be trying to lock things down before she realizes that Rainforest will need to buy Toggle. Am I buying up property on the Monopoly board hoping to improve my chances of winning? Maybe.

But the real point is I don't want to lose Nami. Ever. I don't care how many Park Places or Boardwalks that costs me.

"G-word?" Her eyes grow wide. "You want me to be your goat?"

"No!" I laugh.

"Goofball?"

"Most definitely. You are that." I grin. "Girlfriend. I mean *girl-friend*."

She hushes me dramatically, and glances around the ER. "Hush. Some of your swipe rights might hear you."

I laugh, louder than I intend, and a few people in the waiting room turn. Wrong time. Wrong place. I get it. But I'm impatient. I feel like I've got a lot of ground to make up. And time is running out.

"Are you really sure you want to give up your swipe rights? And all the Instagram models in your DMs?"

I laugh. "You are such a stalker."

She shrugs one beautiful narrow shoulder. "I like to do my research."

She gets me. I get her. We both like to win. It's what makes us work so well together. Unless we're on opposite teams.

"So, your mother mentioned she never wanted to be back here again. What did she mean—'again'?" I ask.

Nami glances up at me, pain flickering across her face. "My dad died here almost three years ago." Her voice is so faint, I have to lean in to hear her. "None of us have been back here since."

"Oh, Nami. I am . . . so sorry." I reach out and gently pull her to me. She sags against my shoulder. I want to hold her up. Now and forever.

Eventually she pulls away. Her eyebrows narrow as she glances over my shoulder. I turn, to see what's making her frown, and see a doctor in a white coat and green scrubs, making his way to Sora, Jack, and her mom.

"There's news," Nami says.

TWENTY-ONE

Nami

Bring back my chair. It's my property. Period. If the police won't
handle this, my lawyer will!!!

DELL OURANOS
PARTNER, CO-OWNER, BUSINESS INFLUENCER, AND
TRENDSETTER
#ALL-HANDS-ALERT CHANNEL
TOGGLE INTERNAL CHAT

I am no one's property. This is why I'm not coming home. Why don't
you want me to be happy?

WEGNER SWIVEL CHAIR

Grandma looks even smaller than I remember in what seems
like her oversize hospital bed, her IV and sensors covering
most of one arm. Thankfully, she's awake, and smiles at us all as we
enter. The monitors beep the steady rhythm of her heart as Mom,
Sora, and I all crowd into the room. I tell myself this time is different. It's not my dad lying in that bed, my dad who would never
wake up.

"Mama, the doctor says your head is okay!" Mom says, leaning
over her bed. Sora squeezes my hand. *Thank God,* she mouths to
me. "You're going to have hip surgery tomorrow!"

"I'm going to Disney World tomorrow?" Grandma asks, confused.

"No! Surgery!"

"Oh!" Grandma shakes her head, rueful. She looks a little out of it. "Too bad. I love Disney World."

"How many painkillers did they give her?" Sora whispers, eying her IV.

"Hopefully a lot," I whisper. I glance back at Jae, hanging in the doorway, Jack hovering nearby.

"Nami!" she cries, seeing me. "And So-dah!"

"Hi, Gram." I dip forward and kiss her on the forehead. Sora squeezes her hand. "This is *not* what you mean by 'fall down seven times, get up eight,' okay? This fall was *too* scary!" She laughs ruefully. "Next time you need a lightbulb changed, you call me. I'll come right over."

"Jack's already volunteered to be on ladder patrol," Sora adds. "So, you call *us*."

Grandma waves a dismissive hand. "I love Jack," she says, waving at Jack. "But I don't want to be a bother!"

"You're not a bother!" Sora exclaims.

Then Grandma sees Jae. "Who is that handsome boy?" she asks me, eyes widening.

I turn to see Jae shrug. "Jae, ma'am. Jae Lee."

"He used to live down the street from us. Remember?" I prompt.

"Come here so I can take a look at you." Jae dutifully comes in. Grandma studies him.

"You *are* handsome. My." Grandma reaches out and squeezes his bicep, and then giggles like a little girl. "So strong!"

I eye her IV. Maybe she's gotten a little too much happy juice. Jae glances at me, a slight blush appearing on his cheek. My grandma still has a vise grip on his bicep.

"Grandma," I say. "Let's let Jae go now."

"Do I have to?" she asks, rubbing his arm. "So many muscles! My! Such a handsome face! Oh! And look at those dimples when you smile! My, oh my. There would've been fights over you at camp."

Sora and I exchange a glance. We know for certain now Grandma has been overserved in the painkiller department. She hardly ever talks about Poston.

"Camp?" Jae looks at me confused.

"Japanese Internment Camp during World War Two," I manage before a nurse in blue scrubs bustles in. "She was just a little kid then."

"Sorry, everyone," he says. "Visiting hours are up in five minutes."

Mom gives Grandma a hug. "I'll be back first thing in the morning, okay, Mama?"

"Will Jae come back? I want to see Jae." My grandma winks at Jae. "Look at you, handsome!" She reaches out, and I swear she's going for Jae's butt. He dodges.

Sora tries to stifle a giggle. "Grandma!" I tsk.

"Time to get some rest, Mama," Mom chides.

I sit in the passenger seat of Jae's expensive Audi, apologizing again, as we drive away from the hospital. "She's really not normally like that. Seriously."

"It's okay," he says, and chuckles. "She's on meds. It's fine."

"You seem pretty calm for having been groped by an eighty-seven-year-old," I add.

"Hey, it's good to know I can expand my dating limits on the apps if I want," he quips. "It's nice to have options."

"With octogenarians?" I stare at him.

He laughs. "Just think about all the early bird specials! And the AARP discounts," he jokes. He flashes me a winning smile. He does have nice dimples. Grandma is right. I embrace the weird floaty feeling in my stomach being crammed into the small interior of his car. Everywhere smells like his hair product. Sweet. Spicy. Awesome.

"Besides, I thought we're exclusive now."

"Oh, right. I forgot." Jae flashes me a smile to show he definitely, absolutely has not forgotten.

My stomach yowls and I realize it's closing in on one in the morning.

"Hungry?" Jae asks me.

"No," I lie.

"We skipped dinner, and you sound like you're possessed by a demon." Jae side-eyes me. "I just got the car detailed, so are we talking pea soup vomit or what?"

"Ha. Very funny."

"I know a great taco joint," he offers. "Not far."

My stomach growls its approval. "It's late . . ."

"They're fast," Jae promises. "And the last thing I want is you fainting in my car. No forehead smudges on the dash."

Jae pulls up to a small taqueria, which is somehow still open in the wee hours of Sunday morning. He pulls around the back alley, and tucks his car into a corner space in the small parking lot.

"You're sure they're good?"

"Mateo's tacos are the best in town." The fact that he has a line at the counter at one in the morning seems to confirm this. Inside the small taqueria, I'm blasted with the smell of amazing goodness. My stomach yowls again and Jae glances at me, quirking one eyebrow.

"You sure there's no alien in there?" he asks as we scoot up in line.

"I'm sure," I grouse, though I cross my arms across my chest anyway. In quick fashion, Jae gets an order of carnitas and tinga tacos wrapped in tinfoil. Two Styrofoam cups filled with horchata follow. Jae lingers at the counter, grabbing a handful of napkins, as I take a seat at a booth near the window. The smell of deliciousness hits my nose, and I can't wait for Jae. I tear into my tinga tacos. The amazing spicy chicken and soft tortilla hit my tongue and I swear, I've never tasted anything so good.

"Careful. You might want to chew before you swallow," Jae jokes as he slides onto the opposite side of the booth.

I take another mouthful. I growl something unintelligible. They're too good to eat slowly. Plus, I'm starving.

Jae flashes me a brilliant white smile. "Told you they were the best tacos in town."

All I can do is nod. It's heaven on my tongue, that's all. Full stop.

"You know, you might want to pause long enough to breathe. I don't want to have to take you back to the hospital. Also, you're wearing half of that last bite. On your face." He grins and I feel like sticking out my tongue, but know it's loaded with carnitas. He slowly unwraps his first taco and takes a delicate bite. I reach for a napkin from the pile he left between us and swipe at my mouth, but I realize I don't even really care if I do have grease on my chin. The tacos are that good.

I devour two and wash them down with sweet rice milk before I even come up to breathe.

"Thank you," I manage. "For today. For taking me to see Grandma. For being such a . . ." I look for the right words. "Good boyfriend."

He grins. "Believe me, 'boyfriend' is only the beginning."

I actually really hope so.

"Here's to a speedy recovery for Grandma," Jae says, and then he offers his horchata up in a toast. We clink Styrofoam cups. Jae drinks, and then finishes a taco. When he sees me eyeing his last taco, he offers it up to me.

"Okay, fine. You sure?" My stomach yowls again.

"We have to appease the demon." He nods to my sternum. "You've got a bigger appetite than Shrek."

I slap at Jae with a napkin. "Rude!" But I actually kind of love it. It feels like we've got a relationship that's just a little more real, a little more honest than most. *Relationship*. That's what this is.

His phone pings, and he glances at it, frowning. I can almost feel his mood shift. I wonder who's texting him, but something stops me from asking. We've only just agreed to be exclusive, and maybe there are people crowded in his inbox he's got to systematically disperse. The thought sends a cold sliver of jealousy through me. The feeling takes me by surprise. I'm used to feeling envious of Jae, and all his accomplishments. But jealousy about losing his attention? That's new.

"Something wrong?" I ask him, eyeing the phone, but I can't see the message from here.

"Just work," he says, frowning at his phone, but then carefully placing it facedown on the table.

The message is late. It makes me wonder if it is actually work-related. Then again, I have heard Rainforest executives don't sleep. Evans certainly doesn't. Imani told me Evans texted her at two in the morning last week just to make sure the signing was still on schedule. "Everything okay?" I ask.

"Yeah." But Jae glances away.

"You know, you don't have to work for Rainforest." Jae meets my gaze then, eyes wary.

"Why not?"

"You're better than that. It's all I'm saying."

"What do you mean? I'm a wolf. Wolves have to work somewhere, and Rainforest pays wolves particularly well."

I shrug, focusing on my Styrofoam cup. I should tread carefully. "You could use your powers for good instead of evil. You don't have to eat Grandma."

"Maybe I prefer little piggies. Bacon is better than seniors."

I laugh. "Fine." I realize I've gone as far as I can. I made my point, and he's deflected me with a joke. I meet Jae's gaze and see there's no hard feelings as he takes my hand reassuringly. "Ready to go, Shrek?" he teases.

"Yeah." I ball up my trash and stand.

"Good, because I've got an eight A.M. meeting tomorrow."

"Does that mean . . . no late-night shenanigans?" I'm suddenly disappointed.

"Oh, there will *definitely* be shenanigans when we get to my place," Jae promises.

TWENTY-TWO

Nami

This is goodbye. I love him. We're going where we can be free.
[attached: picture of Wegner Swivel Chair, a man in a black ski
mask with his arm around the back. They're inside the International
Terminal at O'Hare International Airport]

WEGNER SWIVEL CHAIR
#ALL-HANDS-ALERT CHANNEL
TOGGLE INTERNAL CHAT

I stroll into my office building the next day, and my feet don't even touch the ground. We did indeed enjoy quite a few shenanigans in quite a few positions, and probably got a little less than three hours of sleep, but I don't care. I even smile at Doppelgänger Mitch and his coffee girlfriend on my way to the elevators because I no longer feel envy. Jae and I had coffee together in bed this morning. He has a fancy coffeemaker in his condo, one that makes amazing foaming cappuccinos, and now I realize just why that ad with Doppelgänger Mitch seems so heartwarming. I'm sure he's laughing so hard because one of them probably cracked a joke, and because there's nothing more perfect than waking up to the person meant for you every morning.

Grandma headed into surgery at the crack of dawn and is already in recovery, doing well. Everything went quickly, and the break wasn't that bad after all, and there were zero complications. The doctors were so impressed they thought she's likely to make a speedy recovery. All in all, things are looking up.

The elevator doors open on my floor, and my smile splits my face as I walk by the programmers lobbing Frisbees, their happy voices just a background chorus to the bright musical that is now my life. I'm . . . happy. Everything feels . . . wonderful. As I slide into my chair and boot up my laptop, I'm humming to myself, *humming*. I can't focus on anything. Jae and I are exclusive. This is . . . happening.

In eight short hours, I'll take a rideshare to his condo, and we'll kick off our shoes, and laugh about our day, and share a glass of wine, and cuddle. I'm trying to figure out how best to get clothes from my place and wonder if a quick stop at the dry cleaner's on the way to his place will do. Still, I tell myself I need to focus. I do have work to do.

There are emails in my inbox to read. Voicemails to hear.

Yet all I can think about are replays of a handful of conversations with Jae. The inside jokes. The easiness between us. The way I just feel like I fit in his life. And he in mine.

For the first time in a long time, I'm thinking about the future again. A future that I'm glad doesn't include Mitch. Being with Jae makes me really see how terrible a fit Mitch was. How he barely had an opinion about anything, how he never challenged me. I took it as agreement, not realizing he'd been seething with envy the entire time we were together. Jealous that I'd made something of myself, when he hadn't.

Jae, despite his ego, or maybe because of it, has no time for envy. He's too busy making his own moves, developing his own career. I may not agree with all his decisions (working for Rainforest is on top of that list), but I at least understand them.

When I talk now, Jae listens, with his full body, his whole self, and all his attention focused on me. When I had talked to Mitch, he was usually playing a video game and only half-listened as I told him about my day. The difference is stark and telling.

I'm not even thinking about Evans, about how he'll change Toggle. I'm encased in a bubble of pure love, and everywhere I look, all I see are happy endings.

My phone pings with an incoming text from Jae.

Hey gorgeous. Miss you already.

My toes tingle, and it's got nothing to do with the thin ribbon of air-conditioning across my open-toed flats.

Miss you, too.

Wish I could've lounged around in bed this morning with Jae. But we both had work. We had morning meetings. But being away from him already feels like I'm missing an essential organ. I'm not sure how this happened so quickly, or how he became such an integral part of my life in such a short time.

See you tonight for dinner? I ask, but I already know the answer.

Of course. I've got a new recipe I want to try.

We might need champagne tonight, I write. *I'll buy.*

Least I can do since we're signing the papers for the Evans deal today and making it official. It's the only time I've even obliquely mentioned it. Seemed poor taste to bring up the fact that Jae's losing out on us, and Jae has strategically avoided talking about Evans and Toggle, too, and I figure it's something neither one of us wants to poke too hard. Besides, I got the impression when I brought up Rainforest with Jae that it's not something he's really open to discussing. And that's okay. It's not really my job to tell him where to work.

Dots appear and then disappear on my screen.

I feel the hesitation and the pause. Did I go too far mentioning The Deal That Shall Not Be Named? I shouldn't have talked about champagne. It's like spiking the football.

He's writing something else. Then he stops. They appear again. And disappear. I've never seen Jae hem or haw like this.

Finally, his message comes through. *Don't forget what I said the first time you mentioned Evans.*

What does he mean? That I can't trust Evans? Is he telling me to double-check the fine print? The flirty banter has suddenly gotten serious, and I don't know why. Suddenly, I'm nervous. I want to call Jae and get to the bottom of it all, but before I can, a hard knock comes on my glass office door. I glance up to see an anxious-looking Imani, wearing orange-rimmed glasses and a matching orange polka-dot sleeveless silk shirt.

"It's Evans. Can we talk?" she asks me, and her face tells me it's bad news. I feel a pit form at the center of my stomach. I know then that everything is about to change.

I feel faint and nauseous as I stumble out of Imani's office, still reeling from the news that Evans withdrew his offer. Worse, Imani let me know that right after she got the call from Evans, she got a message from Jae. Rainforest is still in the mix, but they've downgraded their offer. We'll be getting at least one zero less now that Evans isn't interested.

Jae was planning this all along.

A one-two punch.

I can't breathe.

Dell kicks a trash can in his own office, sending it flying across the colored carpet and clanging against the far glass wall. The programmers—my people—are mostly at lunch now, thank goodness, because there's no way I'd be able to hide the disappointment written all over my face.

The betrayal, thick and painful, sits in my throat—a lump that I can't swallow down.

Jae knew about this. I know he did. *Remember what I said about Evans . . .*

Right. I can't trust Evans.

But what he should've told me is that I can't trust him, either.

This was a coordinated attack. Evans withdrawing. Rainforest lowballing us.

And Jae masterminded it all. He knew this was coming and he let me walk right into it, unprepared. He let me have ridiculous dreams about toasting the sale of Toggle tonight with champagne at his place. Maybe going exclusive—or hell, sleeping with me at all—was just a distraction in the first place, so I'd take my eye off the ball.

And the worst thing is: I fell for it.

Hook.

Line.

Sinker.

I've never been so hurt—and so angry—all at once. I'm not sure if I want to cry or scream. Or both. Why did I think after a lifetime of friends and boyfriends and one fiancé abandoning me that it wouldn't happen . . . yet again?

My ears ring, and everything seems slowed down. I grab my bag and head straight to the elevators.

Jae

I've been expecting Nami, and dreading this moment, and yet, now is the time when I can finally, and at long last, come clean. I'm no longer under the restraints of the NDA I signed, really, since she'll know about the withdrawal of Evans's offer, and maybe I can explain everything.

Or maybe she'll hate me forever.

Treely alerts me to her presence, and I watch her storm the stairs, face flushed with anger, quick stride telling me she's coming for me. I take a deep breath. I'll have to make her understand. I'll just have to.

She storms into my office, eyes like molten lava.

"How could you?" she growls.

"Let me explain," I try in my calmest voice. I don't know if I can, but I just want the chance. "Please, sit."

She slams her bag down and sinks into the chair, angrily crossing her legs. That's the first victory. She might just hear me out.

"I'm sorry, Nami. I couldn't tell you."

"You mean you *wouldn't* tell me." She's furious, I can see that. But she's still talking to me. That's good. Keep her talking. Maybe she'll see.

"I couldn't. I'd signed legal agreements."

"You lied to me." Tears brim in her eyes, and I feel I might be undone. I hate this. I knew it would be terrible, but I actually never realized how much I'd hate it. Until now.

"I didn't technically lie. And now I can help you. I can help Toggle."

She cackles a bitter laugh. "You? *You* want to help Toggle? Please. By buying us for much less than your original offer?"

"I had to downgrade the price. Because I plan to keep on your people. It's the only way I can justify it to the higher-ups. I want to help you."

"Please. You never help anyone but yourself."

The criticism stings. She isn't giving me the benefit of the doubt. It's my worst nightmare come true. "Nami. Please, listen—"

She jumps up from her seat. "Stop. Just . . . stop. If I were in your position, I would've just told you."

"And violated all those legal agreements?"

"Yes. Because I care about you, Jae. And it would be the right thing to do."

"Right thing to do?" This is her Hall Monitor streak, the one who thinks everything can be solved with a tardy slip. "Life is messy and gray, and sometimes the 'right' thing isn't easy to figure out. No matter how hard you try, Ms. Hall Monitor. Don't be so naïve."

I mean to make my voice sound light and flippant, a joke, but the words come out harsher than I intend. My words slice like a knife, and she flinches.

"This isn't some stupid tardy slip. You had to know this was wrong. There is *right* and *wrong,* I mean, I can't believe I have to spell this out."

"I'm not saying there's no right and wrong. But it's not black and white. And if you'll just let me explain—"

"Explain what? How you used me? How you never trusted me enough to tell me the truth?"

"If I'd told you, you would've told everyone."

"Why? Because hall monitors can't keep secrets? I'm just a tattletale? You should've let me in. We could've tried to solve this together, instead of *you* figuring you knew better than me, better than everyone."

It's right now that I realize I didn't trust her. No more than she trusted me.

And it occurs to me, in uncharacteristic fashion, I'm blowing it. I need to pivot. I need to make her see. Maybe I can convince her. She has to know we're so right together. Who cares about *business?* It's *just* business. But what we have is different. It's amazing. It's once-in-a-lifetime.

"Nami, none of this changes how I feel about you. What we have . . . it's amazing. Just . . . I tried to warn you about Evans. I really tried. And then, when I couldn't tell you, I thought I could be the one to protect Toggle. Help with the transition."

"I don't want your 'help.'" Anger burns in her eyes. So does hurt. Hurt I created.

"If I told you, I would've been fired," I say weakly.

"You should have quit. Then told me."

"Quit?" I feel like Nami has backed me into the corner, blocked my only escape. I realize right in that second, it never occurred to me to quit. But I could have. She's right. "Who would protect Toggle then?"

"You're telling me when push comes to shove, you won't lay off anyone? Toggle will remain the same."

"Well, no, not exactly, but . . ."

"Then you should have quit," Nami says. "We could have put our heads together to help Toggle. We could've formed a different plan, and with your luck and your credentials, you would've had a better job in a matter of weeks. You probably already have a dozen job offers on your ConnectIn right now." This never occurred to me. Why didn't it occur to me? "So why stay with the Borg?" she continues. "You know they're a terrible company. You know every deal you land them just makes them more powerful, even as they're making the world a worse place. You know they don't care about their employees, or the companies they buy, or their users."

I run both hands through my hair in frustration.

"Again, things aren't so simple. Nothing is all good or all bad. Rainforest does good things, too." But my sales pitch is weak.

"All Rainforest cares about is winning." She glares at me. "*That's* why you stay with them, isn't it? Because ultimately, there's nothing more important to you than winning."

"No," I say quickly, hoping she's not right. "Yes, winning matters. And at the start, yes, that's all I cared about. But with you, Nami, it's always been more than that. You have to understand . . ." How can I make her understand? "It was always about you. I sought you out. I missed what we had in high school. Our competition, our spark. I specifically went after Toggle because I knew you would be there, and I wanted to see you. I called Dell for a meeting because I knew you would challenge me. You, unlike anybody else, are a good adversary. You challenge me in ways that are new and exciting, and you're . . . you're . . ." I struggle for the right words. "You're good for me."

She stops pacing. "I'm good for you," she repeats, hollow.

"I was bored at Rainforest, and feeling unsatisfied, as if nothing mattered anymore, and I just knew, I just knew if I could work with you again, things would be different. That you'd light up my world, and you did—in more profound ways than I ever thought. I never thought it would lead to this . . . this amazing feeling, this amazing . . . *relationship*. I feel more alive than I've ever felt, Nami. That's all because of you."

I blink fast. Nami doesn't move. Maybe it's working. Maybe she gets it.

"You went after Toggle *because* I was there," she repeats.

"Yes."

"Because you were bored. And you thought I'd liven things up for you?" Her eyes glisten with fresh, new hurt. "You upended the lives of all the people of Toggle, people I *care* about, because your job was *not interesting enough for you*? Because you were *bored*?" She spits out the last word.

"No. Wait. I don't mean it like that." And I don't. When she says it, it sounds terrible. Selfish. Myopic. "I wanted to see you again. I missed you. I missed . . . us."

"Then call me. Text me. *Ask me out for coffee.*" She's so angry now. I'm blowing it. Completely blowing it.

"You never would have said yes," I manage, trying again. "You never gave me the time of day, Nami."

"It's still no reason to put yourself above *everyone* at Toggle. God. It's so selfish. So careless."

"But Nami," I plead. I'm desperate now. "I love you."

That's the truth of it. I've loved her for a long time, I realize now. Maybe even since high school.

"It's too late, Jae," Nami says, shaking her head as she tightens her grip on her bag. "It's just . . . all too late. It's over."

And then she snatches up her bag and walks straight out of my office, and out of my life.

TWENTY-THREE

Jae

Sometimes "Live, Laugh, Love" feels too hard. Might we suggest: "Exist, Scoff, Meh."

#DAILY INSPIRATION CHANNEL
TOGGLE INTERNAL CHAT

I never realized that winning could suck so badly.

Nami hates me, and not a good, simmering, flirty hate, but real, cold hate. Nami accused me of being selfish, and I see that she's right. It's no wonder she's not taking my calls. She's probably blocked me. And I deserve it.

I sit in my apartment the following Saturday, dully staring out over Lake Michigan, missing Nami's full-throated laugh and her razor-sharp retorts. I miss her amazing body in my bed, too, but it's her company, her cheerful teasing of me, her annoying, yet definitely right prodding of me to do better that I miss the most. The worst part is it's all my fault. Nami was right. I was careless with Toggle. Hell, I might have been careless with everyone and everything in my life until I met Nami.

Until I really cared about something I could lose.

None of the thin justifications I usually deploy at times like these are working. I've blown down the pig's house, and I feel like shit about it. And the worst part is, there was a right thing to do. I could've quit Rainforest. I could've tried to approach Nami some other way. But I didn't. I assumed I knew best.

My phone rings. I glance at it, hopeful to see Nami's face, but instead, I see the stern face of my father. I almost send him to voice-mail, but as I'm in the mood for punishment, I pick up.

"Jae-Yeon." Dad's serious, no-nonsense voice floats out on speak-erphone. No "Hello." No "How are you?" Classic Dad.

"Hi, Dad."

"Your mother thinks we should make something different for next Sunday. If Nami likes bibimbap, your mother wants to make that. Or maybe teriyaki."

"Nami's not coming."

"Why is Nami not coming," Dad says, less in the form of a ques-tion, and more an accusation.

I sigh. I might as well just get this over with. Rip the Band-Aid off and get the lecture I deserve. Dad will love telling me how he was right about me all along, because I've failed him as a first-born.

"Because I messed it all up, Dad. Because I'm a selfish, no-good businessman son who just likes the sound of his own voice, and doesn't care about anyone else. I'm a crappy son and an even worse boyfriend, and I'll probably never get married or have kids because I'm too selfish to have a family. I'll just be a constant embarrassment to you, so you should probably just give up on me ever doing any-thing else but disappointing you."

Dad says absolutely nothing on the phone. But part of me takes his silence as implicit agreement.

"We are going to Golden Dragon Buffet," he tells me after a beat.

He means the all-you-can-eat Americanized Asian fusion, greasy, serve-yourself restaurant off the interstate that Mom can't stand, where Dad used to take me after soccer practice every Satur-day in fourth grade. Mom thought the neon-orange sweet-and-sour chicken was loaded with too much sugar and food dye, but Dad loved the frugality of it, and didn't much care how long the questionable California rolls sat in the salad bar. I was a kid and greedily took as many fortune cookies as I could fit in my pockets from the giant wooden boat sitting at the entrance. Dad just loved that he could eat whatever he wanted, for as long as he wanted, for $7.99.

"Dad, it's two in the afternoon."

"I'll meet you there. Twenty minutes."

Then he hangs up.

I know from the tone of Dad's voice it's not an invitation. It's a command. I might as well get it over with. I deserve whatever scolding is coming.

A half hour later, Dad and I sit across from each other in a booth, the red pleather seats cracked behind our backs, the air filled with the aroma of old sesame oil. The oversize floor tiles feel slippery, as if it's just been mopped, or maybe years of grease buildup means no matter how often they scrub, it'll never quite be clean.

"Your mother hates Golden Dragon," Dad tells me, as if I don't know. As if the very mention of this buffet won't make her groan, roll her eyes, and reach for a bottle of antacids. He might demand perfection from his own bulgogi, but when dining out, his standards are purely about economics.

Add Dad's unreasonable love of cheap, greasy Americanized Asian cuisine to the list of questionable judgments, but I don't say this aloud.

Dad's plate is piled high with all varieties, as well as some of that risky buffet sushi. Then again, Dad has an iron stomach. I don't think I ever remember him sick. Not once when I was growing up. Even when we all had the stomach flu, somehow, he never fell ill.

I've opted for what I know is safe: fried rice, sesame chicken, and two of their double-fried egg rolls. It's also what I used to get as a kid, plus or minus a dozen fortune cookies. Dad and I fall into silence again, eating, and I begin to hope that maybe this will be the end of it. I'll just stew in Dad's quiet disapproval while we both eat greasy, lukewarm, extra-saucy, extra-fried food. After we've eaten half our servings from the first trip to the buffet, Dad speaks again, but he keeps his eye on his plate.

"I wanted to talk to you about Charlie."

Huh. Not what I was expecting. "Okay," I say tentatively.

"You saw that I was not happy with his engagement."

"Right. About that, Dad. Not cool. He was so upset. And Nick is so great, and I thought we were all past—"

"No," Dad interrupts, holding up a hand. "I like Nick. I am happy for Charlie. I have told them this."

"Why didn't you show it, then?" I'm ready for a fight.

"Because you are the oldest, Jae-Yeon. *You* are supposed to marry first." He keeps his eyes locked to mine. "It is your duty."

"Are you kidding? You were mad at Charlie because he's getting married first?"

"No." Dad shakes his head. "I was upset *with you* for not getting married first."

We stare at each other a beat. And once more it's like the two of us are speaking right past each other.

"I don't even know what you're talking about, Dad. Who cares who gets married first? It doesn't really matter."

"It does *to me.*" Dad points to his own chest. "In my family, it matters."

Once more, I've failed Dad, but I had no idea what I was being tested on. It's like Dad has this secret checklist that I know nothing about, everything that goes into a "good son," and I keep missing boxes that I didn't even know existed. "You brought Nami home, and I thought we were moving in the right direction."

I sigh, my eyes rolling up to the ceiling. Here we go. Another way I disappointed Dad.

"Well, Dad, it'll come as no surprise to you that I messed it all up with Nami." I tell him the entire sad, sordid story, ending with Nami's critique of me being selfish and careless and that I could've avoided this whole debacle if I'd just quit my job in the first place and trusted Nami enough to tell her the truth.

Dad, who has not made eye contact, or stopped eating during the entire tale, grabs a paper napkin from the silver dispenser on the table and gently pats his mouth.

"Nami is right. You should quit your job."

I groan and glance up at the ceiling. "I knew you'd agree. You probably want me to go to med school instead. You think all business is terrible."

He shakes his head. "No," he counters. "I just think *some* business is terrible."

He meets my gaze and I realize that just like Nami, he doesn't approve of Rainforest. Then it hits me: that's why my parents' home is strangely empty of Rainforest boxes. "You don't like Rainforest."

"I read stories about them. Bad ones. They don't treat their employees well." Dad shrugs. "They're not very honorable. I think you could do better things with your life, Jae-Yeon. Just like Nami does." He wads up his napkin in his hand. "You are not a bad man, Jae-Yeon. I am sure Rainforest pays well. It is a well-known company. I understand why you want to work there. I just think you can do better."

I hear Nami again in my head, *You could use your powers for good*.

For a full second, what Dad really means hits home. He doesn't think *I'm* a failure. He doesn't like my choices. That's all. Also, I've fallen victim to those very cartoon bags of money that I sneer at everybody else for taking.

Well, dammit.

"Even if I quit now, Nami hates me."

Dad steeples his fingers above his now-empty plate. "Show her who you can be. Show her you'd put her—and your family—first."

"What if I can't put anyone but myself first? What if I'm just the Monopoly Magnate?"

Dad laughs. "Even the Monopoly Magnate has a family. You used to slip your mother free money on the side."

Wait. He's right. I might have given her an extra hundred dollars whenever she passed Go.

"I didn't think you noticed that."

Dad raised an eyebrow. "I never miss anything."

I laugh. It's true. Dad's like a hawk. And I always took care of Mom.

"You have a good heart, Jae-Yeon. Always have. Taking care of your little cousins, driving them to their dance classes and school. You can make sacrifices when you want to. Nami will see that. If you show it to her." Dad wags a finger at me. "But you have to show her. If you want her to be your family, then you have to treat her like family."

"How do I do that?"

"I think you know how. You're smart. You know what to do."

I kind of do, actually.

"I've been a bad boyfriend, though."

"Be a bad boyfriend, but an amazing husband." Dad raises both eyebrows, his meaning impossible to miss.

"Are you trying to marry me off right now?"

"There's still time to get married before Charlie," he points out.

"Dad." I shake my head. "I'm not rushing Nami to the altar."

"Not with that attitude," Dad chides me. He studies me, and for a minute, I worry he'll find another flaw. "You aren't a bad son."

"I'm not?" I actually think I might be walking into a punchline. As if Dad will say, *You are not a bad son. You're the worst son.*

"You are not a bad son," he repeats, decidedly and with emphasis. "But you'd be a better son if you give me that egg roll." He nods to the uneaten one on my plate.

"There are about a hundred of these over there!" I motion to the giant lighted metal buffet tables.

"Yes, but this one is right here so I don't have to get up."

I have to laugh as I shove the plate toward him. Dad reaches for it and actually cracks a smile.

TWENTY-FOUR

Nami

I feel so alive.
[attached: picture of Wegner Swivel Chair, a man in a black ski mask,
the Eiffel Tower behind them]

WEGNER SWIVEL CHAIR
#ALL-HANDS-ALERT CHANNEL
TOGGLE INTERNAL CHAT

I want to spend the weekend wallowing in self-pity and berating myself for ever, *ever* letting Jae Lee into my life or trusting that he'd be anything other than the self-serving jerk he is. Instead, I head to the hospital to visit Grandma Mitsuye. Her hip is on the mend, and she's doing well in physical therapy, and the doctor says she'll probably be home by early next week. She sent out an SOS call for her favorite soda, since, apparently, while hospital food is better than she expected, she can't get a can of soda to save her life.

Her eyes light up when I deliver the cold can she's been craving. She pops it and her eyes light up at the familiar hissing sound.

"I ask the nurse for a soda, and she keeps saying the hospital is all out," Grandma tells me as she takes a reverential sip, closing her eyes briefly to truly savor the bubbly sweetness.

"She might not be being honest," I admit. "I saw a vending machine right by the elevator."

Grandma's eyes widen. "Oh, that Cathy! I am going to give her a piece of my mind." But Grandma isn't really mad. Grandma never really ever gets mad. She takes another sip of soda and sighs with delight as she leans back against the pillow.

"How are you doing?" I ask as I take a seat beside her bed.

"Oh, fine." She waves a wrinkled hand and smiles. "The doctors say even though I'm old, my bones are strong. This is only the second time I ever broke one."

"What was the first?"

"At camp."

"How?" I tread carefully, because I know if I ask too many questions about the internment camp, she'll clam up. It was the case when my grandfather was still alive, too. Neither one spoke of that time, except to say it's the reason they met: their families shared barracks there. Both families decided to move to Hawaii after the war, as well, because Japanese Americans in Hawaii, unlike on the mainland, were never interned. My mother joked that there were simply too many of them, since they made up a third of the population, but my grandfather spoke more about Hawaii being more diverse and accepting. "Nobody in Hawaii ever asked me where I'm from," Grandpa would often say.

Grandma moved back to the mainland when we were little, so she could help babysit. Grandma now takes a deep breath. "The barracks were poorly built, and the stairs leading to ours were slanted and loose. I fell climbing them, and just landed wrong. There were no doctors or nurses there. I mean, there was barely food, but Dr. Tanaka, next door, set my wrist in a makeshift sling he made from his shirt and someone's ruler. It sounds crazy, but it healed up nice." She stretches her right wrist to show me.

"What was it like there?" I ask her.

"Hot," she says, and laughs. "Dusty." She frowns and waves her hand, as if she's swiping away the memory. "But enough about that." She makes a face, her usual sign for being done with that conversation.

"How are you? I was hoping you'd bring that handsome young man with you."

I sigh. "You probably won't be seeing him again."

Grandma looks stricken. "Oh no. Did I forget something again?" She looks concerned. "Did you already tell me this?"

"No." I shake my head. I relate the whole sordid story, ending with Evans's deal falling through, and Jae failing to tell me, and him orchestrating the whole thing because he was bored. The words feel thick on my tongue, a coating of the bitterness of betrayal. "So, I'm likely going to lose my company to Rainforest, and Jae picked his company over me. I should've seen this coming. I should've known I couldn't trust Jae."

"Oh, I don't know about that. That boy was smitten with you. I could tell by the way he looked at you."

"You were under the influence of painkillers, Grandma."

Grandma Mitsuye laughs, the soft wrinkles near her eyes crinkling. "Maybe. But I know what a boy in love looks like." She presses her lips together. "Sometimes, boys in love have really silly ways of showing it."

I laugh. It's true. But this also hurts my heart to hear. "Maybe. But it's over now. My heart is broken." I feel the tears well up, burning my eyes. I feel like a fool, to be here, yet again. Brokenhearted. Betrayed.

Grandma reaches out and takes my hand and squeezes it. "*Shikata ga nai,*" she says.

"What does that mean?"

"Sometimes, some bad things, like heartbreak, just can't be helped. It's out of our control," she explains. "When my brothers and sisters and I would ask my mother why we were at the camps, and not at home, she'd say, '*Shikata ga nai,*' meaning it just can't be helped. Bad things happen sometimes. We can't control everything in our lives."

I groan. "I feel like my whole life is *shikata ga nai.*"

Grandma laughs. "No, it's not. Remember," she reminds me gently, "you're the one that always gets up eight times." She smiles at me. "You might not be able to control everything that happens to you, but you can control what you do about it."

I sniff away my tears and smile back.

"Knock, knock," Mom gently says from the doorway behind me. I whip around, wondering how long she's been standing there. She looks uncertain as I swipe at my wet eyes. Sora is also with her. "Are we interrupting?"

She glances at me with worry.

"No. Come in!" Grandma says, waving us in. I move to the corner so Sora and Mom can hug Grandma.

"Everything okay?" Sora asks me, in that worried tone she usually saves just for me. But after our run-in in the dressing room, I don't really feel like her fussing over me. I know I shouldn't still be annoyed by it, but part of me is. Plus, I'm just a little bit tired of being the world's hall monitor.

"Fine," I say, shrugging, not meeting her eye.

Grandma glances at me and Sora.

"How are you, Grandma?" Sora asks, taking her turn to hug our grandmother.

"I'll be better if I see a picture of that wedding dress. Your mother says it's a stunner."

Sora shifts uneasily on her feet. "Actually . . ." she begins, glancing at Mom. "I did find one. At the secondhand store on my street."

"You mean you found one at Vogue Bridal. It's gorgeous, look at this . . ." Mom already has her phone out. Running right over Sora's announcement.

"No, Mom. I'm not going to get that one. We talked about it."

"Yes, and *we* decided you'd go with the princess, A-line, one-of-a-kind—"

"No. I'm going with this." Sora shows Grandma and me a picture of a slim white halter-top prom dress, which is very much like the prom dress she wore to her own senior prom . . .

Except hers was lavender, and this one is white.

"It's gorgeous," I say. "It looks like your prom dress!"

"Doesn't it?"

"Sora Reid. We promised Angelique . . ."

"Mom! I am not getting that dress. I cancelled the order. Nami was right. It's too expensive."

I perk up at this. Sora's never so definitively contradicted Mom in front of me. This is new.

"I offered to pay for it!" Mom exclaims.

"*And* I don't want it. And I don't want the Four Seasons, either!"

Mom throws up her hands in frustration. "Nami! Talk some sense into your sister."

I cross my arms. "It sounds like she is talking sense already. This is Sora's wedding. She should get the dress she wants."

Sora mouths, *Thank you.*

"Nami!" Mom declares, shocked.

"Aiko, just let Sora have her prom wedding. It's what the girl wants!"

"She'll regret it later, though," Mom says. "She'll think it's all a mistake!"

"I think the girl is old enough to know what she wants," Grandma Mitsuye says. She waves her hand. "Plus, we have other, more important things to talk about. Nami's boyfriend is behaving badly." I notice the present tense, but I let it slide.

"What happened?" Sora asks. I give her and Sora the lowdown.

Mom looks guilty for a moment. "I should never have given his mom your number."

"Probably not," I agree.

"Well, who cares about him?" Mom, in typical fashion, hurries to cheer me. "Don't even give him another thought. That boy isn't worth your time. Aren't you glad you found this out now, rather than later?"

"Mom, I—"

"Sometimes these things are a blessing, if you think about it . . ." Mom is already rushing to fix the bad feelings. Already hurrying over the painful part. And while she doesn't mean to, it sounds al-most dismissive. *Hurry up. Get over that. It's not so bad. Be happy, so I can be happy, too.*

"Mom—"

But she's still on her tangent. Everything happens for a reason. The universe wouldn't give you something you can't handle. Plat-itudes that she wants to soothe the pain, but really only force it downward, beneath the surface, where no one can see it anymore.

"Mom!" I say, sharper than I intend. Mom's eyes widen. "Please, stop."

"Stop what?"

"You always do that. Rush over the bad stuff. I just want to . . . be in the bad stuff for a second. Not all things can be fixed."

"I don't rush over the bad stuff," Mom says, defensive.

"You totally rush over the bad stuff," Grandma Mitsuye says. "Sweep it under the rug. You know bad things happen. Sometimes, we just have to acknowledge that."

"Do not *shikata ga nai* me right now," Mom says. Clearly, this is a sore spot with Mom.

"But, Aiko, that's life. You can't fix everything."

Mom fumes. "Trying to fix things is better than doing nothing at all."

It occurs to me now that Grandma Mitsuye was always my soft place to land, but in the world of mothers and daughters, there's no shortage of sharp elbows.

"But sometimes when you try to fix things, you cause more prob-lems. Maybe Nami just needs to pick herself up. You can't always be the one picking her up."

"What am I supposed to do? Just *let* her be unhappy?" Mom raises her voice.

"You can't make me happy, Mom." There, I finally said it. Mom looks at me, startled. "And sometimes I think *you* need me to be happy in order for you to be happy. That's too much pressure."

"Why is wanting you to be happy a bad thing?" Mom exhales.

"Because it makes me feel like if I'm unhappy, I'm even more of a failure."

Grandma Mitsuye looks from one of us to the other. "No one in this family is a failure. Sometimes, we're happy. Sometimes, we're unhappy. That's just life."

"Amen," Sora says, squeezing Grandma's arm.

"I swear, if you . . ." Mom threatens.

"*Shikata ga nai,*" Grandma says, and Mom groans, staring at the white tiles of the hospital ceiling.

"I literally hate that phrase," Mom grumbles. And suddenly I see the complexity of mothers and daughters, how Grandma tried her whole life to teach Mom she could only control so much of her life, and how Mom worked her whole life to prove her wrong, that she could control everything. I'm actually more like Mom than I'd like to admit. It's hard, beyond hard, to admit that sometimes we are just pinballs, on a trajectory we can't fully control.

"I think you're both right," I tell them. "Some things we can control. Other things we can't. You can't let my happiness affect yours, or vice versa."

"You're a wise one, Nami-chan," Grandma says, and grins.

"And I still am going to want you to be happy," Mom tells me. "And you, too." She glances at Sora. "I don't know another way."

"I know, Mom," I say. "But sometimes we won't be happy."

"I know." Mom folds me and Sora into a hug, and then she reaches out and takes Grandma's hand.

In the lobby of the hospital, I run into Fatima Bibi, my best friend from high school. We haven't even exchanged a text since she missed my "surprise" birthday party, which seems like ions ago. Her baby is struggling to free itself from the straps of his umbrella stroller, and she's desperately fishing a toddler snack cup of crackers out of her ginormous diaper bag with one hand and adjusting her petal-pink hijab with the other.

"Fatima?" I ask, surprised.

"Nami!" Her face lights up and she folds me into a giant hug. She smells like applesauce and baby wipes. "I came as soon as I heard about your grandma. Is she okay?"

My throat tightens. Fatima came. She hasn't forgotten about me. She's here. For me. For my grandma. "Yes. Thankfully."

"I know how hard this must be. I remember this was the hospital where your dad . . ." She trails off. She doesn't have to finish as she pulls back and studies me. "Are you okay?"

I nod, my throat suddenly too thick with emotion.

"I tried to call you," she says.

"I didn't get the message!" I fumble to grab my phone. I scroll down and I do see a missed call. Just no voicemail.

"I texted you."

"I didn't get those."

Fatima sighs. "I bet Omar erased them. Omar is always grabbing my phone. He almost called nine-one-one the other day." Omar wiggles in his seat, and as if to prove her point, he tries to reach up and grab my phone from my hand. "Omar, no. That's not yours."

Omar has grown so much since I last saw him. When was that? I am struck with sudden guilt. Maybe eight months ago? He kicks his little feet and that's when I notice the sneakers—with worn tread. Since when does he walk? The last time I saw him, he was barely sitting up on his own.

"Do you want to grab a coffee? In the cafeteria?" I ask.

Fatima grins at me. "I'd love that."

We get coffee and pastries and head to a corner table. Omar hops out of his stroller by himself and waddles proficiently to his chair. Fatima lifts him into a booster seat.

"I just can't get over how big he is," I say.

"Me either. I've got crazy muscles in my arms now." Fatima curls her bicep to show me.

"Impressive."

She grins. "Listen, I am really sorry again about your birthday. I didn't want to miss it, but Omar had this terrible fever and Ahmad and I ending up taking him to the ER."

"Oh, Fatima. I didn't know. Is he okay?"

She nods. "Babies just get really dehydrated really quickly, and our pediatrician wanted us to be safe. Two days later, it was like he was never sick. He was back to running around the kitchen at top speed trying his best to find a plug we haven't babyproofed."

"That's good—I guess?" I feel a pang of guilt. Maybe I've been the one not keeping up with Fatima's life, and not the other way around. "I should come out one weekend soon. Maybe we could go to the Brookfield Zoo?"

"That would be nice," Fatima says. "I've missed you."

"I've missed you, too." Suddenly, all the last months and years fly away and we're fourteen again, sharing a package of Sour Patch Kids at a break during a Mathletes marathon. How could I have thought Fatima wasn't my friend anymore?

"Also, Desmond and Ramone wanted me to relay this message to you: they need you to come meet their baby. He's so adorable. You're the only one who hasn't."

It's then that I remember that just last week I got a text from Ramone with dozens of pictures of their baby, telling me we should all get together before the weather turns. I've got a baby towel and matching stuffed elephant to give them, sitting wrapped in my apartment.

"I've been a bad friend, I guess," I say, realizing that maybe I've been the one withdrawing, and not the other way around. "Toggle has taken up all my time."

"How is your work baby?" Fatima asks.

I feel like bursting into tears. "Not good," I admit. I tell her everything: the buyout, Jae, Rainforest, me falling for him and his lies.

"Whoa." Fatima sits back, stunned, and stares at her coffee mug. "You were dating Jae *Lee*. Voted most likely to start his own boy band . . . Jae Lee."

"I know. You can tell me. I'm a fool. I should never have trusted Jae. Jae was always an—" I want to say "asshole" but I pause just in time as I watch Omar take a long drink of milk from his red plastic sippy cup. "A, uh, jerk."

"Jae was always hot," Fatima argues.

"I think you mean he was always full of himself."

Fatima grins. "Maybe. But he was also hot." She shrugs. "Plus, he was always nice to me."

"You cannot be telling me right now that you think Jae is okay. We hated him." I clutch my mug handle a little tighter.

"*You* hated him. I just politely listened to you rant. But I actually thought he was a nice guy most of the time. He was always babysitting his little brothers and his cousins and stuff. It was cute."

"Wait. How did you know about that?"

"Remember I worked at Shake It Up? He'd always drive there after school and buy shakes for the whole carload of kids. He'd make sure they got extra whipped cream and cherries. It was nice."

"Why didn't you tell me that?"

"I think I probably did. You were too busy hating on him all the time. You didn't have room in your brain for contradictory information." Fatima shrugs. "Plus, I know it's terrible to play games with Toggle. But from what you're telling me, Jae basically missed you and jumped at any excuse to try to get back into your life."

"How do you read *that* from him destroying Toggle?"

"He came after it because you were there."

"Because he was bored."

"Because you were the only thing that *doesn't* bore him," Fatima points out. "It's almost, kind of . . . romantic in a backward way."

"It's not romantic," I snap.

"Okay! Okay." Fatima holds up her hands in surrender. "If you hate Jae, I'll hate him. I'm always Team Nami."

I let out a long breath. "Thanks, Fatima. And I'm always Team Fatima." Omar sets down his sippy cup and picks up another fish-shaped cracker. "And you tell me immediately next time something serious happens with this little guy, okay?"

Fatima nods. "Deal," she says.

Seeing Fatima cheers me, but the reality of what's going to happen to Toggle quickly drags me back down. I take the next two days off work. It's not like me, but I also don't have the stomach to break the news to Arie, Jamal, or Priya, or any of the other Toggle employees yet, about the Evans deal falling through. Since I'm pretty sure neither Imani nor Dell is likely to tell them, I have to work out a way to break the news gently. But I don't know how. I spend my two days off in bed, searching for the answer by looking under the covers, wondering how long I can stay cocooned before someone notices I'm missing.

Eventually, I'll have to get up. And level with Arie and the rest about what's going to happen to Toggle. I'm just not ready to see the heartbreak on those oddball faces I love so much. No more whiteboard challenges. No more Frisbee. No more . . . me, frankly. That's what hurts me the most, I think. Toggle will go on, in whatever form Rainforest sees fit, and I won't be a part of it anymore. I can't imagine Jae will let me keep my job after I told him I never want to see him again. Besides, if there have to be layoffs, I'd rather it be me than anyone else I care about. The company—the family—I worked so hard to build will unravel. And there's nothing I can do to stop it.

And, maybe, it is my fault. Maybe Jae offered me that glimpse into a real partnership, a real relationship, a person I want to travel to

Paris with, and for a second, I took my eye off Toggle. That's on me. Jae texted. And called. I've been buried under an avalanche of apologies, but I'm not ready to accept any of them. Because the plain fact is, if he is always going to put himself above everyone, then there's no place for me in his life.

Then again, I realize Jae might have been selfish, but I was selfish, too. I let my own loneliness blind me to his real intentions. I should never have wished for a damn soulmate for my birthday. I should've always kept my eye on Toggle.

I lounge in my plaid flannel pajamas on my too-hard, still oddly new-smelling couch, and wonder how long I can duck out of work. I'm not even sure what day it is: Wednesday? Thursday? Who knows?

Are you coming in today? Imani texts me.

I glance at the pajamas I've spent the last two days in. My apartment is littered with empty takeout boxes and is uncharacteristically messy. Why come in today or any other day? I just can't find the motivation. I've lost Toggle. I've let everyone down. Because I flew off my bike and took everyone with me.

Another ping on my phone. *When are you coming back?* It's Priya. *Please make it this afternoon. I've got money riding on this!*

I have to laugh a little bit.

Am I the whiteboard debate now?

> *You will be if you don't come in this afternoon.*

My phone seems to be blowing up.

Priya is driving me nuts, and won't stop bothering me unless I text you. You need to come in, Jamal texts.

This is your TV Dad. Please come in, Arie writes.

If you come in, we'll tell you who stole Dell's chair, Priya adds.

That's tempting. Very tempting. Although I have a couple of suspects in mind already.

Even Dell texts me.

> *You should come in. There's a meeting*
> *this afternoon at two you're going to want*
> *to be at.*

I cringe at the bad grammar.

> *What's the meeting about?*

> *Some stuff the programmers are doing. I*
> *dunno. The entire board is flying in for it,*
> *though.*

They are? Hmmm.

> *Also, have YOU seen my chair? Seriously.*
> *This has gone on long enough.*

My phone pings with another incoming text. I pick it up, expecting to see Arie or Imani prodding me to come into work, but instead, it's Jae's number.

I should delete the message without reading it. But I don't have that kind of willpower.

> *Namby, I know you've probably blocked*
> *me. But, if you haven't, and you're getting*
> *this, you should come into work this*
> *afternoon.*

My heart thumps in my ears. *Why?*

It's a surprise.

Then I'm definitely not coming. I've had enough
Jae Lee surprises to last an entire lifetime, thank
you very much.

This surprise you'll like. I'll eat two whole
bowls of hell ramen if you don't.

TWENTY-FIVE

Nami

This is the happiest day of my life. We're getting married. Only wish you were here to wheel me down the aisle.
[attached: picture of Wegner Swivel Chair, two black-gloved hands on the back, near the steps of the Cologne Cathedral in Germany]

WEGNER SWIVEL CHAIR
#ALL-HANDS-ALERT CHANNEL
TOGGLE INTERNAL CHAT

I don't know what new games Jae Lee is playing, but I don't care. I don't allow myself to get my hopes up. Fool me once, blame Jae Lee. Fool me twice, always blame Jae Lee.

Somehow, I drag myself into the office. I don't care what scheme Jae has brewing. Whatever it is, it doesn't change the fact that odds are good I'll have to sign over my baby to him and the evil Borg, but before that, I owe it to Arie and the whole team to fess up that I've ruined everything. That I am not, actually, the Best Boss Ever, Meant Unironically. When the elevator doors open on the Toggle floor, and I'm faced with the bright, primary colors of the carpet, the zinging Frisbees over the programmers' desks, and the just barely visible whiteboard through the open door of the break room, marked with a new debate (Who wins a game of Scrabble? Dumbledore or Gandalf?), I feel instantly at home.

And I almost burst into tears.

I'm not ready to let go of this. I don't want to say goodbye. I sniff and swallow, wondering if maybe I could work out some deal with Rainforest. Sell out my portion, but stay on as a consultant? Then I think about Jae. I'd have to swallow my pride and ask him for that favor.

I think about the possibility for a nanosecond, and then realize it would be my worst nightmare. I'd have a front-row seat to see Rainforest slowly dissect and corrupt Toggle until it's just a shell of its former self. Arie and Priya, who are tossing a Frisbee, stop abruptly as I walk by.

"Nami! You're here!" They both run to my side. At the commotion, Jamal glances up from his cubicle and rolls over. The three of them talk at the same time, eager to tell me something, but their words tumble over one another, and I don't really hear a complete sentence from any of them.

"We heard about Evans—"

"We know about Rainforest—"

"It all sounds—"

"One at a time, please," I beg.

"Wait a second," says Imani, wearing bright sapphire-blue-rimmed glasses and matching linen joggers. She marches over from her office. "I thought we *agreed* to do this all together." She stares at the four of them in turn.

"We just couldn't wait to tell her," Priya exclaims.

Dell, wearing his SAE baseball cap, pokes his head out of the door of his office. "What's all the noise?" His eyes light on me and then narrow. "Oh," he says, sounding disappointed. "Hi, Nami. Nice of you to finally make it into the office."

"Any news on the chair?" Priya asks Dell.

"No," Dell growls. "And, about that—"

"Children!" Imani cries, clapping her hands. "Let's be nice." She glances at her watch. "It's nearly two, people."

"To the Fishbowl!" Arie declares.

"Time to take care of business," Jamal adds.

"Come on, let's go," Priya says, and, as if on cue, the programmers nod, drop Frisbees and shut laptops and put down their afternoon snacks. They all hop up and we march directly to the glassed-in conference room. Something is up.

"What's going on?" I whisper to Imani.

"You'll see," she whispers back.

There aren't enough chairs in the Fishbowl for everyone, so the programmers cram into the back, on the opposite side of the presentation wall. Priya slides away from the table and motions for me to sit, and Imani and Dell take the chairs on either side of me. The board members take up the rest of the seats. Arie, Jamal, and Priya take their places at the front of the conference room table. Jamal dims the lights and Arie boots up his laptop. The opening chords of the *Lord of the Rings* music begins, and the oversized screen on the wall flickers to life. Jamal's voice filters through the speakers.

"Once upon a time, in a beautiful place we call the Toggle Shire . . ."

The programmers have cut and pasted photos of their heads on different hobbits, going about their daily business. Most are merrily eating. One cries, "Breakfast Mondays!" and gobbles up second breakfast.

I love this. Absolutely love it. Their faces look so silly on the bodies of *Lord of the Ring* hobbits, and many of them have made ridiculous faces to boot. The animation is clunky but awesome. Jamal's hobbit, in a wheelchair, looks serious and solemn. Priya's has brightly colored hair. Arie's is wearing an argyle sweater, and instead of his face, he has the face of Bob Saget, famous TV dad. There's even a cameo of Dell's Wegner Swivel Chair, dancing to a jig.

"Hey! That's not funny, guys," he groans. "I need my chair back. Pronto."

Arie ignores him. "There were three leaders here. Imani, daughter of the lord of the elvish sanctuary of Rivendell . . ."

Imani's head appears on Arwen's body.

"A dwarf . . ."

Dell's frowning face appears on a dwarf.

"Hey!" he cries, offended.

"And our fearless leader in the galaxy . . . Captain Nami."

They've fused my face on Captain Janeway's body, and there's a brief flash of *Star Trek*'s emblem. The Janeway fans cheer.

"We're mixing mythologies," Jamal explains, as if to apologize. There's no need. It's perfect.

"And the Borg wanted to consume the Shire . . ." We switch to *Star Trek* again, showing the Borg cube with the Rainforest logo.

"The One Who Shall Not Be Named was also interested in absorbing us . . ." They've pasted Evans's face on Voldemort's body.

"Is this a sales presentation . . . or the music video for Nerd Central?" Dell complains.

Several programmers shush him.

"But . . ." Priya jumps in. "There was one force they didn't count on."

Again, we see the hobbits, with the programmers' heads pasted on. Except they're inside the bridge of the USS *Enterprise*-D.

"We had to throw the Picard fans a bone," Arie tells me. I nod, understanding.

"And we had the power of . . ." On-screen, the *Enterprise* fires photon torpedoes that look a lot like NFTs and cryptocurrency, including rotating cat NFTs with rainbow lasers coming out of their eyes. The Borg cube blows up. Voldemort's snakelike face begins disintegrating, flying away into space in tiny flaky bits. The programmers cheer. And a celebration with breakfast sandwiches commences.

Jamal restores the lights, and Imani claps. Dell groans, and I still am not a hundred percent sure what's going on. That's when Arie passes out a stack of papers to each one of us.

"That's just the long way of saying we the hobbits, er . . . I mean, programmers, would like to offer to buy Toggle," Arie says.

I glance at Imani. She nods sagely.

"What?" I sit up straight, scanning the pages in front of me. Yes, it's true. They've formed a special purpose acquisition company called Hobbits Save the Day, or HSD, Inc., a shell company backed by . . . all of the programmers. "I don't understand . . ." I glance at Imani, but she just grins knowingly. Dell grabs the paper and rustles through it.

"This offer is bigger than Rainforest's initial offer." He glances around at all the faces in the room. "Is this a joke?"

"No joke," Jamal says.

"We're actually serious," Priya says.

For the first time since Dell's chair was stolen, he smiles. I scan down to the offer to check it, and see Dell's right. There are so many zeros, I nearly faint. It's above Rainforest's highest offer.

"How . . . ?" I blink up at Arie, Jamal, and Priya.

"I've been telling you about crypto for *literal years*," Arie says, sighing his exasperated TV Dad sigh. "I bought digcoin in 2010 for twenty-five cents. I sold it when it was worth forty-seven thousand dollars a coin."

"Most of the rest of us bought crypto right after Arie. He convinced us to get in. We all sold most of our shares before the crash," Priya says.

"They're all filthy rich," Imani adds.

"What I want to know is why is Priya always stealing extra cupcakes?" Jamal asks the room. "You can buy as many as you want."

Priya shrugs. "Because they're *free* cupcakes, Jamal. You can't buy free."

The people I love so much could buy Toggle over many times. "You don't even have to work here," I say finally. "Why?"

"Seriously?" Priya shakes her head. "Because you're the Best Boss Ever, Meant Unironically. We *thought* we made that clear."

"And because we love Toggle, too." Arie grins. "Fun. Not Evil! Really. We Mean It."

"There's literally no place else like Toggle," Jamal adds. "Where else can we have the whiteboard challenge? Besides, we're not just a company. We're a family."

They all grin at me. My heart feels so full it might burst.

I glance at Imani and Dell. "Are you two on board with this?"

"Completely," Imani says, a sparkle in her eye.

"You had me at a gazillion dollars." Dell grins.

"And the board?" Imani makes eye contact with our investors. They all raise their hands and nod.

"We have only three conditions with this sale," Arie adds. "That a) Dell, I'm sorry but you're out of here."

Dell sniffs. "As if I'd stay among you chair thieves."

"And b) we want Nami and Imani to stay on, as co-CEOs, even as all of us hobbits get seats on the new board."

Tears prick my eyes. "I'd love that." I glance at Imani, who nods.

"I'm in," Imani says.

"And c) we need unlimited cupcakes *per* employee on birthdays," Priya adds.

"Priya, you don't *need* that many cupcakes," Jamal complains.

"But I want them." She glares at Jamal.

"That's fine with me," I say, waving my hand.

"And, even more importantly . . ." Jamal mimes a drumroll. "We extend Breakfast Mondays to every weekday."

"Done!" I say, and the programmers cheer. I hug them all, tears in my eyes. These are my people. We truly are a family.

Priya throws her arms around me. I hug her hard. "You have to give back Dell's chair," I whisper in her ear.

"Do we have to?" she moans. I nod. She glances at Jamal. "Gig might be up," she tells him.

Dell isn't even paying attention. He's at the far end of the conference room with the calculator on his phone out, no doubt trying to fit all those zeros in.

He flashes her a grin. "All good things must end." He glances at me. "Of course, *not* Toggle. Not yet."

Priya and Jamal put their heads together, I assume to figure out how best to return Dell's beloved Wegner Swivel.

"Crazy kids. They grow up so fast," Arie quips as he sidles up next to me.

"Yeah."

"One thing I should mention," Arie begins. "The real hero might be Jae Lee."

My head snaps up at the mention of his name. "Why?"

"He's the one who told us about SPACs. We had no idea we could form a company so easily just to buy another company. He gave us the idea of pooling our crypto, and even offered to invest himself, but that didn't turn out to be necessary."

"He's not so bad, for a Borg," Jamal admits.

"So, let me guess, he told you that you needed to tell me all about it." Jae would never pass up an opportunity to brag.

"No, actually, he didn't." Priya shrugs. "I think he really just wanted to save Toggle."

"Maybe," I say, though I'm still not 100 percent convinced. He picked winning over me. I'm not sure I'm ready to forgive that. "Can you ever really trust the Borg?"

"Actually, he's not Borg anymore," Arie tells me.

"What do you mean?"

"He quit."

"He did?" I don't understand. Why would Jae quit his job at Rain-forest? There's nowhere else he can aggressively continue #winning. Joust—their closest competitor—doesn't have anywhere close to the same market share. "Why?"

Arie shrugs. "You'll have to ask him."

Am I forgiven yet? Jae pings me on my phone. I hate that a single message from him lights a little flame of hope in my chest.

Jury is still deliberating. I can't just let him walk back into my life so easily. He called me naïve. He might not even believe in such a thing as right or wrong. I move out of the Fishbowl, and back toward my office.

Can the jury be bribed? he types.

That's highly unethical.

That's kind of my jam.

I can't help it. I smile.

Much to learn, you still have.

Can you teach me over ramen?

If I don't like what you tell me, can I make you eat hell ramen?

As many bowls as you want.

The first red leaves fall to the ground out in front of Mark Hashimoto's ramen place, beneath the burnt orange elevated train tracks. There's just the hint of chill in the air, a promise of the frigid artic tundra waiting in the wings. Winter is, indeed, coming. I shove my hands into the pocket of my jean jacket as I swing open the door and step inside. Mark is behind the counter, wearing his familiar white apron. He gives me a knowing grin.

"Jae said you might be dropping by. He's over there, in the corner." I glance over, heart thumping hard, and I see the familiar dark hair at the back of his head.

"Did y'all work out whatever was going on between you two? Or do you need a whole bowl of Carolina Reapers to decide it?"

"Not sure yet," I tell him. Jae turns and sees me. My entire chest balloons out at the sight of him, even though he's not wearing his typical weekday blazer. He's got on a soft hoodie and jeans, looking decidedly dressed down. Hope flares in his dark eyes for a second as he rises to meet me, but my expression must be as guarded as I feel, because he aborts his attempt at a hug, and slides back down in his side of the booth.

I'm here to hear him out, I remind myself. I'm here because he did help save Toggle. I owe him this. But I'm not sure if I can trust him. My whole body feels tense.

I slide into the seat opposite his, the table bare in front of us.

"Why did you quit your job at Rainforest?" I ask, curiosity burning in me.

Jae shrugs. "You told me to."

I'm stunned for a second. "Me? But I didn't mean you had to quit. I meant you *could have* quit. I—"

"It's okay." Jae holds up his hand. "I quit because you and, I am sad to admit this, my dad were right. I should do more important work, and I shouldn't be evil. So, I'm going to be a freelance consultant. Help companies do ethical takeovers, help companies not be such . . ." He grins. "Wolves."

"You are going to advise people on *ethical* takeovers." I'm not sure I understand.

He nods. "And help companies *being* bought negotiate with their buyers to get the best outcome for their customers and employees."

"I thought you didn't believe in right or wrong. I thought being a hall monitor was . . ." I swallow. "Naïve. And everything is gray and confusing."

"Often, things are gray and confusing, but you helped me see there is a right. And a wrong. I used 'gray' as an excuse not to take a side. But there's always a right way."

I actually am speechless. I don't know what to say. "What's your angle? You have to have an angle."

Jae shakes his head. "No angle. Just doing good."

I stare at him. "Who *are* you?"

Jae laughs. "Me." He reaches out and gently takes my hand. I let him. "Under the influence of you. You make me better, Nami."

"You called me a grown-up hall monitor."

"Clearly, I need one of those in my life." Jae gives me a rueful grin. "Nami, I'm sorry for hurting you, and for being careless with your feelings and with the people of Toggle. If you'll let me, I want to spend all my time from now on making it up to you."

"Really?"

"I'll eat the Hell Ramen. If you want me to prove it to you."

For a second, I'm tempted. "I'd be a terrible person if I made you do that."

"Or justified." He squeezes my hand. "Nami, I think you're the most amazing person I've ever met. You're so damn smart, you're so loyal to your friends and family, and above all, unlike most other people, you are actually, seriously and without ulterior motive, trying to make this world a better place."

Warmth blooms in my chest.

"I love you, Namby." He grins. And his adoration eyes are back. I love how he's looking at me right now, and I want him to always look at me like that. For a full second, I forget to breathe. "You do?"

"I'm as surprised as you are," he quips, referencing himself. I laugh. "Now, it's your turn."

"My turn for what?" I ask, playing innocent.

"Namby!" he cries.

"I love you, too," I say. "Even when I hate you."

"Oh, I know. *Especially* when you hate me."

"Don't push it," I warn him, standing. Jae tugs me over to his side of the booth, pulling me down on his lap. I kiss him, long and deep.

"Hey, you crazy kids," Mark drawls, interrupting. "So, I take it this means we *don't* need to eat Hell Ramen today?" He's holding a bowl of steaming hot death.

I glance at Jae. "Well . . ."

He starts to look worried.

"Not *today*," I say, and Jae's shoulders slump in relief. "Because I hate-love, or love-hate this man."

"Or how about just love?" Jae suggests.

"I'll think about it," I say as he pulls me back down for a kiss, and right then and there, I know I'll love-hate this man for the rest of my life.

EPILOGUE (1)

Sora and Jack's Wedding
February

Silver balloons and streamers hang from the ceiling of the Evanston Township High School gym, as a DJ at one end of the basketball court pumps out "We Are Family" and one hundred of Sora and Jack's closest family and friends crowd into their prom wedding reception, ready to dance the night away. Sora is wearing the new take on her old halter-style prom dress, which she looks stunning in. Jack is spinning Sora around the dance floor, both of their faces lit up with pure joy. Most of the guests came, as instructed, wearing their own prom outfits—if not the original sequins they wore at prom, then close copies—and their looks run the gamut from the metallic ruffles of the 1980s to cut-out halter dresses from the 2010s. Sora generously let the bridesmaids pick their own dresses, and I went for a sapphire-blue bare-shoulder A-line and dyed-to-match strappy heels.

"Is prom everything you wanted it to be?" Jae asks as he hands me a cup of definitely spiked punch. I watch my Honolulu cousins bob and weave through the crowd. Mom, who has at long last surrendered to Sora's wishes, is also dancing with Great-Uncle Bob, and there's a genuinely festive vibe in the air. The wedding is 100 percent Sora, and I couldn't be happier for her.

"Better than I could imagine," I say, taking the plastic cup from him and taking a big sip. I'm so happy, genuinely happy for Sora and Jack. But I'm also genuinely happy for me. Jae and I have been nearly inseparable the last six months. I'm letting my lease run out next month, and I plan to move in with Jae. It's a big step, but also a natural step. We spend every night together, anyway. Sharing a mailbox won't be that big a commitment.

Jae has been the puzzle piece in my life that I never knew was missing until he clicked right into place.

Grandma Mitsuye, using a cane, sways to the beat, and gives me an approving nod. She winks at Jae, and I make a mental note to keep her far from him in case the spiked punch gives her ideas.

"Are you ready for this?" Jae asks me, taking a gulp of punch and nodding to the dance floor.

"Are *you* ready for this?" I threaten to do the sprinkler and Jae barks a laugh.

"No one is ready for that, Namby," he says, but he grins, and he's got that adoring but teasing look in his eye, the one he saves especially for me. He's also looking particularly dashing in his sleek designer tuxedo, which fits his lean, muscled shoulders perfectly. The fact is, we're an amazing team, and when we're on the same side, we're unstoppable, just like we are in the tennis league we play every other Saturday.

The song fades away and the DJ, AKA my Honolulu cousin Niko, takes the mic. "Eh . . . sistas and aunties," he drawls in his slow Hawaiian pidgin. "You no like wedding? Don't get married. You want own wedding? Bouquet toss!"

The crowd on the dance floor cheers, and Sora heads to the raised stage mid-bleachers, her white roses in tow.

"You'd better go elbow your way to the front. Some of your cousins are desperate for this," Jae warns me.

"Are you just secretly hoping I catch the bouquet, so I'll fight Isabella for your grandmother's ring?"

"You would *definitely* win that match," Jae says. "And you'd make my dad a very, very happy man. He keeps leaving me messages telling me there's still time for us to get married before Charlie next month. He's still holding out hope."

"Where would we ever find a reception spot in one month?"

"He recommends the Golden Dragon."

"Of course he does." We've been there more than once to meet his dad for a quick weekend lunch. It's amazing the difference in mood when Mr. Lee is faced with an all-you-can-eat buffet.

"I realize you're dying to discover just what Korean names my parents have picked out for our children, but trust me in that you don't have to catch that bouquet."

"Why not?"

"Because I plan to marry you anyway. I'm not leaving this up to fate." He flashes me a cocky grin, and I tug on him close and kiss him.

"I love you."

"Love you, too." I blow Jae a kiss as I move through the crowd toward the grouping of single cousins, two divorced aunts, and Jack's little niece, Allie.

"I'm going to catch the bouquet," she tells me, her sparkling light-up sneaks flashing bright purple.

"I am sure you will," I tell her. Allie's a feisty little one, and she took her petal-dropping task at the small ceremony near the bleachers very seriously.

Sora turns her back to us, taunting us with the bouquet. "One . . ." she says, winding up. "Two . . ." She winds up some more. "Three!" she shouts, sending the bouquet sailing above the eager hands. I see the flowers, in slow motion, moving right to me. Then, at the last second, Jack's niece leaps into the air, snagging the bouquet right out of my hands. That kid has an amazing vertical. I glance over the heads of my disappointed cousins to see Jae literally doubled over laughing.

"You should've boxed her out," Jae scolds as I return to him.

"Now your dad will be hopelessly disappointed."

Jae takes my hand. "No, he won't. I told you, I'm going to marry you anyway."

"Is that a promise . . . or a threat?"

"Both," Jae teases.

Kesha blares through the speakers.

"'Tik Tok'? Did *you* request this?"

"I might have," Jae says, grinning.

"Are you ready to dance?" I ask him.

"I'm not sure I'm ready for whatever *you* call dancing," he teases as I take his hand and drag him out to the dance floor.

"Shut up and dance with me," I tell him.

"I'm trying," Jae says, moving gingerly about. "I just don't want to lose a toe. Or a leg."

"Don't be so dramatic," I chastise, whipping my hair back from my face. "You know you love my moves."

"They're memorable," he says, and grins. I bounce into his chest, and he wraps his arms around me and holds me tight. "I love you, even if you dance like . . ."

"Like no one's watching?" I offer.

"Like you might be having a medical emergency," he finishes.

"I love you, even though you *totally* rip off all your moves from Justin Timberlake."

"Are these our wedding vows? Because they're awesome," Jae deadpans.

"I vow to honor and cherish you . . . through Carolina Reapers . . ." I begin.

"And scorpion peppers," Jae adds. "In bad dancing . . ."

"And super, tripped-out egos . . ."

"And in writing detention and tardy slips . . ."

"And in acing you on the tennis court without even trying . . ."

"Because we're perfect together," Jae finishes as he pulls me to him tight. I couldn't, actually, agree more.

"Yes, we are."

He looks at me with those amazing adoration eyes, and I know I'm looking up at him with the same. I've never been so thankful to Artemis.

Jae dips down and presses his lips to mine, and a whole future together opens up before us. I can't wait to meet it.

EPILOGUE (2)

Today we signed the papers, and Toggle is officially owned by the HSD (Hobbits Save the Day)! I'd like to say . . . so long, suckers!

I do want to thank you for returning my Wegner Swivel. I was relieved to hear you didn't actually send my very expensive, very rare chair to Europe and that the interns just Photoshopped the background. I'm glad I didn't actually have to sue anyone. Could've been a real nasty business, given how rare and expensive Wegner Swivel chairs are.

DELL OURANOS
FORMER PARTNER AND CO-OWNER, STILL BUSINESS
INFLUENCER AND TRENDSETTER
#ALL-HANDS-ALERT CHANNEL
TOGGLE INTERNAL CHAT

Pleasure working with you, too, Dell. Good luck in your future endeavors!

[attached picture of Arie in Wegner Swivel Chair, waving]

ARIE BERGER
DAD HOBBIT

Wait. Is that my chair?

DELL OURANOS

> FORMER PARTNER AND CO-OWNER, STILL BUSINESS
> INFLUENCER AND TRENDSETTER

That's Arie's chair.

[attached picture of Priya in her Wegner Swivel Chair]

> PRIYA PATEL
> COOL HOBBIT

Are we talking about chairs?

[attached picture of Ameer and two other interns, also sitting in
Wegner Swivel Chairs]

> AMEER QAZI
> INTERN AND HOBBIT-IN-TRAINING

Hans Wegner truly was a genius.

[picture of front office receptionist also in a Wegner Swivel]

> ARPA PRAVAT
> RECEPTION HOBBIT

WHAT THE HELL IS GOING ON?!

> DELL OURANOS
> FORMER PARTNER AND CO-OWNER, STILL BUSINESS
> INFLUENCER AND TRENDSETTER

Everyone now has a Wegner Swivel Chair, Dell. The hobbits bought
each employee one. Thanks, HSD! These are SO comfy.

[photo of Paula, also in her own Wegner Swivel]

> PAULA HERNANDEZ
> HEAD OF HR

You have got to be kidding me. They gave all of these plebes a
$12,000 chair?! Why?!

> DELL OURANOS
> FORMER PARTNER AND CO-OWNER, STILL BUSINESS
> INFLUENCER AND TRENDSETTER

Everyone deserves a piece of Modern Danish Luxury in their lives.

I'm using mine as a plant stand.

[picture of Wegner Swivel Chair near Jamal's desk with a plant on
the seat]

> JAMAL ROBERTS
> HOT WHEELS HOBBIT

I hate you all.

DELL OURANOS
FORMER PARTNER AND CO-OWNER, STILL BUSINESS
INFLUENCER AND TRENDSETTER

We love you right back, Dell! [kissy face emoji]

ALL HOBBITS
THE SHIRE

Wait. Did one of you set my ringtone to 50 Cent?!

DELL OURANOS
FORMER PARTNER AND CO-OWNER, STILL BUSINESS
INFLUENCER AND TRENDSETTER

[Video of all Toggle employees, rolling in their Wegner Swivel Chairs, sunglasses on, to the beat of "In Da Club"]

ALL HOBBITS
THE SHIRE

ACKNOWLEDGMENTS

I have so many people to thank for helping me write this book! First and foremost, I'd like to thank my agent, Deidre Knight, and everyone at The Knight Agency, who have stuck by me for more than twenty years. In a publishing world that's often fickle, Deidre is anything but—she's the most loyal and supportive agent, period.

Thank you to my thoughtful and brilliant editing team at St. Martin's Press: Alexandra Sehulster, Mara Delgado Sánchez, and Cassidy Graham. Thank you for helping me take this manuscript to the next level. To the amazing marketing staff at St. Martin's Press (because no one will read a book if they don't know it exists): Marissa Sangiacomo, Katie Bassel, Kejana Ayala, and Brant Janeway.

I'd like to thank my North Shore Ladies: Hillary, Gretchen, Julie, Dani, Beth, and Annie. A special thanks to the indominable Elizabeth Kinsella, who suffered through employment with me at the Evil Spam Company (All Evil, No Good). Thank you to all the amazing friends you introduced me to: Carroll, Kate, Kelly, Jane, Stina, and Linda. Thank you to the Laniers, Moriaritys, and Lewises, for always being up for celebrating a book launch!

Thanks to Jerry Won, and all he's doing with his amazing podcast, *Dear Asian Americans*. (Jerry, you've been to the White House so many times, they are going to name a bedroom after you! Seriously.) And I have to give a shout-out to Reera Yoo and Marvin Yueh, hosts of *Books & Boba*. Thank you for all you do to promote Asian authors.

Thank you to my Tanamachi family: Mom, Dad, Patty, Matt, and Jill. To my kids (biological and bonus): Hana, Miya, Pete, Sarina, and Sophia. You awe, honor, and inspire me every day, and I'm so proud of all of you!

And, last but by far not least, to my soulmate and husband, PJ Benoit, the best listener, supporter, cheerleader, and partner anyone could ever ask for. He is the personification of the ultimate wish granted . . . in this life and the next.